LOVE IS DEAD

A ZOMBIE ANTHOLOGY

EDITED BY
ANTHONY GIANGREGORIO

OTHER LIVING DEAD PRESS BOOKS

JUST BEFORE NIGHT: A ZOMBIE DUOLOGY
BLOOD RAGE & DEAD RAGE
BOOK OF THE DEAD: A ZOMBIE ANTHOLOGY
BOOK OF THE DEAD 2: NOT DEAD YET
BOOK OF THE DEAD 3: DEAD AND ROTTING
END OF DAYS: AN APOCALYPTIC ANTHOLOGY VOLUME 1 & 2
DEAD HOUSE: A ZOMBIE GHOST STORY
THE ZOMBIE IN THE BASEMENT (FOR ALL AGES)
THE LAZARUS CULTURE: A ZOMBIE NOVEL
DEAD WORLDS: UNDEAD STORIES VOLUMES 1, 2, 3 & 4
FAMILY OF THE DEAD, REVOLUTION OF THE DEAD
RANDY AND WALTER: PORTRAIT OF TWO KILLERS
KINGDOM OF THE DEAD
THE MONSTER UNDER THE BED
DEAD TALES: SHORT STORIES TO DIE FOR
ROAD KILL: A ZOMBIE TALE
DEADFREEZE, DEADFALL
SOUL EATER, THE DARK, RISE OF THE DEAD
DARK PLACES, DEAD END: A ZOMBIE NOVEL
VISIONS OF THE DEAD

THE DEADWATER SERIES

DEADWATER
DEADWATER: Expanded Edition
DEADRAIN, DEADCITY
DEADWAVE, DEAD HARVEST
DEAD UNION, DEAD VALLEY
DEAD TOWN, DEAD SALVATION
DEAD ARMY (coming soon)

COMING SOON

DEAD HISTORY: A ZOMBIE ANTHOLOGY
THE WAR AGAINST THEM: A ZOMBIE NOVEL by Jose Vazquez
DEAD WORLDS: UNDEAD STORIES VOLUME 5
THE CHRONICLES OF JACK PRIMUS by Michael D. Griffiths

LOVE IS DEAD: A ZOMBIE ANTHOLOGY

Cover Illustrated by Andrew Dawe-Collins

Table of Contents

STUPID CUPID

JESSY MARIE ROBERTS

Prologue

Venus and Mars exchanged glances, each standing on opposite sides of their son's bed. Cupid was tangled in a mass of sheets and blankets, one bare, pale cheek peeking out from amidst the pink and red bedding, his face buried under a heart-shaped pillow.

Venus sighed and sat down on the edge of the plush, over-stuffed mattress. "Come on, now, love. You have important work to do today."

Cupid groaned and buried his face further under the hand-stitched pillow. "Go away. I'm not getting out of bed."

Mars frowned and yanked the pillow from his pouting son's head. "Get up, sport. It's Valentine's Day, *your* day. Humans are counting on you to make their dreams of romance come true."

"And what do you care of romance and love, father? Usually you're too busy watching the war channel at Club Mount Olympus to care what I'm doing!" Cupid whined as he sat up in bed and leaned against the plush headboard.

It was Mars' turn to sigh. "Romance and love are important to you and your mother, *Cupido*," the God of War said, patience etched into the wrinkles of the deity's face. "Now, tell us what bothers you so we can help."

Cupid pursed his lips and shook his head.

"What is it, son?" Venus asked gently, brushing an errant tuft of wispy blonde hair out of Cupid's cherubic eyes. "You can tell us anything."

Cupid drew in a deep breath and blurted out a name. "Psyche."

Mars' eyebrows drew up toward his hairline and his face exploded in blotches of red. "Psyche? For the love of Pete, *Cupido*, haven't you gotten over her yet?"

"Mars," Venus hissed through clenched teeth, casting a warning look at her lover, "stop yelling at him. He's *sensitive.*"

"Sensitive is an understatement, Venus. Look at him, chubby and naked, lazing about in bed on *his* most important day of the year! And all because of that harlot, a girl who dared be as beautiful as the goddess of love!"

Venus harrumphed and muttered, "Almost as beautiful," before turning her attention back to her son and stroking his plump, flushed cheek. "Your bow is waiting for you, my pet. You know you derive such joy from poking the humans with your love-tipped arrows."

Cupid clenched his fists and smashed them into the bed, fat droplets of water leaking out of his large round eyes. "I don't want to prick the humans with love today, mom!" A mischievous leer curled the corners of his mouth. "Father, as I have dominion over the living on Earth and the dead in Hades, I wish to use my new bow today, the one given to me by Pluto for my birthday. It was a much better gift than that hand-sewn heart pillow," he added under his breath, loud enough so his mother, the talent behind the pillow, could hear.

Mars looked to where two bows, one red and one black, and two separate quivers of arrows, both the same color, rested against the wall by the front door of Cupid's studio loft. "I'll tell you what," Mars said, striking a deal with his son. "If you do your sacred Valentine's Day duty, I'll go with you to Hades and we shall torment the dead together."

Cupid's eyes grew wide and a smile of pure joy replaced the malicious twist of his lips. "Truly, father? Just you and I, damning the damned? Will Pluto allow it?"

Mars laughed, his thundering boom rattling the walls of the apartment. "Of course, my son. I'll offer him front row tickets to The Middle East. Pluto loves to see war up close and personal—it gets him out of his underworld doldrums!"

"Okay!" Cupid agreed, jumping out of bed, his fleshy belly jiggling from his efforts, his morose thoughts of Psyche erased by excitement at a father-son day in Hades, "This is the best Valentine's Day ever!"

The son stood up on his tippy toes and brushed a quick kiss on Venus' cheek before grabbing his red bow, the wrong quiver of arrows, and rushing out the door to find a nice, fluffy cloud to drift through on his journey to Earth.

1

James sucked on a mint-flavored wooden toothpick and surveyed the dim room. He grimaced as a skinny twenty-something in a frilly red and white dress pranced by, batting her fake eyelashes and blue-encrusted eyelids in a gruesome attempt at flirtation.

"You owe me more than a drink," he said to David, his cousin and best friend, as they leaned against the shiny bar, "This whole scene is...*revolting*."

David laughed, his perfectly even teeth blaring white in the soft lighting. "It isn't *that* bad, James. Besides, you owed *me* one. That's how I roped you into coming along in the first place."

"True," James said, cocking his head to the side, "but I never imagined it would be this bad. A singles retreat? I must have been out of my mind to agree to such a thing!" He made a sour face, as if tasting something vile. "Remind me again why we're here."

David tilted his champagne glass to the far left corner of the banquet room, smiling when he caught the attention of a well-appointed blonde. "Michelle," he sighed, taking a long swig of his bubbling refreshment.

James smirked. "That's right. You brought me to a singles retreat to stalk your co-worker. Why didn't you just ask her out at the office?"

David shot James an irritated look. "I tried. I asked her if she had any Valentine's Day plans and she said she was coming here with her best friend. I was lucky to score the retreat tickets. A last minute cancellation. I couldn't come alone. That would seem desperate."

James cackled into his whiskey sour. "As if this," he mocked, gesturing to the room with a sweeping arm, "doesn't already reek of desperation."

David thumped James on the upper arm. "Stop complaining. A luxury weekend, your own hotel suite with pay-per-view and Jacuzzi bath, free food and an open bar—all at my expense. Shut up and enjoy yourself."

3

James filched his room key from the pocket of his borrowed slacks and jingled them in front of David's face. "I'm heading up to my room. I'll see you Sunday morning for the long drive from here, the corner of Hell and Timbuktu, through the middle of nowhere, until we're back in Chicago."

"You were supposed to be my wing man," David cried as James weaved his way through the throng of tittering singles to the hotel's elevator.

Turning around, James flipped David the bird, and then leaned against the up button until the elevator door chimed and parted.

* * *

Michelle felt David's eyes following her everywhere she went in the banquet room and she regretted telling her co-worker her weekend plans. While he was nice and good-looking, she wasn't interested in a relationship with him and had thought he would get the hint when she told him she was spending Valentine's Day weekend with her best girlfriend.

"Do you want another drink, Michelle?" her friend, Alison, asked as Michelle slurped up the last of her fuzzy navel. "I'll go get it from the bar for you. I know you don't want to deal with David."

Michelle, sighed, feeling like a jerk. "Maybe I should just tell him I'm not interested in him. Maybe he could find someone else here. There are plenty of single ladies who would die for his attention."

"It's pretty obvious he only has eyes for you."

Michelle furtively glanced over at the bar where David was speaking with a handsome man in a white button-up shirt and dark slacks. "Let's just forget about David and have fun! It's been forever since we've spent a weekend together!"

"Deal," Alison said, clinking her wine goblet against her friend's glass.

"Tell you what, you grab us more drinks and I'm going to run upstairs to my room to touch up my make-up. There are twenty-five single men here—well, twenty-four, if you don't count David—and I want to talk to each and every one!" An overweight man with a stained *Show Me Yours And I'll Show You Mine* t-shirt walked

4

by, tossing the girls a tongue-wagging leer. "Except him," Michelle giggled.

"Another fuzzy navel?" Alison asked, rattling the ice in Michelle's empty glass.

"Yes, please. And ask the bartender for an extra shot of vodka."

Alison smiled, approval stamped over her freckled face. "Thatta girl! I'll see you in a couple of minutes."

"Sounds good!" Michelle scampered to the elevator, barely squeezing through the doors before they closed.

* * *

Cupid hid, unobserved, in the top corner of the elevator. He pulled back the red bow's string, peered down the shaft of the one remaining arrow from his last romantic mission to Earth, and let the heart-tipped instrument fly through the air.

The arrow was shot with such force, at such close distance, it went straight through the blonde female's shoulder and embedded itself within the brown haired man's shoulder blade.

"Two birds with one stone," Cupid giggled, levitating, his invisible, diminutive form obscured from human perception. Pricking each of the humans with the same love arrow would make their love stronger than usual. Though he wanted to stay and watch the inevitable fireworks, he was eager to finish his Valentine's Day duties. The son of Venus and Mars buzzed out of the elevator, rigging the bow with one of the twelve arrows from his quiver.

Once he had delivered all twelve arrows to lonely fools, he could return to his bed in his apartment and order take-out.

"Ouch!" the woman cried, pressing her hand against her shoulder.

"Bloody hell!" the man shouted, pulling at the collar of his white shirt and looking down at his clavicle.

At once, they looked at each other, the stinging pain forgotten.

"I think I love you," the man whispered, bringing his hand up to brush against the woman's pink cheek.

"I know I love you," she answered, covering his hand with her own, nuzzling into his palm. Overwhelmed with passion, the couple embraced, their mouths meeting in love's true kiss.

Panting, he broke away for just a minute to groan, "My room is on the ninth floor. Come with me there."

"No," she argued, wrapping her arms around his neck and wiggling her body closer to his. "My room is on the seventh floor. It's closer."

The elevator door dinged, signifying their arrival on the seventh floor. The couple stumbled, lost in adoration's first embrace, to her suite.

On the ground level of the hotel, twelve other arrows were embedded into humans, only those arrowheads were forged in the bowels of Hades and intended for underworld necromancy play rather than romance. By the time Cupid discovered his mistake, his quiver was empty.

With an unconcerned shrug of his shoulders, Cupid teleported to his room and switched on the reality plasma screen television on his dresser to watch the ensuing chaos with glee.

2

James rolled on to his back, spent from an energetic bout of lovemaking. "My, God, girl, I don't know how I've lived without you," he admitted, pulling her to rest against him.

She laid her head on his shoulder, her fingers sliding through the thick mat of hair decorating his hard chest. "I feel the same way. I can't believe my feelings for you. It's like I've never known love until I looked into your eyes."

"I know exactly how you feel," he said, contentment oozing out of his pores. "I'm James, by the way. James Williams."

She raised up her head and dropped a quick kiss on his lips. "I'm Michelle Summers."

He feathered kisses down her cheek and neck. "I have a confession. I know who you are. David's my cousin."

Michelle grew still. "David from my office? Oh, that's right, I saw you guys talking at the bar. He has a bit of a crush on me. Do you think he'll understand?"

James thought of his cousin's long-standing romantic affection for Michelle and dismissed the worry. "He'll have to. We're in love."

A sharp knock at the door distracted him from trailing kisses down the length of her body. "'Michelle? Are you in there? Hurry and open up!" a scared voice cried from the hallway, followed by additional pounding thumps against the door.

"It's my girlfriend, Alison," Michelle said, hurrying out of the bed to the door, wrapping the damp, white top sheet around her body.

James scooted out of the bed and pulled on his boxer shorts and slacks, barely fastening the top button before Michelle swung open the door. Alison pushed Michelle aside and ran into the room, slamming the door behind her and fastening the deadbolt. "We need to get out of here!" she screamed, tears of terror streaming down her ashen face.

"Calm down," Michelle said, ushering her weeping friend toward a chair. "Tell us what happened."

"Us?" Alison asked, looking confused. She spied James on the opposite side of the room, buttoning his white shirt. "Oh my God, Michelle, are you naked?"

Blushing, Michelle tightened the sheet. "Forget about that. What's going on?"

"It was terrible," Alison whispered, lost in horrific reverie. "Something happened downstairs. A dozen or so people fell to the ground, their bodies convulsing until...until they stopped moving. One of the women is a doctor and she pronounced twelve people dead at the same time. Nobody knew what to do. The doctor suggested poison and we all threw our drinks onto the floor, but the...then they *woke up.*"

Michelle sputtered, trying to get words to come out of her mouth, but only succeeded in making small, stuttering false starts.

James knelt down in front of Alison, forcing her attention to him. "They *woke* up? What the bloody hell do you mean by that?"

Alison covered her face with her hands, her red hair spilling onto her lap as she hunched over, wailing. After a couple of moments, she wiped her blood-shot eyes and grabbed James' forearm. "They woke up, sat up, stood up...they staggered around, their arms in front of them, groaning...we tried to help them, to ask them what we could do, but they started biting people!"

"Biting people?" James echoed, getting to his feet and pacing the hotel room's plush carpet floor. "Like biting them and running away?"

"No," Alison screamed, once again on the verge of hysteria. "Like biting and eating people!"

"Is this a fucking joke?" James barked, pulling his loafers over his bare feet. "Are you drunk?"

"Go see for yourself, if you don't believe me," Alison shouted, pointing at the door. "But don't expect to come back in this room, you jerk!"

Michelle, snapped back into reality, slapped Alison across the cheek. "Calm down, Ali. James is always welcome in my room!"

Alison looked stunned, then confused. "What're you talking about? You barely know the guy."

Michelle smiled sheepishly and stood next to James, sliding her arms around his midriff. "We're in love," she blurted, a girlish giggle punctuating the statement.

James rubbed his hand up and down Michelle's arm. "That's right, honey. We're getting married."

"Married? What!" Alison screeched, her fists balling up in her lap. "Has everyone in this hotel gone completely crazy?"

James turned to Michelle, ignoring Alison's outburst. "You stay here with your friend and lock the door behind me. I'm going to go see what happened downstairs and find my cousin. Don't open up for anyone but me. Okay?"

"I don't know if I can bear a minute being apart from you," Michelle cried, burying her face against the crook of his neck.

"I know, love, but we have to know what's going on down there. It breaks my heart to see you cry. Dry your tears, I'll be back soon."

"Oh my *God*," Alison wretched from her seat, watching the scene with obvious disbelief. "Are you guys on something?"

James and Michelle walked, hand in hand, to the door. "I love you," he whispered against her lips before giving her a tender goodbye kiss.

"And I love you."

* * *

James decided not to wait for the elevator and ran down the seven flights of stairs until he was in the lobby of the hotel. Mad chaos surrounded him, half-dressed men and women shrieking and sprinting, chased by the slow-moving, grunting undead.

Across the room, perched atop the shiny bar, James spied David. His cousin had a bottle of Jack Daniels in one hand, and a bottle of Jose Cuervo in the other, as he fended off a moaning onslaught of attackers. James picked up a wooden chair and smashed it against the hard floor, splintering it into small, sharp points of wood. He leaned over and picked up the largest and pointiest piece and charged the bar where his cousin was surrounded by man-eating monsters, their blue-lipped mouths clicking and clacking as they snapped their jaws, trying to get a piece of David's flesh.

Wading through the hungry crowd without incident, James jumped onto the bar beside his cousin, his thick stick held before him as a knight wields a broadsword. "Are you okay?" he shouted over the mutinous cacophony of the aggressors.

"For now," David said, hopping to the side to evade the crooked teeth of a snaggle-toothed spinster enemy. "Do you have a plan?"

James brought the chair leg down over a man's head. "Get upstairs, get Michelle and her friend, and get the hell out of dodge."

David smiled, his relief evident. "Thank God you want to help me rescue Michelle. I was worried you'd be a selfish prick about the whole thing."

"Umm," James said, uncomfortably. "I wouldn't dream of leaving her behind." He resolved to tell his cousin of his new relationship at a different time, when they weren't being chomped at by salivating, undead fiends.

A stiff hand, still locked in the throes of rigor mortis, swept James' feet out from the bar and he fell backward, off the oak counter, and onto a squishy, black, non-stick mat. The bartender cowered next to him, shielding his face with his arms, a cry of alarm escaping his trembling, spittle-coated lips.

"Shhhh," James sounded, putting his index finger to his lips. "You'll be okay. We need a gun."

The bartender nodded and pointed a shaking finger at the shelf to his left. James squinted and saw a shotgun and a box of shells hidden behind rows of glasses. "Why do you have a shotgun?" James asked, incredulous. "This isn't the Roadhouse, for God's sake!"

The bartender shrugged. "I didn't put it there. Are you going to use it or what?"

James thought about it for less than a second. He swiped the glasses onto the floor, the crashing tinkle temporarily muting out the howl of the hungry dead. He cracked the weapon, found the gun loaded, and handed the box of shells to the bartender. "Get ready to hand me more shells," he said, clicking the gun back together. "Ready?" James asked.

The bartender nodded.

James bellowed a battle cry and jumped to his feet, firing the shotgun at the first biting face he saw. The bullet drilled straight through the zombie's head, brain matter and tissue exploding out the exit wound. He saw an assailant attack David's ankle and fired the second shot through its head.

The bartender handed him two shells and James wasted no time in reloading the gun. "Follow me!" he yelled and made his way out from behind the bar and into the maddening, vicious circle of shambling-dead cannibals.

Out of the corner of his eye, James saw David scramble down from the counter top to fall in line behind the bartender. James emptied the shotgun's rounds through the eyes of two other growling gentlemen as he stormed toward the elevator, determined to get back to the seventh floor to assure himself Michelle was unharmed.

Their backs to the elevator door, the shotgun out of ammunition and no time to reload the firearm, the three men kicked and hit in an effort to protect themselves from the encroaching semicircle of bloodied, outstretched arms. When the automated door chimed open, they backed into the space, surprised and disgusted to find a middle-aged man leaning over a small woman, scooping bits of her entrails into his gnawing, filthy mouth. Bile erupted at the back of James' throat and he forced himself to swallow the rancid liquid as he swung the shotgun like a baseball bat and connected with the ravenous ghoul's chalky-white face.

A long strand of small intestine hung out of the zombie's mouth. He was no longer moving, his crushed skull resting against the eviscerated belly of his victim, enshrouded by the wet membranes of her seeping innards.

"Is it dead...again?" the bartender asked.

"Give me a shell. We'll make sure."

With steady hands, James loaded the shotgun and took careful aim, firing a bullet through the smashed cranium.

"What about the lady?" David asked, blanching when he looked at the macabre splatter of bone and gray matter painted on the elevator walls.

James barked a dry laugh. "He's eaten half of her insides. I think she's beyond our help. Hit the button for the seventh floor," James instructed David.

His cousin looked puzzled for a second. "We're on the ninth," he said.

"Forget our stuff. Let's get Michelle and her friend and get out of here."

David's finger hovered over the circular button labeled seven. "How do you know what floor Michelle's room is on?"

Looking away from his cousin, James muttered, "I rode up with her earlier. Now, press the damn button and let's get on our way before this guy's friends figure out how to get into the elevator."

Satisfied, David pressed the button.

The three men were silent, the elevator lifting them to the seventh floor, when a low keening wail echoed through the confined space. They looked at each other, trying to ascertain the noise's origin.

Undead arms pushed the man off her body and the dead woman sat up, her organs spilling out of her stomach to splat against the tiled floor.

"She's alive...again!" the bartender shouted, curling up into a small ball, and wrapping his arms over his head.

Without hesitation, James put the barrel of the shotgun against the woman's head, her teeth chattering in anticipation of human flesh, and pulled the trigger.

3

James pounded on Michelle's hotel room door. "Open up, it's me!"

"It's me?" David mimicked, his eyes tightening in suspicion.

James ignored his cousin's glare and looked around the empty hall, the shotgun in his grip. He heard the safety chain jangle and then the door creaked open, Michelle's blonde head peeking into the hall to take a look. "James? Is that you, my love?" she asked a second before throwing herself into his arms and pressing small, open-mouthed kisses along the length of his jaw.

"What the f…" David started, his epithet cut off by Alison grabbing his wrists and pulling him into the safety of the room. When the five of them were securely ensconced within the ivory walls of the luxury suite, David curled his fist into a ball and swung at his cousin.

James easily deflected the blow with the shotgun.

"How dare you!" Michelle screeched, kicking David in the shin.

David hopped up and down on his good leg, shaking his smarting hand in the air. "Someone give me an explanation about what the hell is going on in here?"

"Good luck," Alison slurred, slugging back a miniature bottle of gin and tossing the empty container with a clatter against half a dozen other small, empty bottles. "One minute she's coming to the room for a second to put on make-up, the next she's naked in bed with *him*. Can't figure it out for the life of me." Alison hiccupped and reached for another travel-sized bottle of liquor.

James swatted the gin from her hands. "Enough is enough. Michelle and I are soul mates. We can sort out the details of our love lives after we escape the undead hordes trying to turn us into their next supper. Let's calm down and figure out a way to get from this room to the parking garage without getting eaten alive, all right?"

"Oh, James, you're so smart," Michelle cooed, lifting up on her toes to kiss the tip of his nose.

"Oh, darling," James breathed, twirling a handful of Michelle's golden tresses around his finger. "You're so beautiful my heart skips a beat when I look at you."

"Oh, brother," David groaned as he watched the two love birds. He trudged over to where Alison leaned against the hotel mini-refrigerator and tore a half-opened bottle of bourbon out of her hand, then chugged the liquid. "Somebody shoot me," he croaked around the burning liquor.

"Are we going to try to escape or are we going to stay up here, cuddling and drinking, while the zombies come after us?" the bartender yelped, wiping a chunky piece of brain out of his hair and whipping it to the floor.

"I can't bear to look away from you, my sweet," James cried, dropping to his knees and burying his face against Michelle's thighs. "I love this woman!" he declared at the top of his lungs, tilting his head back to look up at her, droplets of joy leaking from his blue eyes and running down his love-struck face.

Alison yanked the shotgun from James' hand and pointed it at his head. "Shut up, you moron," she sputtered, swaying back and forth, sloshed out of her mind. "They'll hear you!"

David grabbed the shotgun by the barrel and tore it out of Alison's grasp. "Stop waving that thing around, you drunk," he growled, resting the shotgun against his shoulder, butt in his hand, barrel toward the ceiling.

James bounded to his feet and took possession of the gun. "This thing is useless to you, David. You've never shot a gun in your life."

David let James take control of the firearm. "True. I studied books through my misspent youth."

"Hello!" the bartender screamed, waving his hands above his head. "Can we focus on getting out of here?"

"Yes!" James, David, Alison and Michelle shouted in unison.

"I'll take the lead," James said after a moment of awkward silence. "Michelle, you and Alison go right behind me, followed by David and the bartender."

"Andrew," the bartender muttered.

"What?" James asked, irritated by the interruption.

"Andrew," the bartender said louder, his eyes shifting around the room. "My name. It isn't 'bartender'. It's Andrew."

"Fine," James said, "Michelle, you and Alison go right behind me, followed by David and *Andrew*," he said, stressing the bartender's name. "I only have two shots and we won't have time to stop and reload, so we need to move as fast as we can. We go down the stairs, through the lobby, and straight into the parking garage. David's blue SUV is on the first floor of the parking garage. We get in, we drive like hell, we get help. Got it?"

"How many are there?" Michelle asked, worry flooding her voice.

"I don't know, baby," James answered, running his fingers through her blonde locks. "We saw one dead lady come alive in the elevator after being snacked on. We need to assume everyone's been infected."

"There's about fifty of those things?" Michelle shouted in panic.

"Yes. We'll be okay. Just keep moving. They're slow and stupid," James said, giving Michelle a small smile before looking at the rest of the group. "You guys ready to do this?"

4

The shotgun was emptied before they reached the stairwell. "Run, run, run!" James shouted to his four companions as he busted through the exit door and raced down the first of seven flights of stairs. A pretty little undead thing in a mini-skirt looked up at them from the landing, bloody drool dripping off her bleached teeth, letting loose a horrendous groan. James heaved the gun through the air, connecting with her temple. The woman's body smacked against the concrete stairs with a *thwack*, her head splitting open, revealing a seeping fissure. After a second, she twitched and rolled over, her teeth snapping as she bit at the ankles running past her salivating mouth.

"She's still alive!" Michelle squeaked, sprinting past the animated corpse.

"Don't look at her! Keep going!" James shouted, skipping down the steps.

They maneuvered down the stairwell with no further incident. James tore through the door leading to the lobby, the mayhem more dramatic than on his first visit to collect David. The floor was slick with blood and other fluids James was too squeamish to identify and every person in sight was either feasting or being feasted upon, the occasional undead devouring parts of their own bodies if nothing else was available.

The five of them ran across the large room toward the heavy exit door to the parking garage. One of the zombies lurched at the group, tackling Andrew and tearing a large chunk out of his neck. Andrew screamed, his feet pumping as if he was still running toward safety instead of lying prone on the floor, a famished being atop him, swallowing hunks of his skin.

"Bartender down! Bartender down!" Alison yelled, reaching down and pulling her stiletto pump off her slender foot and beating the attacking ghoul about the neck and shoulders with it. David tried to grab Alison as he ran by, to drag her with him toward the garage, but she tripped and fell, her equilibrium unstable from the large quantities of alcohol she'd consumed.

"Andrew. My name's *Andrew*," the bartender said hoarsely as the thing bit off his lip.

A second zombie, a female, dropped beside Alison, pulling the inebriated girl's hand to her mouth and biting through her pinky, severing the finger at the base of the joint.

"Keep going, David!" James shouted, sparing a quick glance behind to see Andrew and Alison down, zombies munching on their limbs.

"I'm sorry!" David cried, then caught up with James and Michelle.

James opened the door to the parking garage and forced Michelle through the opening ahead of him, pointing at David's SUV. "The dark blue one. See it? Run and get in. The doors are unlocked. I'm right behind you."

Michelle hurried toward the oversized vehicle, James at her heels. Behind him, James heard David grunt and spun to see his cousin on the ground, undead hands wrapped around his legs, pulling him toward a gaping mouth.

"David!" James cried, gripping his cousin's wrists and pulling him toward the SUV.

"I've been bit, James. Save yourself!" David screamed.

James hesitated for a moment, looking at his cousin and then to where Michelle waited, frantic, in the passenger seat of the SUV.

"What are you waiting for, man? Run!" David shouted, his eyes rolling back in his head from pain as the zombie bit through his Achilles tendon.

"The keys, David. I need the keys!" James yelled, dropping David's hands.

As the ghoul pulled David back into the building, David managed to fish his keys out of his pocket and toss them to James. "Take care of her," he choked, his voice barely recognizable.

"I will," James vowed. "I love her."

James raced to the SUV and slid into the driver's seat. The engine hummed to life as he turned over the ignition, and minutes later, they were driving out of the parking garage, making their way down a winding, isolated road toward the nearest town to report the outbreak.

Michelle smiled at James and clasped his hand between hers. "I'm sorry about your cousin. David was a nice guy," she said after a moment.

"I'm sorry about your girlfriend," James replied, a bright smile plastered across his face.

"I love you. I can't wait to marry you, to spend the rest of my life with you."

"And I love you. You're my best friend, my everything," he gasped.

Without a care in the world, the couple kissed, their passion overwhelming them until James let go of the steering wheel, possessed by the insatiable need to touch his beloved's body. The vehicle skidded across the median and over the side of a cliff, plunging the lovers to their death at the bottom of a rocky ravine.

When the SUV finally struck bottom, it erupted in a blazing fireball that incinerated anything within its confines. Scorching the love sick couple to ash.

Epilogue

"*Cupido!*" Mars shouted from outside his son's one room flat at the base of Mount Olympus. His lover, Venus, stood next to him, her delicate foot tapping with impatience and ire.

Cupid opened the door slowly, his chubby arms raised above his head as he yawned. "Hello, father, mother," he said, a delighted grin slicing through his fleshy face.

"What have you done?" Venus stammered, pushing aside her son and stepping into the apartment, Mars a step behind her.

Cupid looked at the ground, faking shame. "It isn't *that* bad," he began, "Pluto had a meeting with Zeus and they sucked all of the zombies into the underworld. Earth and all her precious little humans are safe once again. It's no big deal. Honest."

Mars backhanded his son, hurling the overweight bundle against the wall. Cupid slumped on the floor, cowering from his angry father. "You are a menace," Mars snarled, his powerful features blotted with rage.

Cupid touched a chubby finger to the cut at the corner of his mouth. "Does this mean we aren't going to have a father-son day in Hades after all?"

BLOODY HEARTS FOR MY VALENTINE

KEITH ADAM LUETHKE

"**D**o you remember the day I asked you to marry me? It was this time last year on Valentine's Day. That was a terrific day. I rented that row boat and we ate lunch on the river. And me, stupid me, dropped the ring into the water. Do you remember? Of course you do, you must. I jumped in after it, and my clothes were soaked all day, but I was happy. We were happy. And that engagement ring sparkled even brighter. It makes me feel better knowing you're still wearing it," he said, and buried his head into his hands.

Across the bedroom, Lacy, his future bride to be, was tied to four corners of the bed. Her flesh was gray. Her gums and teeth were black. A gaping hole in the side of her chest showed parts of her rib cage and maggots squirmed in and out. And, worst of all, her once sky-blue eyes were now a milky white. She thrashed her limbs but couldn't break free of her bonds. Flies buzzed around her head and flew in and out her ears.

"What can I do for you? What will ease your pain?"

She gave a single groan and gnashed her teeth at him.

"You're hungry," he said, and went to the corner of the room and grabbed a green backpack. "I'll see what I can find. I won't be long."

He turned on the television for her before leaving the room. Newscasters were babbling on about the end of the world. How the dead had rose to claim the living and what the Army, Marines, and National Guard were doing to stop them. He made sure not to close the door all the way because she didn't like it when he did that. Well, when she was alive, she didn't, now, it didn't seem to bother her that much, but he did it out of habit.

"I'll be back soon, honey."

He walked out of the apartment and locked the door behind him.

The streets were a mess of wrecked cars and dead bodies either being eaten by crows or the living dead. He hadn't seen anyone like him in a week and was beginning to think everyone had escaped.

"Don't worry, honey. I'll find someone for you. I won't let you starve to death," he said to himself, looking back at the place he called home for almost five years.

He unzipped the backpack and withdrew a machete and a police issue service revolver. The cop had been kind enough to hand over the gun after Malik chopped off his arm. His fiancée had taken her time chewing away the flesh from the limb and even snapped the bones and sucked down the marrow. His only regret was that the rest of the officer had gotten away. He'd followed the blood trail to the end until it stopped at a gas station at the end of the block. He never dared to venture into that area though, as the roar of a singing chainsaw kept him at bay.

Ready for action today, he shouldered the backpack and went on his way.

The first zombie he ran into was munching on the head of a boy whose legs were torn from the knees.

Malik brought his machete across the zombie's neck, slicing through flesh, tendons, and bone. Dark blood spurted from the wound. The head was hanging from sinew so he struck again, severing the head from its shoulders. He kicked the head down the road and whistled a hapless tune as he continued on his way. Other zombies spotted him and took the up the hunt to consume his warm flesh. He quickened his pace, kicking the head harder and sending it flying down the road. The zombies lurched forward, shuffling after him as fast as their rotting limbs could carry them. As he continued, he spotted where he wanted to go; a suburb neighborhood consisting of five large houses and a dead end.

One of the zombies, a man wearing a faded 'Shell' hat, got close enough to rake his long fingernails across his back.

He spun around and planted the machete's blade through the hat and down its cheek. The zombie's head was split down the middle and it crumpled over like a puppet losing its strings.

He ran to the nearest house and banged on the door.

"Help me, please! I'm being attacked!"

He waited for a response. Inside, the house was quiet and nothing stirred.

The few zombies which had followed him shuffled onto the overgrown lawn and came after him.

He ran to the next house and the next, banging and screaming for aid until a slender, strawberry blond answered the door and let him inside.

* * *

Kelly rocked back and forth, shivering. The house was extremely cold for February and she didn't take well to it. Her family had moved on when the local police wanted to get everybody in town to the fire department. She had hid under her bed when they came, and had cried as her parents called out for her to no avail. But she couldn't join them. She wouldn't. She'd urged them the day before to stay behind, to fight off the growing zombie hordes, and survive like they'd always do together. Only they didn't agree. They saw protection in numbers, and when the police came, they quickly joined them. She didn't regret going with them then. The house was quiet and she could finally get enough peace and quiet to get some reading done. But as the days slipped into weeks, she grew tired of the solitude and struggled with leaving the house and attempting to reach the fire station on her own. She packed her backpack with canned goods and found the longest, sharpest kitchen knife in the house to join her quest.

Today, the day she planned to leave, a man being hunted by a handful of zombies, ran into her neighborhood and banged on her door. He didn't look dangerous so she let him in, and it was the biggest mistake of her teenage life.

* * *

"Thank you," Malik said. "I didn't think anyone else was left."

Kelly locked the door behind her.

"We're not safe here. They'll break down the door now that they know we're in here."

"Yes, you're right. We should deal with them right away. Are you alone?"

The question caught her off guard. "My mother's asleep upstairs. Let me go wake her up."

As she darted around the man and headed for the stairs, a loud *thump* struck the door, it was followed by another and another as the zombies outside tried to claw their way in, the door already giving way under their combined weight.

"Get your mother and let's get out of here. Do you have a car?"

"I...no, we don't have a car."

"Go upstairs," he ordered, "I'll deal with them."

She raced up the steps quickly and headed for her mother's room where she kept her backpack and the knife. Downstairs, she heard gunfire and hungry moans.

"Hurry up, girl. I'm running out of bullets!"

She slipped through the backpack's arm loops and carried the knife downstairs. When she reached the bottom of the stairs, she saw that the front door was torn in half, and dozens of walking corpses poked through, eager to get inside.

He spotted her and motioned for her to join him.

"Is there a back door?" he asked.

She raced down the steps and into the kitchen. "This way, follow me."

He fired the rest of his bullets, splitting a few skulls in the crowd just before they broke completely through the door.

"Where's your mother?"

"Hurry up," she called to him.

He ran after her. They trekked through the kitchen, living room, and to a sliding glass door.

"Through here," she ordered, and pushed the door open.

The zombie horde trampled into the house, knocking over family pictures on the walls, fouling the air with a rancid stench, and ceaselessly following the pair.

They ran into the backyard and into the woods bordering the home. The dead chased after them, but once they reached the forest, they were slowed down by the dense underbrush.

"Let's get onto the road. I know a safe place to go."

They crept out of the woods and found the road without a problem.

"What's your name anyway?" she asked.

"I'm Malik, pleased to meet you."

"I'm Kelly, likewise," she said. "Where do you have in mind? Is it the fire department?"

"No, I don't know where the fire department is. What happened to your mother?"

"I was by myself. I just said that so you wouldn't think I was alone. My mother and father left a while ago. They went with the police to the fire department. I stayed behind. I thought it was safer. I was going to find them today when you came."

"Well, I'm glad I found you in time then. Do you mind coming with me? My wife's sick and needs medicine. I was searching for some when I got surrounded. I have food and water there, too, and the place is safe, they can't get us there."

"I don't think I should. My parents probably miss me."

"Please, I want to go with you, but I need to see to my wife. Maybe if she feels better we could go to the fire station together."

"That sounds okay, I guess."

He led her to a brick apartment complex and they climbed three floors of stairs.

"Shouldn't we look for some medicine first?" she asked, confused.

"Not yet. I think she'll perk up when she sees you. We haven't had company for a long time."

Kelly put her kitchen knife into her belt. He unlocked the door for her and let her inside. She walked into the living room and covered her nose with her hand.

"Oh, wow, what's that smell?"

Malik locked the door. "Honey, I'm home."

A low grunt came from the bedroom.

He watched Kelly take off her backpack and put it on the floor. She faced away from him and was looking around at the messy apartment.

"When was the last time you cleaned this place?"

She wasn't paying attention as he put the gun to her head and pulled the trigger.

The bullet bore through her skull and popped out her left eye socket. She tumbled to the floor, leaking crimson.

He walked over her body, careful not to step on her.

"I'm sorry," he told her and said a silent prayer.

From the bedroom came a low moan. His wife was hungry. He took Kelly by the wrists and dragged her down the hallway. Blood leaked out of her shattered eye socket, making a long slick river of crimson on the floor. He opened the door and tossed her inside.

His wife grunted and thrashed in her bonds.

"Hi, honey, look what I brought you. Are you still hungry?"

She jerked back and forth and snapped her jaws.

He yanked Kelly onto the bed and pushed her beside his wife. Once the body was within range for her to take a bite, she did something strange. She sniffed the corpse and jerked her head back.

"What's wrong with it? She's fresh. I just shot her a minute ago."

The zombie made no more advances on the dead body.

"Dammit, you're not going to waste her. She was a descent kid. Don't tell me I just killed her for nothing."

His wife slumped back in bed and produced a low guttural moan.

Sighing, he pulled the body off the bed and sat her down against the wall. A long serrated kitchen knife fell from her belt.

He picked it up and put it on the dresser beside his machete.

"You want me to cut her up like I did with the last one, don't you? You know, you're getting really picky lately."

He snatched the machete and grabbed the dead girl by her strawberry blond hair. The first swing chopped into her neck, creating a two inch gap. He chopped again and again as blood and bits of flesh splattered his clothes and seeped into the rug. Once her head was off, he tossed it to his wife. It landed beside her own head, close enough for her to munch on the appetizer. But instead of sinking her teeth into a chewy morsel, she ignored it.

"What is wrong with you?"

He cut off an arm and severed a leg. He offered both limbs to her as gifts but they were refused.

"Dammit!"

He threw the machete against the wall in frustration.

"You need to eat something, please, honey, do it for me."

She gave a hungry moan in reply.

Malik grabbed the knife from the dresser and stabbed his corpse in the chest. He cut through the sternum, broke through the rib cage, and pulled out the heart. To his astonishment, it was still warm. He sat beside his wife and offered her the bloody heart.

"Here, eat this."

His wife jerked her head forward, tearing the heart from his hand and chewing on it with pure ecstasy.

"You liked that, didn't you?"

She licked the blood from her lips and gave another long moan.

"You're still hungry. Why don't you eat the rest of her?"

He shoved the severed head at her but she wouldn't touch it.

"Fine, you want hearts, I'll get you some fucking hearts. My baby isn't going to starve, no way."

He picked up his machete and the knife.

"I'm going to go clean up, then I'll go out again. That girl said something about a fire station not far from here. There should be more people inside there. I'll check the maps and the phone book in the living room before I go."

She grunted her approval.

"I love you, dear."

He blew her a kiss and changed out of his bloody clothes. Within ten minutes he was ready, armed, and willing to kill again.

* * *

The fire station was two miles away and surrounded by zombies. The way there was easy. Malik only had to use a handful of bullets and the machete took care of the rest. He looked up the fire station in the phone book and used his local map to find the exact location. Everything was going smoothly until he discovered the place crawling with at least a hundred dead freaks. Some ceaselessly beat on the doors while others paced back and forth, waiting out the inhabitants within. He needed a plan to get inside if he was going to get to them.

Circling around the perimeter, he spotted a truck with a zombie hunched over a man in a flannel shirt. Upon closer investigation, he discovered it was a woman gorging herself on a long haired man slumped over the driver seat. Had the world been what it once was, he would've thought she was doing something besides tearing out his lower intestine and stuffing it into her gore-speckled mouth.

"Hey, ugly, you want some fresh meat?" he called to her.

She tore her attention away from the corpse and slumped out of the truck. She shuffled toward him, dripping bloody chunks from her mouth. Malik waited until she got closer and shot her in the face. Her head exploded like confetti.

He went to the truck and searched the disemboweled man for his keys. Both of his pockets were empty. From the corner of his eye, he saw the keys already in the ignition.

"You poor bastard, I bet you almost made it out of here."

He dragged the man out and slid behind the steering wheel. The seat of his pants got wet as he sat in a pool of cooling blood.

"Oh, shit, that's gross."

He tried to ignore the wetness creeping through his jeans and twisted the key in the ignition. At first, the truck grumbled and black smoke poured from the exhaust. He tried a second time and the engine turned over and started.

"All right, now here we go."

He put it in gear and headed for the fire station. Once he was about a hundred feet from the building, he revered the engine and honked the horn.

The zombie horde turned to look at him, their vacant eyes staring at him with keen interest. They moved together with a shuffling gait and headed for the truck.

"Come on, you slow fucks, come on."

Once they were far enough away from the building, he released the break pedal and slammed on the gas. The truck plowed into the undead crowd of rotting flesh, knocking a handful to the pavement, and crunching the remains under the tires. He drove straight through them and didn't bother stopping, picking up speed as he headed for the entrance to the fire station.

Someone peered out the front window and quickly moved. He raced for where the figure was and braced himself for the impact.

The truck crashed through brick and glass, creating a sizable hole in the building and curling the hood of the truck up like crumpled tinfoil.

He noticed a limp hand sticking out from the rumble and a wicked grin appeared on his face. He was completely unharmed.

He leaped out of the totaled vehicle and raced through the entrance he'd made. Inside, the fire station was a mess of broken glass and pieces of brick. He found a vacant room with an open door. Hurried voices came from the other side.

He kept his handgun pointed toward the doorway and advanced.

"Help me, please. I'm hurt," he groaned. "Please, I'm bleeding to death."

The voices fell silent, then footsteps raced away. He darted through the door and witnessed two people running down a hallway. One was a heavy set man, the other a woman.

His first shot dug into the man's upper thigh, bringing him down. The woman turned back and cried, "Please, don't kill us. We surrender."

He quickly advanced on them. The man was bleeding heavily from the gunshot and cursed at him. The woman was older than he expected and had fine wrinkles on her face.

"I didn't mean to shoot you. I thought you were one of them."

"Bullshit, you fucking asshole. You piece of..."

Malik interrupted him by firing a bullet into his stomach, and another one in the side of his neck for good measure. The woman screamed and wrapped her arms around the dying man as he bled out and grew lifeless.

"Get up. You're coming with me."

"You're a monster. Why are you doing this to us? He was my husband."

"Hurry up, lady, or you'll be next on the list."

She slowly stood up and raised her hands in surrender.

"Do you have a car somewhere?"

She didn't answer at first.

"Do you have a car?" he repeated.

She sucked in her lips so he shot her in the shoulder.

The woman cried and bled. "Yes, we do. It's down the hallway and in the garage."

"Okay, lead the way."

She gripped her shoulder and wept as she forced herself to walk on weak legs. He followed her closely, the gun trained on her head. Behind them, the corpse of her husband stirred. He shoved her forward, turned, and sent a bullet into the newly formed zombie's head.

"How close are we?"

"It's...not far," she sobbed, and led him to a thick double door. "Through here."

"Open it," he ordered.

She pushed through the door and revealed the garage.

"The car's in there. It's all gassed up and ready to go. Just take it. You don't need me."

He sneered and brought the gun across the side of her head, the blow hard. She collapsed on the floor, unconscious.

"You're wrong, you know. I need you more than you know."

He carried her to the only car in the garage, a sleek black Mercedes. The keys were sitting on the dashboard and it had a full tank of gas just like she said. He shoved her into the passenger seat and smashed her head in again just in case she woke up.

There was a garage door opener on the console and he pressed one of the black buttons. The garage door lifted, revealing dozens of zombies.

"Shit!"

He started the engine and drove toward the crowd, but he didn't get enough speed and the zombies quickly overwhelmed him. They pawed at the glass and pounded on the Mercedes with their rotting fists. He twisted the wheel and forced them backward. Soon, he made his way through them and onto the road. Before long, he was driving far away from the fire department and towards home.

* * *

"Honey, I'm back!" Malik called as he dragged the unconscious woman through the doorway. Just as he locked the door, his victim moaned. Instead of striking her a third time, he continued to pull on her until he reached the bedroom.

His wife struggled with anticipation when he walked in. He dropped the body and turned the television off.

"Happy Valentine's, baby. I brought you another one."

The woman's eyes fluttered open. She looked at him first, then the zombie tied to the four posts of the bed, and then saw Kelly's dismembered corpse, especially the head, and cried out, recognizing the face immediately.

"My baby... What have you done to my baby girl?"

He paused suddenly. "You're her mother?"

The woman leaped forward, knocking him over. She dug her fingernails into his eyes, pressing them in deeply.

Malik screamed as the nails popped his corneas. He managed to punch her in the face before she could reach his brain matter. Sightless, he crumpled to the floor, screaming in agony. Unknown to him, the woman snatched his machete and swung it at his head. The blade bit deep into his temple and cracked his skull. He slumped over, motionless.

She looked around at the pieces of her daughter and wept.

The zombie strapped to the bed grunted and made wet smacking noises with her mouth. The woman stared at Kelly's torso and her missing heart. With rage filling her, she focused her attention on the man who brought her to this terrible nightmare place.

"You want him?"

The zombie seemed to nod her head as it jerked back and forth.

The woman yanked the machete out of Malik's head and swung the blade down into his chest. After a grueling ten minutes of cutting muscle and breaking bones, she found the prize she was looking for--his heart. She tossed the warm organ to the zombie and left the room.

She could hear the dead woman feasting on the heart greedily, tearing each valve apart and sucking down the warmth. A part of her wanted to go back into the room and finish off the poor soul, but another just wanted to leave.

She chose the latter, racing out of the apartment complex and all the madness it conveyed.

It was the worst Valentine's Day she ever had.

ONE TOO MANY

MICHAEL D. GRIFFITHS

It was all the same on every channel. Normal programming had ceased and was now replaced with endless speculation as to what was causing the massive plague of hungry, walking corpses. No one had any answers and things were only getting worse.

David always had a hard time believing the zombies would take over so easily, like he had grown up seeing in the movies, but somehow it was happening, and there wasn't much anyone could do to stem the tide.

His house was a deathtrap, with its sliding glass doors and multiple windows. His only bit of luck was that he had taken the situation seriously early on and had maxed out his credit cards by buying supplies.

Supplies which were already loaded into the back of his forerunner. A good thing, too, for less than twenty-four hours later, all credit cards became useless.

David knew a good place to hole up. It was one of his favorite campsites and it should be somewhere he could be able to hold out for a while. It had cliffs and water, as well as wide-open fields where it would be hard to sneak up on a man. He figured as long as he had water, he had a chance, and zombies might be able to do a lot of things, but they couldn't surprise him halfway up a cliff.

He only had two problems.

One was that he was married to Tracy. His second problem was his girlfriend, Jessie.

He knew he was a bastard for cheating on his wife, and it had happened a lot more than once. He still loved Tracy, but he had to admit that he loved Jessie, too.

He was so screwed.

The affair had been going on for nearly a year now. There had been some close calls, but he'd never been caught. Now here he was, about to leave with Tracy, when he got a frantic text on his phone. It had said, "Please help me, they're already walking around outside. I can't make it to my car. I'm so scared."

He felt like the jagged claws of the walking dead were already pulling his mind apart. He loved Jessie and couldn't leave her to die. But how could he tell Tracy that they had to pick her up before heading to the campsite? Even if he somehow could pull that off, how could he live out in the woods with his wife and his mistress? Rubbing his forehead, he almost laughed. After a year of being careful, it took a plague of flesh-eating zombies to expose his secret.

Damn, David thought as he snatched up his rifle, *what am I going to do*? He patted the Desert Eagle on his hip. After scanning his front yard, he figured there would never be a better time to go. It would be dark in an hour and he wanted to be well away from the city before then.

After taking a long pull of his beer, David finished it off and then quickly opened another. He was still putting off leaving, putting off heading into the growing horde of undead, but especially putting off telling Tracy about their first stop. He hoped getting a few beers into his system would help him stay calm, and now even though he might have had too many, he wasn't about to stop.

"There are more out there," Tracy said with a quiver in her voice. "Don't you think we should go?"

"Yeah, I was thinking the same thing," he said as he shoved his open beer bottle into his back pants pocket. "I want you to grab that last crate and go straight to the car. No matter what happens, once you're inside the car, you don't get out. Got it?"

She nodded that she did. Peeking out the door, he saw his neighbor, Larry, stumbling painfully close to David's car. The man was now quite dead. "One of them is close. I'm gonna go take him out. As soon as I do, it's go time." He didn't care that the zombie was his neighbor. He'd always hated Larry anyway.

He cracked open the door carefully. Taking aim with his gun, he smiled when his shot was on target.

"Hot damn, a head shot. Okay, Tracy, let's go!"

He hadn't counted on how the noise of the gunshot would attract other walking corpses. A foul moaning filled the air as half a dozen zombies began to shuffle towards them. Tracy uttered a quick shriek and raced for the car. David had to go to the far side, but another neighbor, that jerk who always played heavy metal at three in the morning, was lumbering towards him. Streaks of gore covered his Iron Maiden shirt. He was snapping his mouth like the dead metal head already had his teeth in David's flesh.

David stopped to fire. He aimed for the head and missed completely. Now the zombie was too close for him to make it to the car door. He shot again, but the bullet went too low and took the freak in the side of the neck. It stumbled back, but despite its neck losing a quarter of flesh, the bloody zombie kept coming at him. Tracy began to scream his name as the zombie closed on him.

David didn't have time for another shot. The zombie lurched at him as the other ones grew closer. He had no choice; he had to use his rifle. But the corpse grabbed it. Soon he was pushing David against the side of his car, while teeth snapped inches from his face. The beer bottle in his back pocket shattered against the car and showered his pants with glass and cold beer. He could see the others were almost on him. He figured if even one more of them joined the fray he was done for.

"Damn it!" he shouted as he pushed with all his strength. The zombie stumbled back, lost his footing, and fell. This also caused the zombie behind it to stumble and fall. His Desert Eagle was out of his holster, and a second later, he clicked the safety off. Another zombie, in an EMT uniform, was almost on him, but this time he didn't miss, and its head exploded into a red fountain of bone and brain matter. Abandoning his rifle, he got into the car. Tracy locked the doors instantly. He fumbled with the keys as flopping hands smeared bloody handprints down the windows with meaty smacks. He had the key in the ignition when his own rifle hit the driver side window, forming a spiderweb of cracks. He and Tracy shared a brief, wide-eyed look and then the car was racing away from the undead crowd, leaving more mangled bodies in its wake.

* * *

The walking dead were everywhere and they couldn't make it a block without seeing at least one. More often however, it was far more than that and in many places they gathered in the dozens.

Passing through their neighborhood, they hit a main road. David wanted to drive faster, but this wasn't possible. The roads were clogged with abandoned vehicles, victims, and zombies. "This isn't good," he said quietly. Tracy didn't bother to reply.

After driving another mile, David was forced to come to a stop. A semi had rolled over onto its side and was blocking most of the road. There might have been enough room to get around it on its right side, but a delivery truck blocked the area.

"Why did he park there?" Tracy sounded like she was three seconds from completely losing it.

"He's probably dead," David said, but was already checking his gun. "I'm going to have to move the delivery truck."

"Are you nuts? You'll be killed!"

"What other choice do we have? We need to make it to the woods. Do you wanna walk through all this?"

She had no answer for that, but David was already scanning the area. This stretch of the road was removed from residential areas. Looking around, he only saw three zombies and they were still far off, but were also already moving towards them.

Checking his gun one more time, he jumped out of the car and sprinted for the delivery truck. He made it safely, but before he could enter the cab, he heard a sick, tearing sound. Fearing the worst, he wasn't disappointed. Behind the driver's seat, the deliveryman was on his back while two zombies tore at his mangled guts. Blood and viscera was everywhere, splashing the once pristine white boxes with strings of gore and clinging bits of bloody flesh.

The sight startled him and gave the zombies enough time to spot David. With wet groans they lurched towards him. He might have cried out, but the first one's head was exploding before he realized he was firing. He was aiming at the second one when something grabbed at his leg.

Tracy was screaming.

Looking back, he was just in time to see the thing's teeth about to close on his calf. Wide-eyed with horror, he pressed the pistol against the zombie's skull and fired. Blood and brains sprayed over his pants, painting them a sick red.

Now however, the second zombie was on him. It stumbled and they both went toppling out of the truck. His elbow smacked the unforgiving pavement and sent his pistol flying from his grip.

The zombie was now on top of him. The zombie opened its mouth, and a stream of gore fell onto David's cheek. It was trying to bite at his face, but he quickly slammed his forearm into its throat. Tracy was screaming something, and he didn't need to understand her words to know that other walking corpses were approaching. He could hear their moaning growing louder.

Worse yet, he could hear one of them shuffling up behind him. But he had more immediate issues. The zombie was clawing at him as it tried to clamp its teeth down on his arm. With his free hand, David began to fumble for his utility tool. His palms were slick with blood and he was struggling to pull it out of its case.

He cried out when another zombie grabbed a fistful of his hair and jerked his head back.

He wasn't going to make it!

That was when he heard the squeal of breaks and his skull was suddenly on fire as the zombie that had his hair went flying over him, taking a half inch of his scalp with it. It hit the other zombie off balance and that was all David needed to pull the pliers free. He flipped it open, like a butterfly knife, and before the zombie that was over him could recover, he stabbed it in the eye with one end of the tool. This wasn't enough to kill it, but David kept pushing. He used the pliers to force the thing off of him. He kept it up until the walking corpse finally went limp.

David thought it was Tracy who came to his rescue and was surprised to hear a man's voice say, "Stay down!"

Shots from David's gun rang out, and the other zombie, the one that still clenched a fistful of his hair, was taken down. For a moment, David stayed where he was, just trying to catch his breath, but soon he was scrambling to his feet. Yet, before he could get a good look at his rescuer, the man was screaming.

A zombie had his rescuer from behind and was biting out his throat. The man was already dying when David fired his gun. He gave each of them a headshot and then rushed back to the truck. More zombies were approaching, but David didn't let this slow him down. There were no keys in the ignition, but he found them in the center of the driver's pooling guts. Just when he went to grab them, the driver's hand shot out and closed on his wrist.

"Damn it!" David cried out, pulling away. Despite his mangled body, the driver was trying to close his teeth over David's arm and he was forced to use another bullet on the ruined corpse.

With keys in hand, he rushed over to the driver's seat, only to be confronted by yet another zombie in the doorway. "Damn, why are there so many around here?" he snarled through clenched teeth. When he went to shoot the thing in the face, the gun just clicked.

"Crap!" he shouted as he kicked the zombie in the chest. It fell backwards and landed on its back, but David saw there was already another behind it. His hands fumbled with the bloody keys, and finally drove them home.

Gnarled hands were reaching in for him as he tried to get the big truck into gear. Then, with a roar, he threw it into reverse. Both zombies were knocked off their feet and he made sure they didn't get up again, and feeling their heads explode under the tires was the best thing to happen to him all day.

After running over another three zombies in the road, David abandoned the truck and sprinted back to his car and a frantic Tracy. A few seconds later, the car rushed through the passage he had made and continued to head through town.

* * *

"Oh my God, they're everywhere," Tracy gasped. "How could this have happened so fast?"

"I don't know," he said softly as he swerved the car around a group of zombies already eating a man. Their victim wasn't finished screaming as he was pulled apart.

They rode in silence, letting the horror speak for itself, until somehow they made it through the center of town. "We have one more stop to make before we head out to the campsite."

"What...what do you mean?" she was nearly hysterical.

"Jessie sent me a text. She's all by herself. She needs someone to get her."

"What, are you crazy? Doesn't she know anyone else? Why can't someone else get her?"

"She's our friend, Tracy. We can't just let her to die."

"She isn't my friend. I don't even like her. And I don't want to risk my life for her!"

"Fine, you can stay in the car."

"What's going on, David? Why do you want to rescue her? Why is she so important to you? Why aren't you worrying about Matt and John?"

"I did contact them. They're supposed to be meeting us out there. Jessie doesn't have anybody and she's on the way. Do you want to be the only girl out there with a bunch of men?"

It must have been the right thing to say, for she stayed silent as he turned down the road leading to Jessie's house. When he looked over, he saw Tracy staring out the window while her white knuckles flexed over the armrests.

Jessie lived in a new housing complex at the edge of town, but the zombies were taking it over like everyplace else. They passed a police car awash with blood. On the street, nearly a dozen zombies were fighting over the few remaining pieces of the officer. "We're losing," he said in a whisper with his dying breath.

Tracy looked like she wasn't sure if she should be horrified or furious as he neared Jessie's house. David finished his new beer and opened another. He took a long pull before he reached her driveway.

As he neared, David said. "Lock the doors as soon as I leave. I'm gonna keep the motor running." Around ten zombies began to lurch their way. "Shit, they've already seen us. I might as well honk the horn for her so she knows we're here."

He backed the car into her driveway, getting as close to her front door as he could. They had only waited five seconds and already the zombies were nearing them. "Where is she? Is she too stupid to run out, I say we leave her here," Tracy said as she crossed her arms over her chest.

"She's probably too scared," he said while opening his door to leave the car. One of the zombies was at Jessie's front door, slamming against it with its fists. He paused, aimed, and went for the headshot. Its forehead jerked back and the twice-dead body toppled violently to the walkway.

"Jessie!" he shouted as he ran up the front steps, jumping over the fallen zombie with half its head missing. After quickly trying the doorknob, he took a step back and kicked it open. He slowed at the threshold, not knowing what might be waiting for him.

"Jessie, baby, you okay? Jessie!"

On the floor was a large bloodstain. He nearly lost it when her little dog went flying by him, heading outside, barking continuously.

"Jessie come on, we have to get out of here!" He heard something moving in her bedroom. Rushing towards the bedroom door, he said, "Baby, I'm here, didn't you hear me honk? We need to get going."

Her back was facing him and he moved towards her and grabbed her arm. As she spun around, a spray of blood hit him first. For he saw to his horror that one side of her throat had been torn out, the teeth marks apparent.

He was so shocked to see her like this that he hesitated.

She didn't.

Her teeth clamped down on his forearm, and with a savage tear, she took a huge piece of flesh out of him. With a horrified shout, he pushed her away and started running.

"Oh, no, oh, no. It's not true, it's a mistake."

He reached the living room just as the first zombie began to enter the house. From outside, he heard the sound of his car pulling away. He shoved the zombies aside and stopped at the front door.

"Oh, Tracy, no, don't do this to me! Come back!" he screamed after the car, but all he got were flashing taillights as Tracy slowed to turn the corner. Then she was gone.

He brought up the Desert Eagle and was able to take out two zombies before Jessie came up behind him. David was still screaming when she sank her teeth into the side of his neck.

SHE LOVES ME, SHE LOVES ME NOT

MARC WIGGINS

"Fuck you, Dad," Sean said again. The first time was out of jest but now a growing bitterness lined his voice.

"Come on, boy," replied a grainy voice after a long hackle. "Can't you take a joke? I'm just busting your balls. I didn't raise you to be a pussy."

Sean stood at the bathroom sink while shaving with his straight-edge razor. That's what his old man always used and he found himself liking the feel of the blade, too. It wasn't because he admired the old bastard, chalk it up to genetics. Besides, he had no fond memories of the man when he was a boy, no recalled moments of himself as a child watching his daddy shave and wanting to copy him. No, there was nothing to equate their shared preference or any of the other numerous traits he got from him. It had to be in the genes.

"What the fuck are you talkin' about? Mom brought me up. You didn't show up again until I was thirteen." *And it was bad timing*, he thought to add but didn't.

"I had shit to do, kid," was the easy reply.

"Yeah, yeah, yeah," Sean leered back at him through the mirror. This was his dad and he loved him. He hated him, too. Most of what he knew about him was from his mother when he was a kid. She would only talk about him when she was drunk and that was often. Stories of his old man and Vodka went hand in hand. After her fourth or fifth glass, he'd hear how he was just like him, looks and all. Sean glared in the mirror and had to admit that much. He was his father, minus the gray hair and deep crevices in the forehead and laugh lines. Both of them had the face his mother regarded with both admiration and disgust.

"All I was saying," the gray version of him explained, "is that you can't trust those bitches. Watch your ass. And cover your pecker when you want to get it wet, or one of those bitches will own you. They're all cunning whores. Always calculating and plotting."

"You mean like with Mom? You should've worn a rubber," Sean accused.

Those eyes in the mirror turned dark at the recrimination, "Don't give me that, boy. I came back."

And that he did, Sean remembered. Three weeks after his thirteenth birthday.

"And don't forget, it was just in time to save you from that bitch." The older eyes continued. "Do I need to remind you of how I found you? What you were doing…"

That tone of condemnation and salvation nearly caused Sean to flinch and cut himself with his razor. His otherwise steady and creative hand with sharp objects was troubled with the memory. Not just *that memory*, but several memories, all exquisite and shameful.

It all really began one night when Sean was twelve. They both sat at the table like any other night. She just drained her sixth glass and he nursed a cherry cool aid while dutifully listening to her rants like he always did. He remembered specifically how it began at the end of her sixth drink. He used to always count her rounds while he sat there taking in her unique perspective on everything in the world, most of it revolving around his long gone, *deadbeat* father.

That sixth drink was the last one he observed with a child's eye. The emptied glass slipped out from her sloppy lips and clanked to the table. The ice cubes barely had time to settle when she poured her next. She didn't immediately pick it up. Instead, she stopped talking and stared at him. Her eyes were glassy and hinted with bloodshot, yet she seemed to have more command over her gaze on him than she normally would at this stage of her evening.

"Sean, you're growing up so fast. You remind me so much of your father…" she said in a tone starkly different than the harshness that marked her darkening mood so far. Her words were now soft and careful, though still slurred. "The good parts, you know," she followed with a cooing purr.

She took her drink and moved across the table to the chair next to him. Her hand, not the one holding her Vodka, eased under the table and touched him. He cowered at that and then again when she called him by his father's name.

His alarm, however, gradually eased and he began to stir while she continued to rub him and repeatedly call him by *that name*, each time with mounting passion and certainty. She knew he wasn't him and he knew. Nevertheless, that night, the first of many, ended in her bed.

He both loved and pitied her. She was everything to him and he'd do anything for her. On those nights, and they grew in frequency after he gained the skills to give her what she wanted, he learned the most profound love. If he had any friends back then, his secret was something he wouldn't share with them. They wouldn't understand.

Shame was an abstract concern until *he* came back. His first actual memory of his father, not those conjured from his mother's accounts, was on that night, three weeks after his thirteenth birthday. The man didn't knock on the door. There was no grand entrance, no embraces or tender greetings. No, the man had snuck in and Sean met him for the first time while he and his mother were in bed. She never saw him; she was too distracted by a mouthful of his young manhood. Sean had to lift his head for a better look past the bobbing of her dirty blond wig while the man walked over and stopped at the edge of the bed. He instinctively knew it was his father and didn't panic from the strange entrance. Their eyes locked for the first time.

She was right. His father did look just like him, only more self assured and fully grown. There was something else and Sean didn't see it until the man's eyes broke free and looked down at his mother. He wrinkled his nose at the smell of alcohol wafting through her mess of blond hair that rode up and down in excited rhythm. His features shifted into an expression that Sean's adolescent face had never known or formed. It was a look of hate, disgust and judgment.

His father never said a word. He simply glared at her while they continued on with their various acts of intimacy. His mother never took notice of him while she moaned and grinded away. Sean tried many times to close his eyes and pretend he wasn't there, but there he stood with his ominous stare each time he opened his eyes.

Just before Sean climaxed, his father turned and walked out of the room. After they were done, his mother breathlessly flopped to her side of the bed and giggled while referring to Sean by his father's name and telling him how good he was. She soon passed out, but the name she used seemed to echo throughout the room, or at least in Sean's head.

Sean didn't understand why his father didn't speak or stop him and his mother to announce himself. In fact, he didn't see the man again until the next time he and his mother were in bed. It was strange how the man had such good timing for his visits or why he chose to only come at those times and without comment.

There were many such visits.

Sometime later, his father finally came to visit Sean when he was alone in his own bedroom, after he left his mother's bed. That's when he finally heard his voice. During those first conversations, his father seemed nicer and more understanding. He didn't joke back then. His deep voice filled the darkness with confidence and reassurance. It told Sean that he didn't do anything wrong but his mother did and they had to fix the problem. At first Sean didn't think there was anything wrong but, over the course of several more visits, the voice convinced him otherwise. It told him what to do.

That was a long time ago and now Sean was a man. His father now lived with them. It had taken some convincing, but his mother finally came around to accepting the man back into their lives, though not happily so. Sean no longer made love to her and he didn't know if she or his father ever did. Like anyone else, he didn't want to think of those kinds of things about his parents. However, she was often moody and he sometimes wondered if it was because he had cut her off.

He had to be his own man.

"Are you with me, boy?"

"Huh?"

"Are you listening to me? Jesus Christ what's with you? Sometimes I think I'm talking to myself with you."

"Yeah, Dad. Hey, I don't want to talk right now. I have to get ready."

Sean heard the clank of ice cubes within a full glass of Vodka. He saw her in the mirror just as he was finishing up with his shave. The reflection of the bathroom doorway filled his mirror. His father slumped against one end of the door's frame while his mother stood as far away as she could on the other.

"So what are you going to do for them on Valentine's Day?" the soft but not quite feminine voice asked.

"I don't know, Mom. I've never had three girlfriends at the same time," Sean answered, wiping away remnants of shaving cream from his face.

"Well, I can't say I'm proud of you," his mother's voice said. "You shouldn't be playing the field and you should have only one girl at a time. But then again, you're just like your dad. One's not enough."

"Chip off the old block!" the deeper voice cried with pride. Sean wondered if he was just antagonizing his mother or if he was genuinely proud.

"I dunno. They're all nice girls and I feel bad. I can't decide which one's the best for me. I don't want to hurt any of their feelings." He was sincere as he buttoned his perfectly pressed white dress shirt and tucked it into equally considered slacks.

"You should pick one of them and get a really nice present for her. Let the other ones go," he heard her say.

"Fuck it, boy, take your time. Play the field. You're young and you've got time," the other voice countered. Again, Sean wondered, was he mocking her or was he serious?

As if to break up the possibility of another argument, Sean heard the heavy foot falls of construction shoes approaching along the hallway's wood floor. Matheson, his trusty handyman, appeared at the door between his parents.

Sean looked at him through the mirror, when the man said, "Hey, Sean. I'm done with the addition to the basement. You want to check it out before I take off?"

"Nah, that's okay." Sean said while fastening his leather belt. Matheson had worked for him for years. He was always meticulous. Sean knew he could trust him and he didn't have time for formalities.

"Okay, boss. See ya later." Disinterested shoes walked off through the hallway and out the front door, leaving his two parents at either end of the bathroom door. They stared back into his reflection, each continuing their opinions with wordless expressions.

Sean answered both of their mute advice, "Okay, I don't know what I'm going to do yet. But no one's going to get hurt."

He turned around and walked through the door into the hallway. *It's Valentine's Day*, he thought, *I don't want to blow it with any of them.*

His first girlfriend was Amber. He had met her in a grocery store parking lot. Charmed by his practiced lines, she was easy to pick up. She was his longest standing girlfriend. They had been going out for a little over seven months. She was feisty and he liked that about her but he knew she loved him by the way he was always able to calm her down. The only thing better than sex, is make-up sex.

The next girl was Becky. A very sweet and shy young woman, he couldn't resist introducing himself to her along the street about five months ago. It was almost too easy to convince her that she needed a ride so late at night. Of the three, he was the least sure about her. She always seemed to go along with whatever he wanted to do and he sometimes found that boring.

His most recent girlfriend was Susan. She was the youngest and he met her in front of a high school a few weeks ago. She was young and impressionable and he adored that about her. She always had this wide-eyed look about her while taking in his every word. He had so much more to teach her.

He loved them all and he knew they all loved him. But he knew his mother was right. He would have to choose. Which one of them would get his heart? He wanted something true and he was tired of playing the game. But which one would it be?

Just then he realized the answer. This was Valentine's Day and a gift was expected. A cheap thought formed in his mind. *What if I didn't get any presents?* he wondered. *Which one would love me, anyways?*

It was a crazy thought but it made sense. Which girl would love him more than the things he could buy her? That would tell him everything. He started humming to himself, pleased with his own genius. A solution only he could come up with and not from either of his parents.

He had a few minutes to kill before his first date; the first of three dates, all carefully planned that night. He was good at the game and he had gotten away with the crazy schedule so far. But by the end of tonight, he'd find out which one was his true love.

He went into the living room and grabbed the remote to turn on the television. To his dismay, the cable was out. He half heartedly flicked through a few channels that all returned the same dead screen. Under normal circumstances, he would have called the cable company to complain but he didn't have time. Instead, he moved to the couch and sat down, daydreaming about which girl would pass his test and thus fulfill his dreams.

She loves me, she loves me not, he bemused humorously. Tonight was going to be a big night.

While his mind went over the possible outcomes, he didn't pay attention to the sounds drifting in from outside. From varying distances, sirens wailed and sporadic gunshots peppered the air like muted firecrackers. Isolated instances of those sounds weren't so unusual for his neighborhood but Sean didn't care to think they were more frequent and intense than usual.

To further distract him, his parents came in. He watched their dark glassy reflections on the defunct television screen while they sat on the other end of the couch.

The clock chimed. It was time for his first date. Sean had no way of knowing it would be the last chime of the clock since power would go out within the hour. But for now, he was happy and sprung into action. Where had the time gone? He must have been in a daze. No wonder, he had a lot on his mind with such a big decision to make tonight.

He stood from the couch, straightening his shirt and slacks. "Showtime!" he announced. "How do I look, Mom?"

"You're very handsome. Please, dear, be a gentleman. Do the right thing."

A mocking snicker from his father erupted throughout the room. "What the hell are you talkin' about? Let the kid have his fun. Who wants to get pinned down with some hog? Once one of you bitches land a man, you blimp up and do nothin' but bitch and suck the joy of life out of the guy you trapped."

Sean sighed. He wasn't going to allow himself to get caught up in it with them again and he turned to leave.

The grainy voice continued. "Instead of worrying about my kid, why don't you get off your fucking ass and make yourself useful for once in your miserable life. Look at this shit hole! Looks like you haven't picked up a broom in years."

The criticism was dismissed by a sloppy clank of ice cubes within a glass as it tilted into tired lips.

"Bitch..." was the worn out conclusion.

A more upbeat, "Give 'em hell, boy!" carried with Sean as he left the room.

"Oh, shut up, you old bastard!" echoed his mother's slurring 'last word' through the kitchen as Sean made his way in.

Sean loved his mother and would never criticize her but his old man had a point. This place was long overdue for a good cleaning. He rarely thought to pitch in and help her out with the household duties. What little he managed to do seemed to be the only things that ever got done. His justification would be that he simply didn't have enough time to do more, given his busy schedule with the girls and he was the only one in the house who earned a paycheck.

He walked through the kitchen, a mess only slightly filthier than the rest of the house. All cups, dishes, utensils and cookware were exhausted into chaotic heaps in the sink, on the counters and stove, with several of them sprawled and discarded on the floor. Whatever foodstuffs left within them were long past rotten. Some were so ancient that they now seemed fused to their forgotten containers with varying shades of black, and no longer gave off any smell. The ugly odor in the room came from a greater assortment of leftover fast foods left to fester in their throwaway cartons or bags. Flies hovered over their more recent finds with sickly and bloated speed.

Sean completed his trip through the kitchen, passing a somewhat massive heap of garbage bags he kept meaning to put out. He kicked aside a paper container, letting week old Chinese noodles to spill out into a smear across the dirty tiled floor. Flies scattered and buzzed in angry protest.

He came to the door and paused to pass reassuring hands over his carefully greased hair and to double check the pristine arrangement of his starched shirt and slacks. A spot of noodle sauce tarnished the tip of one of his shiny black dress shoes and he bent down to rub it away.

With a smile, and now confident in his presentation, he knocked on the door that led into the basement.

There was no answer.

To Sean, this wasn't unusual. One thing all of his girlfriends had in common, they were shy. He opened the door and peered into the darkness. The only things visible were the first steps illuminated by the kitchen light. After that each one was progressively dimmer until midway down blackness swallowed everything.

"Yoo-hoo, Amber!" he teased while stepping into the darkness. She was his first date and she lived below in the first chamber to the right, directly off from the base of the stairs.

He was greeted with the scurrying of chains that were latched to the ankles of all his girlfriends. He wasn't surprised by the racket. He knew that to be the sounds of his ladies shuffling back to their cots so they could wait for him. They were all so easy going and giving to his every whim. He appreciated how they always made time for him, whenever he wanted. Each of his girls almost always patiently waited on her cot in anticipation while he made his rounds.

Sure there was the occasional argument but he was always able to soothe them into compliance.

He easily made his way down the steps, and slipped his hand into his pocket. In it, he gripped his folded, straight-edge razor. But this was Valentine's Day and he sincerely hoped he wouldn't have to bring it out, at least not until much later tonight after he made his choice. He had a hard decision ahead of him. Which one would be his true love? Which one would pass the test? Who among them would be the one he'd keep?

His mind was not yet ready to consider the fate of the other two. Breaking up was hard to do but it needed to be done. He sighed. But that wouldn't be until later tonight. At least the unfortunate two could enjoy one last quality evening with him.

The only other sad aspect was how disappointed Matheson would be when he found out his underground structures wouldn't be needed anymore. He'd really done a marvelous job at constructing the cubicles in the basement. The ankle grips and locks on the chains were top notch and he did a masterful job in ensuring that the bolts never loosened from the concrete, no matter how they could be wiggled and worked on. Oh, and the fourth cubicle he just worked so hard on. Well, *Se La Vie*. Sean was ready for a new chapter in his life.

Matheson was a God send. If it wasn't for him, he doubted he could juggle three women at once. Matheson was a handy guy to have around. Smart too. He was the one who gave Sean *the idea*. Just keep all three of them in the same place. It saved on time and expenses. God knew gas was too damn high nowadays to mess with all the traveling.

However, Matheson wasn't that great of a plumber and the toilet the girls shared constantly backed up. Still, he'd throw him a bone and have him build suitable accommodations in his bedroom for the true love he chose tonight. The bathroom up there worked just fine.

He was now completely engulfed in darkness midway down the stairs. He raised his hand to scrape his fingernails along the side of the wall and called out playfully. "Aaaambeeer, I'm coming to get you."

He liked to tease her and she was fun in how she always played along. She really could be convincing in how scared she acted when he *did* the boogeyman. He especially loved that wheezy tone in her squeals and pleas.

She was a good sport and made it so much fun. Maybe she'll be the one.

When he reached the final step, he became aware of something strange. By now, the rattling chains should have stopped with the girls already back on their cots. He knew, how they knew, that he didn't like the sound of them. He expected them to be in their place.

Three sets of chains still rang out in chaotic chime. More than that, there wasn't the hurried scatter that usually marked his entrance. Instead, the chains continued to scrape along the pavement in slow, lazy and broken bursts. They were still loud and underneath the echoing clatter, Sean thought he could hear something else. He wasn't sure, but were those the sounds of moans he heard?

His anger grew. Though he liked to play games, only he was allowed to make up the rules. No, whatever they were up to, he didn't like it. They would pay.

He was a generous man and allowed each girl twelve feet of chain as to give them enough freedom to the common toilet. His rage mounted. They knew the rules and he'd given them plenty of time to be where they were supposed to be. The first thing he taught each of them was to keep her chained foot motionless while she waited in her cot. Yes, he could forgive the unavoidable rustle while he had his way with each of them. But this was insulting. The metallic rustle continued to echo throughout the basement in contempt of his rules.

"You girls got some explaining to do," he icily warned while making his final step onto the basement floor and pulling the string to the overhead light. He was ready to charge at the first girl he saw but his brand new dress shoes slicked over a horrendous pool of blood that covered the smooth concrete surface. After a faltering dance, he fell over and landed hard into the red mess. There was so much of it that his impact ended in a small splash.

"God damn it," he groaned at the sting of his fall. "I told you women to clean up after the toilet!"

He looked down and realized he wasn't in a puddle of toilet water; the red not immediately registering with him. It was inconceivable there would be this much blood spilled on the floor. He didn't care what it was, he was pissed. His rules had been broken.

In a growing fit, he moved to get up. His palms slipped a little in the massive body of gore while he lifted himself to a sitting position. He examined himself. The entire front of his outfit was drenched and ruined, and he began to feel a wet stickiness wherever he saw red on himself.

"What the..."

Finally, he recognized the coppery smell. It was something he knew very well from other ex-girlfriends he'd kept down in the basement. *No! Why don't I remember! I didn't blackout again, did I!* he wondered.

Unfortunately for Sean, this wasn't a discovery of something he'd done recently. The blood on him wasn't from his doing. When he looked up, he learned as much.

Amber was the first one he saw. Her skin was gray though most of it was bathed in dark crimson. Standing next to her was his second date, Becky. She was likewise adorned in gore with less of her gray peeking through. However, she hunched over to compensate for a huge gash in her stomach. She suffered a violent tear across her gut with bite wounds marking the edges. The only parts of the wound not drenched in red or black were the dull yellow of her intestines that slopped down to the floor and dragged along her steps with the ends sweeping along side her foot chain in the bloody pool. Behind her was his third date, Susan. She was the most disfigured. He only knew her by process of elimination. Her face was completely torn away, revealing her stained skull with a single grotesquely large orb that served as her eye. She leaned to her right to compensate for the flesh eaten from her leg and calf.

Sean looked on in horror. The three ghouls were just now realizing his presence after adjusting to the light he had switched on before falling. Until now, they only knew darkness in their new undead lives.

The women didn't remember the numerous horrors Sean had brought on them in their previous existence. They didn't remember how starved they were, and that Amber finally died of weakness the night before. They didn't remember her rising and killing Becky. And what used to be Susan, didn't recall the two of them going after her. None of them remembered they were once afraid of Sean.

They only knew one thing. They still felt starved. Yet this was a brand of hunger new to them. Susan, perhaps more so, since she was the last one to die and still virgin to the taste of her new drive.

Sean knew nothing since his mind locked in disbelief and terror. He dumbly watched his captives turn to look at him. Always first, Amber shambled towards him with her chain in tow. The other two followed, though somewhat hindered by their wounds.

"No, no, no," Sean blubbered. He still had time to get away. Unlike the girls, he didn't have chains to lock him in place. His cowardice did that for him. The three ghouls took their time to reach him, not unlike the leisurely pace he once inflicted upon them.

"Please..." he begged and finally started to scoot back towards the stairs. He was too late. His first date, Amber, met him at the base of the first step. He raised his arms protectively to cover his face. She fell over and landed on his legs.

He squirmed more forcefully, going nowhere. His traction vanished between her weight and the slippery floor. Amber was always the feisty one and that was still true in her death. She looked into Sean's eyes and snarled before launching her head into his thigh. Her teeth might as well have been as sharp as a scalpel. They ripped into his bloodied slacks and, after some twisting and haranguing, she lifted her head to look back at him with a piece of his flesh hanging from her mouth. It dripped with his blood between her teeth and a sandwiched tatter of cloth from his trousers.

She began to chew while digging her stiffening fingers violently into his wound.

Still in a state of disbelief, Sean feebly whimpered when Amber pulled at the ends of the jagged hole in his trousers. A wide rip ran down the length of his leg. The cloth in her mouth didn't agree with her and she spit out the mangled chunk.

He finally screamed the first time when Amber dove in again into his bare leg. Her unhindered bite into his soft flesh allowed her to dig in far deeper and she pulled away with a slab that would have been enough for three casual-sized mouthfuls. She barely bothered to chew this time and gulped it whole. Her throat expanded to accommodate the unnatural size of her swallow and that lump traveled down her neck while she lifted her head upwards and shook it side to side to foster its progress. Once the grotesque bulge had disappeared into her chest, she looked at Sean again with a dismissive glance. Her dull eyes somehow took on a gleam and then she shot back down to drill further into his leg.

The pain he felt nearly gave him the strength to break free. However, Becky landed on his chest and Susan crashed in behind her. Had Sean taken the time to really get to know Becky, he might have discovered she was once a meticulous person in life. This translated into her death. She took care to slowly rip away his shirt before she decided to eat into him. With each giving break, Sean saw buttons fly into the air from the force of her pull. After the pop of the last button, his shirt ripped completely open to expose his bare chest. However, Becky was momentarily distracted from launching into him by Susan.

Susan, at one time the youngest and most inexperienced of the girls, lumbered over Becky's back and flopped down to meet Sean face to face. Once the most beautiful of the three, nearly all of her face was torn away and now resided in the bellies of the other two girls. Sean looked inches away into the perfectly round eye within in her naked socket and he hiccupped into shocked silence.

The next screams were not his own.

"Fuuccckkkk! Oh, Gawd!" the voice of his father cried as Becky finally landed her first bite into Sean's belly. She didn't lift up with a mouthful. Rather she bit and chewed in quick successions while she mined her way into his large intestines.

Amber grew tired of his leg and pulled more at the torn edges of his slacks. The cloth ripped up to his beltline and revealed his penis. Sean never liked underwear. It would have been an annoyance during the heat of the moment when he made love to his entrapped girls. She grinned almost into a smile as if she appreciated one less thing to rip away.

"Oh, please. No!" the voice of Sean's mother shrilled just before Amber descended and bit away the flaccid organ. An incoherent falsetto roared out of Sean while Amber rose and chewed with delight. But, the meager tube of meat wasn't to her satisfaction and she wound up spitting out the mangled mess. She lowered her head again to assault the two other parts of his manhood.

The youngest and faceless Susan clumsily scoured at a thin layer of skin from his forehead. The scrape of her teeth against his own bone was agonizing to him. Yet that assault competed with the cacophony of searing pain he felt everywhere else and he rapidly grew weak from blood loss. Most of his blood had already drained into the spreading pool on the floor to mix in with the other girl's.

Sean now only had the strength to protest with moans and grunts, his tone becoming a weaker version of Matheson. Yet, his laboring sounds were far from the cheerful ones the handyman once made while he worked so diligently to construct the chambers.

The girls continued to devour Sean after he drifted away. They didn't stop until his eyes opened again without pain and his body twitched with a new purpose. Only then, they lost interest with him and stood to shamble about the basement with the clatter of chains to follow their senseless paths. Sean was too disfigured to rise, as much as he tried. He was condemned to repeating the same stupid and failed attempts in an effort to get up.

He'd continue to do so mindlessly for a very long time, until he eventually rotted away to the point of immobility. Had he been an optimist, he might have found that Valentine's Day had paid off beyond expectation. None of them could get out of the basement and he didn't have to choose after all. They were all together forever.

All living voices within the house were now silent. Beneath the awkward swipes of chains were moans and grunts from bored ghouls with nothing to do and nowhere to go. Most of those sounds wafted throughout the house from the basement.

No one would ever come to investigate the horrors that took place in the house. Everyone else had their own problems to deal with, and soon, with very few exceptions, the rest of the world would be as dead as those in the house.

Had one the luxury of curiosity, had one bothered to enter the house, one might have noticed something.

Not all sounds came from the basement. There was other, though extremely feeble and weak from years of decay.

In a bedroom once claimed by Sean's mother, there was a large cedar hope chest at the foot of the bed. The thing inside it protested with moans and grunts not at all human in nature. If anyone really cared to open it, the only recognizable thing within the soupy and twitching mess was a dirty blond wig.

A LITTLE NUMBER NINE

SEAN GRIGSBY

"Welcome to Ms. Otha's. Can I help you wit anyting?"

"Oh, I'm just looking," Danny said.

The thick presence of incense stung his eyes as he fumbled his way around large, porcelain elephants and a stack of ethnic walking sticks, standing upright in a dusty cauldron.

"Well, now, what exactly are ya lookin' fer?"

He held back his laughter. Her Jamaican accent had to be fake; a gimmick.

"I want to get something for my girlfriend, for Valentine's Day."

"Ah, the day of love. What's ya name, boy?"

"Danny Stallward," he said, approaching the cluttered counter.

"I'm Ms. Otha. So what's ya girl's name?"

"Lisa."

"And what do she like?"

"She's really picky. It depends on what kind of mood she's in, I guess." His eyes kept glancing upward, to the shelves on the wall, high above the counter.

Ms. Otha smiled. "How 'bout some nice jewelry?"

"Yeah, that might work; something special."

His stare was now fixed on two crystal bottles on the top shelf. Their contents, one pink and one blue, sparkled even in the gloom of the store.

"Ev'ry ting we got special. But I see ya got ya eye on some of my potions up 'ter."

"What do they do?"

"Ah," she drew it out in a whisper Danny felt was canned. "Da pink one would suit ya good on da Day of Love. Give ya girl a few drop a dat and she be all over ya like meat on da bone."

"How much?"

Danny's rapid excitement in asking sent Ms. Otha into laughter. "Dere's a first time fer ev'ry ting, now ain't der, boy!"

She continued laughing and when she caught her breath, she answered.

"Tree-hundred,"

"Three hundred!"

"Dey not sellin' dis at Wal-Mart, now is dey?"

"What about the blue one?"

"Dat one even more expensive, and more powerful. You don't wanna be messin' around wit it, ya hear?"

"Well, I don't have three-hundred. Fifty is pushing it."

"Den why don't we look at some jewelry?"

Danny sighed and nodded. Ms. Otha pulled out several black boxes filled with necklaces, rings, and bracelets.

"She doesn't like gold, just silver," he said.

Ms. Otha removed all of the yellow-tinted pieces and smiled back at her customer.

"This one looks nice," he said.

"A fine necklace to hang round ya pretty girl's throat."

Danny scrunched his brow at such a strange comment. Ms. Otha held the necklace up and continued smiling.

"I give it to ya for twenty-fy."

"Okay. Do you have any charms to put on it or anything?"

"Shore! We got nuff charms to put fear in da butt of da devil himself!"

"Uh, okay," he said. "Nothing spiritual though. I mean, nothing religious."

"I tink I might have sometin' in da back."

She disappeared through a curtain of hanging beads, leaving Danny in the storefront, alone. The cold, seeping in from outside, mixed with the smell of incense and dusty relics. The combination was inappropriate and made his stomach turn. As a distraction, he rubbed his hands together and stared again at the crystal bottles.

He listened for Ms. Otha. She still bumbled around in the back. Grabbing one of the walking sticks and coming around the counter, he reached toward the bottles with the stick and nudged them toward the edge. He needed to hold one, to smell it.

They both fell.

He reacted quickly enough to catch the blue potion but the pink crashed into the counter, sending shattered crystal and the smell of sex and candy through the air.

"*Ya break it, ya buy it, boy!*" Ms. Otha screamed from the back.

Danny jumped the counter, grabbing the silver necklace and slamming his fifty dollars in its place. He pocketed the bottle and rushed out into the snow. The adrenaline pumping into his system made him feel jittery and his face red while he tried to take steady, measured steps until the next block.

That's when he ran.

He had planned on taking a cab but that notion was left back on Ms. Otha's counter, along with the smashed bottle and his fifty remaining dollars. His cheeks started stinging and then became numb. Removing his pocketed hands, he touched them to his cheeks, trying to warm them and bring back some feeling as he slowed to a jog down the sidewalk. Piles of charcoal-colored slush lined the pavement. The overcast sky became darker as cars splashed by bars and bookstores, where icy patrons had decided to hole up for the better part of the night.

Danny's lungs felt tight and he decided to walk the rest of the way. The steam and wheezing continued with each exhale as he climbed the steps to his girlfriend's apartment building. Once inside, he stepped up to the elevator and a door opened behind him.

"You know, you wouldn't wheeze if you worked out once in a while," a voice said from behind him.

Danny turned around to see a man, a little older than him, wearing a tank top and leaning against the door frame.

"Mind your own business, Melanie."

"I've told you before, it's Mel!"

"Whatever," Danny said, turning back around and calling for the elevator.

"I don't understand what she sees in you. You got no style, you work in a freakin' pizzeria, and you don't treat her the way she needs to be."

"And you're a dirty, old creep that talks like Sylvester Stallone and you're her freakin' *landlord*! So back off."

The elevator opened and Danny stepped inside.

"You're too pathetic to take me on."

"Yeah, well, at least my parents didn't name me Melanie."

The doors closed before the disgruntled landlord could get to him. Danny smiled. Pissing Melanie off was just one highlight of visiting Lisa.

* * *

"Baby!"

The door to apartment 402 swung open and a short brunette jumped into Danny's arms, wrapping her bare legs around his waist and kissing his mouth. He walked in with her still around him and shut the door.

"I know it's a day early," she said, hopping to the floor and skipping toward the kitchen. "But I wanted to make you dinner."

She had her curly hair up and wore a t-shirt and tight, short shorts. The fabric was like skin around her backside and there were illegible letters spread across it that made the slight, yearning ache inside Danny's core grow even larger.

"Great," he said.

"And, I got this box of wine. Some people at work said it's just as good as the pricey bottle stuff."

Lisa poured two glasses and handed both of them to him.

"Can you put these on the table?"

"Goin' all out, huh?" Danny said, doing as she asked.

"It's Valentine's Day! Well, close enough, and I wanted to do something special for you. Don't you like it?" She made a pouty face from where she stood in the kitchen.

"Of course! I love it. And I love you!" She was so damn cute.

"I love you, too!" she said and blew him a kiss. "Set our drinks down and I'll bring it out in a minute."

Danny sat in his usual spot and folded his coat over a chair next to him. He stared at Lisa's glass and fiddled with the potion bottle in his pocket.

Might as well use it, he thought.

You don't know what that stuff does!

But that lady said she'd be all over your meat or something!

He pulled it out and removed the top, putting his nose to the rim. It had no smell. He didn't understand. The pink potion had been so sweet, so invigorating. This one could have been colored water.

Clark, Lisa's fat Siamese cat, hopped onto the table and rubbed his face against Danny's hand, purring loudly.

"Hey, buddy."

The cat moved towards the bottle, moving against it at first, then sticking its snout into the opening. Danny moved it, holding it away from the animal.

"Watch it! This is expensive."

Clark pawed and swiped toward the bottle, howling a deep, impatient meow.

"Chill out."

"What are you doing to my cat?" Lisa called from the kitchen.

"Nothing."

He scooped the cat up and placed it on the floor beside him. Clark stayed and stared up at Danny as he poured a few drops of the potion into Lisa's glass. The cat began to howl again.

"Be quiet, sweetheart," Lisa said, walking in with two full plates in hand.

Danny returned the bottle to his pocket.

"Did you pet him?"

"Yeah," he said.

"I guess he just craves attention. Just like his mommy!"

She leaned over and kissed Danny's lips before setting the plate in front of him.

Corned beef and cabbage. His favorite.

"I thought I smelled something good," he said.

"I take care of my baby."

She took a sip of wine, and after placing the glass back down and swallowing, her eyes widened.

"Whoo! I'm already feeling it."

"Lightweight."

"Screw you!"

They laughed.

"Your landlord was giving me shit on the way up here," he said.

"What did he say?"

"How he doesn't see why you're with me." Danny felt a lump in his throat. It hadn't affected him when Melanie had said it, but coming out of his own lips, it hit him low.

"Then he must be the blindest man in the world. Besides, I see a lot in you and I'm the one that counts."

This drew a smile from Danny's lips.

Lisa gulped down the rest of her wine and slammed the glass down on the table, almost to the point where Danny thought it would break.

"Damn," he said.

"It's good stuff!"

She began digging into the corned beef and shoving large bites into her mouth, ignoring the cabbage. Danny watched in confused awe as his girlfriend degraded her eating habits to that of an ill-mannered frat boy.

Lisa looked up and noticed the puzzled look on his face. "What? I'm hungry."

"You always get onto *me* for smacking."

"I cooked this all day for you. And I'm not smacking. Do you want my cabbage?"

"Hell, yeah!"

She scooted it onto his plate and sat back in her chair, watching him finish. Danny glanced up at her several times, smiling and wondering if the potion would work or if it was a rip-off; if he had actually purchased it.

"I want you."

"What?" he asked over the last bit of food still being chewed in his mouth.

"I want you inside me."

Clark meowed in between the tense silence, but Danny was excited.

"Are you sure? I mean, didn't you want to wait?"

"I know, but...I don't know if it's the wine or Valentine's or what. I just...I want you!"

She giggled and walked toward him as he smiled. Picking his hand up in hers, she led him into the bedroom. He had been in her room before but it never looked as new as it did now. She left the door open and threw him onto the bed. He was surprised by the hostility but enjoyed it. He pulled stuffed bunnies and bears out from under him.

She jumped on top of his waist and pushed her face hard against his while she moved her tongue around like a ballerina inside his mouth. The cool of her lips increased his ache. She pulled at her clothes and Danny mirrored her, both of them stripping down to enjoy the act he had wanted since first talking to her on the phone.

Seven months was a long time.

Her body was more beautiful than he had imagined and he appreciated her short stature and that her parts were close so he could take everything in at once. Lisa rolled him on top of her, grabbing his thighs and pulling them toward her with an energy and strength he had never seen in her. But it didn't matter. The thrill was so great; his rational mind took a much needed vacation into the softness of her form.

She kissed him all over, scratching her nails softly against his back, thrusting in his rhythm. Her nails began to dig deeper into his skin, increasing his pleasure so much that she shook him alert when her kisses turned into hard bites.

"*Quit it*," he yelped in pain.

"I'm sorry, I'm sorry!"

"That hurt!"

"I guess I was just getting into it."

She sat on him, making her pouty face and rocking back and forth on his groin. Danny smiled and leaned up to kiss her.

He tasted blood. Putting his fingers to his lips, he brought them back to see they were red.

"Holy shit! You really got me."

She touched his chest and stomach, moving her fingers against the teeth-shaped wounds she'd put there, her lips now stained a deep red with his blood.

"Do you wanna stop?"

"Hell no! I've waited too long for this."

They both giggled as he turned her over.

* * *

Rolling over in bed the next morning, Danny was surprised to see Lisa still asleep beside him. He remembered she was usually up before him and her snores continued as he left the bed and entered the bathroom. Coming out after his shower, she was still asleep. He worried about her being late for work but decided not to disturb her and let her sleep for a while longer. After putting on the clothes he had worn the night before, he heard her cough several times behind him. He could hear the gobs of mucus breaking up and the slight moan of agony with each one.

"Danny."

"Are you okay?"

"I feel horrible."

He stepped closer to her, close enough to see her but far enough not to catch whatever it was she had. There were dark circles under her eyes he hadn't noticed before and her lips were a strange purple color. He took a step back, hoping she didn't notice.

"Will you call in sick for me?"

"Of course. Did you go out without your coat?"

"You know I always bundle up. Maybe I caught something."

Maybe it was the wine, he thought.

"Okay, I'll call in for you, baby. After I get off work, I'll pick up some clothes and come straight here to take care of you."

"I'm glad I have you," she said.

"I'm glad I have you, too."

"Wonderful way to spend Valentine's Day, huh?"

"At least we started a day early. See you later," he said.

"I love you."

"I love you, too."

* * *

"You finally hit it?"

Chris hoisted him up and swung him around like someone who won the lottery. Danny didn't think anyone could be happier than Chris was about it.

"Yeah, now my poor girl's at home sick all day without me."

"You probably did her so hard, it threw her immune system outta whack," Alfred said, loading dough into the cooler.

"Hey! Watch that kinda talk in my place. That's Danny's future wife you're talkin' about," Chris said.

"It's all right. That's just his way of sayin' he's happy for me, too," Danny said.

"So how was it?" Alfred asked.

"Well, I'm not goin' into details with the two of you but…it was great!"

"Did you do the thing I told you about, with the thing?" Chris asked.

"Chris, I'm not gonna take advice from a sex-crazed Italian. You like chicks with moustaches."

Alfred cracked a loud laugh from inside the cooler.

"Hey, now. I'm your boss. And those ladies got character!"

"Let me ask you, though. What do you know about Spanish Fly and aphrodisiacs and stuff like that?"

"Ah, man! You don't wanna mess around with that stuff. You got a free pass at home. Had a cousin who tried it. Thought it would spruce up his sex life. We found him spread eagle on his living room floor, dick just as stiff as the rest of him," Chris said while shaking his head.

"He died?"

"Yeah. Stuff's toxic."

"Does it make you go crazy? You know, like biting the other person and scratching 'em up?"

"Never heard of nothing like that. You didn't give Lisa any of that stuff, did you?"

"No! No way. I was just curious."

Alfred stepped out of the cooler with a black, plastic container he put under Danny's nose.

"Hey, did it smell like this?"

Danny grunted a disgusted noise and backed away with his hand over his nose.

"Quit jerkin' around with my mushrooms, Alfie!" Chris joked.

They all cracked up.

"Now go throw those things away," Chris said.

Alfred took the container to the back and Danny grabbed his boss' arm.

"I did want to ask you something, though, Chris."

"Oh, yeah?"

"I was wondering if you thought about promoting me to assistant manager."

"Ah, I don't know, Danny. I mean, things are tight right now with the economy and all that."

"I'm gonna ask Lisa to marry me."

"What? Are you kiddin' me? That's wonderful!"

"That's why I was hoping you might consider the promotion. I want to get her a nice ring and..."

"Look, man. If you really want to marry this girl, the first thing you gotta do is get the hell outta this pizzeria. I mean, *I'm* here but it's my place. I own it. Alfred's got no responsibilities or a woman or anything. Guy lives with his freakin' grandma."

"But I like it here," Danny said.

"If you want to provide for her and get her a nice ring and all that, you gotta make a little more than minimum wage and lousy delivery tips. You get me?"

"Yeah, I get you."

"Then as your employer, I suggest going out today and applying somewhere else."

"Okay," Danny said, walking toward the front.

"Hey!" Christopher handed him a mop. "*After* you mop the back."

* * *

Danny took an early day and returned to Lisa's apartment building a quarter after two. He'd never been inside so early and the cold silence blanketed him as he made his way through the foyer. Melanie didn't even open his door to stare in disapproval. Danny smiled and pulled himself up the stairs along the handrail, happy to take the long way.

Reaching the fourth floor, he walked down the hallway, smelling the mildew that festered under the carpet while flickering, yellow light coated the narrow path. Melanie still hadn't replaced the bulbs, although every tenant had complained since December. Danny knocked against his girlfriend's door. Giving her a few seconds to get out of bed or off the couch, wherever she might be, then he knocked again.

Still nothing.

He tried the knob and it opened. Preparing a lecture on the dangers of unlocked doors in the city, he stepped through the entrance and found Lisa standing in the living room. Blood covered her from head to toe. It seemed to have poured from her mouth then down the front of her pajama top. She was standing in the middle of the living room with Clark in her hands. The cat wasn't happy about it.

Clark struggled and growled in her grasp as she brought him closer to her mouth. Danny darted toward them, pulling her arms apart and letting Clark drop to the floor.

"Run, Clark. Run!"

The cat howled as he raced out of the open door. Lisa snapped her head up to see him. Her eyes, no longer dull, now overflowed with comprehension. She looked even worse than when he'd left her that morning. The putrid color that had been confined to her lips now covered her entire body. Danny held her arms. They were cut all over with long, deep scratches from Clark's defensive swipes. He looked them over with concerned eyes. No major arteries had been sliced but Danny knew it was still bad. He could almost feel the pain himself.

It's like it didn't even faze her.

"Where did all this blood come from?" he asked.

She looked down and her head bobbed as if she was drugged, then her head rose again to meet his eyes.

"I don't know...."

"What the hell were you doing?"

"I was asleep...on the bed and...."

Danny lifted her up and carried her to the bathroom. Sitting her on the toilet, he remembered the front door and ran to lock it.

"What's goin' on in here?" Melanie stood in the doorway with his arms crossed. "Neighbors have been buggin' the shit outta me, sayin' it sounds like World War Three is goin' off in here."

"Look, I just got here and Lisa's sick, so I don't know what they're talking about," Danny tried to explain.

"Sure. I bet. What's she got?"

"I don't know. Maybe the flu or something. But I..."

"Maybe I can take a look at her. Give her some medicine."

"No. I got it under control. I'm about to give her a bath so, if you don't mind..."

Danny waved his hand towards the hall. Melanie looked, as if there were something there.

"Okay, but if I hear anything else, I'm callin' the cops. But they're not the ones you gotta worry about. Understand?"

"Do what you have to, Mel."

Mel stood there for a second, a look of confusion draped across his face. "All right then. Don't use the elevator. Somethin's wrong with it," he said and walked off.

Danny shut the door and locked it. He figured Clark would come scratching when he forgot about the incident in the living room, if something like that could be forgotten. Danny knew *he* couldn't forget and that it was probably all his fault.

Lisa slumped on the toilet like a drunken prom date. Danny started the bath water and peeled the blood-drenched pajama top from over her head, throwing it into the small wastebasket. Lisa wrapped her arms around him and began kissing his neck and arms. Her skin was cool and damp except for where Clark had torn her open. Danny could feel heat rising from the wounds and surrounding skin. He thought about infection.

"Hey, hey. We've got the rest of our lives for you to kiss me," he said, pushing her back. "I've got to give you a bath and bandage you up. Then, we're going to the hospital."

"No...no hospital. We don't have the money."

"I'm taking you to the emergency room. They have to treat you."

"Please...just give me till tomorrow."

"Are you sure?"

"If...I don't feel better...you can take me then."

Danny sighed. "Okay but if I see any more crazy stuff; I'm kidnapping you and taking you somewhere to get help."

She tried to crack a smile and Danny lifted her into the tub. After wiping her down, he let her soak in the warm water while he went into the next room. He returned with the silver necklace.

"Happy Valentine's Day!" he said with a smile.

Danny held out the necklace, as if attempting to place it around her neck. Lisa raised her brow as much as she could under the weight of illness and her lips parted.

"But...I didn't get you anything."

Her hand lifted to grab the necklace but dropped back against the tub as her eyes closed. She still breathed, as hard to detect as it was, and Danny knew she had passed out. Laying the necklace on the sink, he drained the tub and carried her into the bedroom. He dried her off and dressed her with a pair of panties and a large sweatshirt.

Danny imagined doing this for their babies somewhere in the future, when they were married with kids, and the thought made his throat tighten and his eyes water. He hoped they would at least make it through the night.

He closed the door behind him and stepped into the bathroom to wash his hands. While drying them, he stared at the silver necklace and remembered his escape from Ms. Otha's store the previous night. Only one person knew what would help Lisa. Danny just hoped the lady would.

He found the store's number in a phonebook and dialed.

"Ms. Otha's."

"Ms. Otha, I know I'm the last person you wanna talk to but I need your help."

The sound on the other end was so quiet that, at first, Danny thought she hadn't heard him but it soon swelled into a roar of laughter.

"I knew your thieving ass would come crawling back for help."

The Jamaican accent was absent.

"Your voice...."

"Nothing illegal about having a fake accent but what you did, that's a textbook felony," she said.

"I'm sorry. I freaked out. I'm gonna pay you back, I promise. I just need to know what chemicals were in that bottle."

"Boy, my accent might be fake but the shit that was in that bottle is pure, real magic. That's not something the Poison Control hotline can help you with." She laughed again. "And as far as payback is concerned, don't worry about it."

"Oh, thank you..."

"'Cause I'm already getting it! I told you not to mess with that blue shit. You gave it to your girl, didn't you?"

"Yes! Please, help me."

Danny started to cry as Ms. Otha laughed harder.

"Ain't nothin' can help you now, boy. Your girl's gonna die and that ain't the worst of it. If she's been acting strange, believe me, things are gonna get a whole lot stranger and everything around you is gonna be ripped apart. Karma's a bitch." She hung up.

Danny slammed the phone against the kitchen counter repeatedly. His mouth salivated with anger. The pattern of his inner organs froze and tightened. His lungs quit working. Everything in him stopped and focused on removing the pain in the form of salty streams from his squeezed eyes and short gasps of misery from his lips.

Straightening up, he slapped his hands together, trying to collect himself.

Ms. Otha was just screwing with him. Lisa would be fine.

Someone's voice echoed in his head about denial being the first phase of dealing with death.

No.

He pushed the thought away. She just needed to let it pass through her system. In the meantime, he would need to take care of her. Juice, medicine...

The medicine!

Grabbing her keys from a bowl on the coffee table, he locked the front door and rushed down the hall towards the elevator. He had already pushed the call button when he remembered what the landlord said. As soon as he turned to walk toward the stairs, the doors chimed and opened behind him.

Melanie must have fixed it.

Turning back around, his stomach churned and sent him into a fit of dry heaves as he covered his nose and mouth to block out the stench. Blood was splattered all over the walls and the floor, mixed with chunks of hair and tissue. A middle-aged woman, from what Danny could tell from her mangled head, lay in pieces inside the elevator. Most of her was gone, like the remnants of a devoured rack of lamb. He had seen her in the building before, wearing the same neon-colored jogging suit.

Lisa did this. All that blood...

But it wasn't her fault.

He had to get rid of the body or, more accurately, its parts. Hurrying back into Lisa's kitchen, he found only one garbage bag left in the box under the sink. He grabbed a pair of rubber gloves and listened for Lisa. After hearing nothing, he ran back to the elevator.

The severed hands, legs, and arms filled the bag along with the scoops of guts and bloody hair he fed in with his gloved hands. Neither the torso nor the head that dangled from it would fit. He moved to the key switch and saw the key had already been turned and broken off, realizing it was why the elevator wasn't working on the other floors.

Hoisting the bag over his shoulder, he headed down the hall to the garbage chute.

His eyes darted from each side, watching out for exiting tenants as he moved his legs faster. The bag started bouncing against his back and he could feel the gory contents squishing against his skin. He held it away from him like a bag of soiled cat litter. Making it to the garbage chute, he threw it in and spun around, flinching at the sight of an elderly woman exiting her apartment.

"What are you wearing?" She eyed him as she locked her apartment and pointed towards his red-stained gloves.

"Oh, these. I spilled some punch on the floor. Valentine's Day, you know."

"Hmm," she said and began walking the other way.

"You can't go that way!"

"Pardon me?"

"Melanie, er, the landlord said the elevator isn't working."

"I swear, every day something else is falling apart. Does he expect me to walk down four flights of stairs?"

"I could carry you."

"I'm not a cripple! It's just going to take me a bit longer. Excuse me." She moved past him and under her breath said, "Weirdo."

Danny waited until the gray tip of her head was out of sight and ran for the elevator. He pressed the call button, hoping no one else would attempt to come his way. The doors opened and he was relieved to see the head and torso still there, and then became confused as to why he was relieved to see such a horrible thing. He snatched the parts up, steadying the head, and charged back down the hall to the garbage chute.

No other tenants blocked his way. He did his best to make sure no blood fell to the carpet, not that it would have been noticeable. When he reached the garbage chute, he tried to figure out how to shove the rest of the body down the hole. He knew he couldn't set it down, that would cause a mess. Taking a deep breath, and holding down his bile, he held the torso against his chest with his right arm while the head slumped on his shoulder.

A moan came from behind.

He whipped around but the hallway was empty. He listened again but nothing else came except the random pops and creaks of the old building.

Then, another moan.

This time, Danny realized it came from the head against his shoulder. He jerked open the garbage chute door as the mass of meat and bone began to squirm in his arms. His cries met with more moans from the corpse. He pushed it into the hole but it became lodged, its mouth snapping at Danny's face. Screaming, he pulled the door up. The thing remained in place, doing its best to take a bite out of him. He jerked the door harder, again and again and again. Blood and gore splattered across his face each time but the corpse didn't budge.

Danny sighed and the creature growled.

He turned around and saw a fire extinguisher hanging on the wall a few feet down. Pulling it from the hook, he ran toward the corpse and bashed its face in with the extinguisher's bottom. Its teeth crumbled, flowing out with the red stream escaping its mouth.

The right eyeball swung loose from its socket as the skin around it ripped apart to reveal a smashed skull. It continued to writhe.

Letting out a frustrated growl, he slammed the extinguisher downward, into the torso, pushing it deeper into the chute. The thing began slipping as more of it flew against his clothes and mouth. Giving a long push, the body dislodged from the opening, taking the fire extinguisher down to the pit with it.

He sank to the floor against the wall and looked down the hallway. No one looked out of their doors. No police came storming up the stairs. It had returned to the silence.

Lisa!

The door was cracked open and he wondered how long it had been that way between his sprints to and from the elevator. Returning to the apartment, he saw that Clark was hidden under the side table next to the couch, grumbling and focusing on the closed bedroom door. Danny stepped toward it. An unknown sound came from the room, soft and rhythmic. He took a step back and began to scan the apartment.

Rushing to the kitchen, he grabbed a bread knife and saw a small, novelty baseball bat hanging from a nail on the side of the cabinet. He thought about the night he bought it for Lisa on their first date at Tucker Stadium. Grabbing it, he prayed he wouldn't have to use either weapon.

He slid the knife into his belt and pressed against the bedroom door. The hinges whined in a squeaky vibrato and he gripped the bat tighter. Melanie lay on his side against the floor, a rose in his hand and a pool of blood gathering under him. Lisa knelt behind him, burying her face into the gory area under his arm.

"Melanie, you *idiot!*"

Lisa looked up from her meal, a chunk of meat still hanging from her teeth. She flipped the body onto its back, continuing to chew, and plunged her fist into the chest.

"Stop it! You're tearing him apart, *Lisa!*"

She forced her hand out, clutching Melanie's dripping heart.

Danny staggered back, shaking his head. "My God, what have I done to you?"

She held the heart out to him like a gift, rising to her feet, stumbling over her landlord's lifeless body. Danny backed into the living room, holding the bat in front of him. She followed, carrying the heart in both hands and shaking it toward him, making her pouty face. His back hit a wall. Lisa inched closer. Blood dripped in slow beads against the floor, making a trail from the bedroom.

Lisa pushed the heart near Danny's face. He turned his head away from the disgusting organ. Pushing it against his lips, she moaned.

"Quit it," he said.

He could taste it. His guts began twisting, ready to heave. He raised the bat. His heart began to beat faster, aching at the thing he was about to do. Clark hissed behind them and another, louder noise followed. Danny looked over Lisa's shoulder to see Melanie's tattered form limping from the bedroom. His eyes were bloodshot and strings of blood and drool poured from his gnashing teeth. Limping closer, he raised his arms and moaned again.

Clark flew from under the table and clawed into Melanie's leg.

Melanie began swinging around, trying to kick the cat loose. Clark's growl shook with each jerking motion. Danny pushed Lisa aside and ran toward the two warring creatures as Melanie's bloody hand grabbed around the cat's scruff and lifted it into the air.

"Leave the cat alone!" he screamed.

Danny shoved the bat into the dead man's open mouth, pushing him backwards. Clark ran off into some dark place of the apartment. The animated corpse grabbed at the bat with one hand and reached for Danny with the other. Danny pulled the knife from his belt and swung it toward Melanie's head.

Lisa's hand stopped Danny's attack with a tight grip around his wrist, squeezing until he dropped the knife. Blood covered her face. Soft bits of Melanie's flesh still stuck to her lips. Danny couldn't deny it any longer. The thing in front of him was no longer his girlfriend. He ran from the apartment, the sounds of their staggering footsteps and Lisa's screams echoing behind him.

The building's tenants, recently home from work or an errand, stepped out from their apartments, curious about the horrible noises coming from 402. Lisa and Melanie burst from the apartment and fell upon them. A couple stood in their doorway, the man ate chocolates out of a heart-shaped box while the woman stared over his shoulder. Melanie grabbed the man by the throat, chocolates spilling onto the floor as his girlfriend shut the door behind him and bolted the lock.

The undead landlord began pounding the man's head against the door. His face smashed into the wood, breaking his nose and smearing the number plate with blood. The last hit with the human battering ram broke open the door as the man's skull caved in. Melanie dragged the body into the apartment so he could find the woman and feed on them both.

Lisa lumbered down the hall after Danny. Most of the tenants shut and locked their doors at their approach. An elderly woman tripped as she rushed to her door. Lisa's feet crushed down on the old woman, the old woman's bones cracking under the determined weight of Lisa.

Lisa grabbed the suit collar of a fleeing man's jacket and snapped his neck into a distorted 'L' shape as she continued her pursuit. Melanie stumbled out of the apartment and followed, only stopping to rip an arm from the business man's body, chewing on the end of it as he lurched down the hall.

The janitor's closet reeked of chemicals that burned Danny's throat. The moldy mop and gathering dust did nothing to help him remain quiet. Every time he breathed in, he had to fight the urge to cough. He heard nothing but the hum of the radiator above his head. He remembered hearing screams on his way down the stairs but they had disappeared when he stepped off onto the second floor.

They're slow enough. Just have to wait them out.

He wondered why he didn't head for the exit. He was only one floor away. Why had he hid in the closet? Why was he still here? The only reason he could think of was that some part of him, defying all sense of logic, didn't want to leave Lisa. Maybe there was still hope to save her.

Too late to change my mind, now.

A mixture of different noises came from outside the door. They were far away. Danny closed his eyes to focus, to make them out.

They were screams.

It came from the third floor. They grew louder. He could hear heavy breathing and then, a loud thud followed by another and then another, like someone had dropped a sack of potatoes that burst and continued to roll down the stairs. The sound stopped near the door and Danny could hear whimpering. The breathing was closer, heavier. Familiar sounds of exertion came from someone's mouth and then a thump against the floor.

Steady footsteps in the distance grew louder. The person's whimpers grew with them as something moved closer.

"No! Don... The plea was cut short and replaced with a thick, wet squish.

Danny backed away from the door. The air around him was cool and gave him a feeling of vulnerability. He moved back to the door. It made him feel protected, if only in the slightest way.

They're going to find me!

An apartment door swung open close by.

"Freeze!" a man yelled.

A garbled moan answered the man. Danny heard the click of a firearm.

"Easy, Mel. You know I'm a cop. I can get you some help. I need you to get on the floor...Stop!"

The echo of two gunshots sent Danny to the ground. The smoky, metal burn crept into his nostrils from under the door. The policeman screamed over grotesque sounds of sloshing and cracking that reminded Danny of a tree branch snapping in the wind. Something kept pounding. He looked at the crack under the door. Although he couldn't see a thing, he hoped for some sign the cop was okay or that at least Melanie was gone.

Another gunshot ripped out, followed by the clanking of metal against the floor.

Silence.

Danny gritted his teeth and placed his trembling hand on the doorknob. His whole body shook and jangled the knob as he turned it. Poking his head out, he saw the policeman was on his back with Melanie hunched over his legs. The cop's eyes were wide and stared at the ceiling. Blood continued to pump from a gash in his throat. His left arm was gone and Danny saw it sticking out from under Melanie's still body.

The gun lay right in front of Danny. Keeping an eye on the dead policeman and the prone Melanie, Danny opened the door some more and picked it up. The heat of the metal made him flinch, and with both hands he pointed the weapon at the cop's head. The man didn't move.

Using his left leg, Danny kicked Melanie off of the officer. The zombie's brains poured from its skull like rotten oatmeal. They both lay still.

It only spreads from Lisa's bite.

He moved his aim from the policeman's head and dropped the gun to the side, turning to face the stairs.

Lisa stood in front of him.

Her skin hung on her face, drooping on the right side like a Picasso. Aside from the blood that drenched her limping body, a wetness covered her that shimmered on her purple skin. Danny could even smell the death that oozed from her pores.

She swiped at him, her arms grazing his head as he ducked and ran for the janitor's closet. Slamming the door behind him, he began to pound his fists against his thighs in frustration.

Why are you back in here?

His knuckles chipped against something hard in his pocket. He winced from the sharp pain and pulled the object out. It was the potion. The door knob began to turn.

She can open doors, stupid!

He set the crystal bottle on a metal shelf unit to his left and grabbed the doorknob, pulling back with his entire weight so the door couldn't open. Lisa threw herself against the wood, pulling on the doorknob as she backed away for another impact. Danny's eyes darted around the small closet, over paint cans and bottles of bleach for something to hold the door closed.

Two black bungee cords were attached to the metal shelves, hooked to braces in the brick wall behind.

Danny unhooked one and the shelf jerked forward, sending the bottle into the air. He dove towards it, slamming onto the floor elbows first. The potion landed into his open right hand. His elbows felt like shattered glass and something stabbed into his gut. He got to his knees and saw he'd dropped the policeman's gun and landed on top of it.

Leaving the potion on the floor beside it, Danny jumped to his feet and began to wrap the bungee cord around the door knob.

Lisa ripped the closet door open.

Danny punched her between the eyes and she staggered back into the wall.

"Oh, God! I'm sorry, I'm sorry, I'm sorry..."

He shut the door and hooked the bungee cord back into the brace that stuck out from the wall. The rubber made a tense stretching sound and Danny could tell it was old. It wouldn't hold up. Lisa pounded against the door and this time she screamed. Danny grabbed the gun and the potion from the floor and backed deeper into the darkness of the closet. He thought about how he had never struck her before, even if under the present circumstances it was understandable. He could hear her growling. The anger and frustration came with every hit, with every scream.

A hand broke through the wood.

"Shit!" The bungee cord snapped. Its hook whipped across his face, drawing blood from a large cut. Lisa continued her frenzy. The stale yellow light shot through the hole and Danny had to squint. He lifted the gun and aimed it at Lisa's chest.

That's not gonna work. And what the hell are you doing? She's your girlfriend!

He could see how strong she was. The door crumbled as she continued to punch and claw her way through it. She would have no problem removing his head in the same fashion. The skin around her arms peeled back, revealing dark, wet tissue.

A thick gob of mucus had built up in his throat as tears dribbled from his eyes. He could see her face and redirected the gun's sight to it. Through all the blood, all the rotting skin and eyes, he saw the way she used to be.

She was still his. He cocked the gun.

The cool crystal of the potion bottle felt good in his left hand, much gentler than the blocky heat in his right. He lowered the weapon and looked at the bottle. Then he slid the gun away and opened the potion. Lisa crawled through the broken door and he raised the bottle to her, like he was at a dinner party and he was toasting the host.

"Happy Valentine's Day, baby."

Pressing the open bottle to his lips, he tossed his head back and swallowed deeply.

Brutal Killing in South End.
Police See Connection
By Latricia Burroughs

Investigators are still on the hunt for suspects involved with last night's homicide in the south district. Shortly after 9 P.M., police dispatched officers to Ms. Otha's Voodoo Boutique on Hopson St. where neighbors were complaining of a loud disturbance within the shop. Upon entering the business, officers discovered the remains of the store's owner, Otha Tenenbaum. "It was the worst thing I've ever seen," said Officer Terrance Ladley, one of the first patrolmen on the scene. Tenenbaum's body had been disemboweled and spread across the front counter. The business owner's arms and legs had also been torn and, along with the rest of her remains, had strong indications of cannibalism. "There were multiple bite marks covering her body and limbs," says Detective Gabe Shepard.

"Enormous amounts of flesh had been bitten off and the perpetrators took every effort to damage the victim's brain and top area of the head." Police are convinced the same individuals, being labeled "The Cannibal Couple", were involved in the Valentine's Day apartment massacre three days prior. "These individuals are ruthless and have no compassion for human life," Detective Shepard stated. Eye witnesses claimed to have spotted a young man and woman, covered in blood, holding hands and walking from the crime scene just minutes before police arrived. Chief Robert Andrews is suggesting a mandatory curfew to city officials until the murderous couple is apprehended.

VALNETINE'S DAY CANDY

ANTHONY GIANGREGORIO

Gene Watterson opened the main door to the Hallmark store on the corner of 8th and Main and nodded to an old woman with a walker. But the old woman barely looked at him, her face filled with fear and concern as she hurried to exit the building.

Not understanding what might be wrong with the woman, he merely shrugged and entered the store, figuring she was just acting senile like most old birds he'd met in his twenty-two years of living on the Earth.

It was Valentine's Day and he was in the store to get candy and flowers for his best girl, Sandy. They had been going out for almost three months and he was head over heels in love with her. They'd had sex a total of six times so far and each time was better than the last.

He was confident when he gave her the flowers and candy; he would be in line for number seven, too. As he entered the store, he heard some muffled screams and yells, the voices all male.

Stepping with trepidation down the center aisle, ignoring the cards on display for the moment, he slid up to the counter at the back of the store.

As he moved to the edge of the aisle, he saw what looked like a scuffle between a homeless man and two policemen. It was just as Gene poked his head around the corner to see what was going on, that he saw one the cops pull out a stun gun and zap the shit out of what had to be a bum-- a homeless man.

The bum danced a jig as he was filled with electricity, his nerves freezing up, and Gene could swear he saw smoke come out of the bum's ears. Then the man dropped to the floor, and no sooner did this happen, then the cops were on top of him, handcuffing his arms behind his back. In the scuffle there was a soft crack, like a neck snapping, but no one heard it, or if they did, they didn't give it much thought.

"Get 'im cuffed, hurry the fuck up," the first cop snapped at his partner.

"I am, hold on a sec," the second cop yelled back. As he leaned down to use the cuffs, the bum's eyes snapped open and he took a small chunk of flesh from the cop's arm.

"Son of a..." the cop screamed as he punched the bum in the head and pulled his arm back. "The piece of shit just bit me, Carl, what the fuck!" the cop screamed.

But Carl the cop wasn't listening, instead he was finishing the job his partner began, and he handcuffed the bum. With blood-red lips, the bum snarled like a wild animal as Carl pulled the raving lunatic to his feet. No one seemed to notice the bum's neck was broken, after all, the bum was still moving so he was alive...right?

"You okay?" Carl asked his partner who was cradling his arm against his chest with a handkerchief."

"Yeah, I'll live. It looks worse than it is," he said as he checked the wound. It was already slowing, the blood clotting.

"Come on, you asshole," Carl said to the growling bum. "We got a room with your name on it down at the precinct." He turned to the store clerk who was watching in shock. "Sorry about the mess, pal, but we had no choice."

The clerk, a pimply kid in his late teens, only nodded. "Sure, Officer, you did your job. Thanks for coming so fast." The voice was high and nasally.

Carl nodded and yanked the bum towards the front door, his partner right behind.

"Sure, pal, protect and serve, that's our motto."

Then the two cops and the bum were moving and soon were out the front door as pedestrians paused to watch them drag the bum to their squad car.

Gene watched them go with his mouth hanging open. He had never seen such violence. Well, not in real life, anyway. Sure the television was full of that stuff but not right in his face. He walked over to the clerk who had begun picking up the items knocked to the floor by the scuffle.

"What was that all about?" Gene asked.

The clerk shrugged, as if what happened was no big deal.

"Not much. Another bum wandered into the store so I had to call the cops. I tell ya, though, this guy was on somthin'. Did you see the way he got zapped and he was still kickin'? Shit, my uncle got tasered once and he was out for almost the entire night. That bum must have some constitution."

Gene only nodded, not knowing what else to do.

The clerk stopped cleaning to look over at Gene, where before he had been concentrating on working. "So, mister, can I help you with something?

Gene blinked and nodded once more. "Huh? Oh, shit, yeah, I need a box of heart-shaped candy and flowers."

The clerk pointed to the west side of the store. "Sure, whatever's left is over there. Man, you sure waited for the last second, huh?"

Gene scratched his head. "Yeah, I guess I did. I work a lot and well, you know..."

The clerk stopped cleaning and stared at Gene, crossing his arms. "No, not really, I don't. I sure wish I did, though," he said.

That was when Gene realized from a female point of view, the clerk was pretty nerdy looking, not the first pick for a boyfriend.

"Oh, sorry, man, yeah, I get it. Maybe next year," Gene said ruefully. "So, I'm gonna go see what's left."

The clerk watched him go for another few seconds, made an annoyed face behind Gene's back, and got back to work cleaning the store. Greeting cards and other miscellaneous items were strewn about, knocked from the shelves from the fight. Gene was forgotten from the clerk's mind as soon as he walked away.

Gene made his way to the section where the Valentine's Day items were stored. The shelves were all but empty, only a few stray and open candy boxes strewn about like wreckage from a plane crash. With no choice but to try and find something, he began pushing items aside. He searched for almost ten minutes, and was about to give up, when he found an unopened heart-shaped, bright red box of candies on the bottom shelf. By the looks of things, it had gone unattended by pure luck.

Taking the box off the shelf and holding it up like he had found the Holy Grail, he beamed with delight.

"Now for flowers and I'm good," he said to himself, feeling like a kid finding the last Easter egg at the hunt.

There was a refrigerated glass case in the next aisle and this section was more trashed than the Valentine aisle. Metal shelves with serrated racks stared back at him like a Communist peasant's refrigerator, the entire scene bathed in a pale white light from the two anemic bulbs mounted to the ceiling of the glass case.

More metaphors of deserted cupboard and shelving units came to mind but he refrained from using them, as he didn't want to become redundant.

Opening the glass case, he felt the rush of cool air and began picking up a flower here, a stem there. By the time he was finished, he had a haphazard bouquet, filled with carnations, baby's breath and three roses, two red and one white. A couple of pedals were missing but in the arrangement it wasn't immediately noticeable.

Carrying his finds to the counter, the nerdy clerk glared at him.

"Wow, you found somethin', huh?"

Gene nodded. "Yeah, this is it, though. The next guy is shit outta luck."

He handed the clerk the flowers who began to roll them with paper decorated with little hearts. When he was through, Gene had to admit the bouquet didn't look half bad. The clerk rang up the box of candy and then the flowers.

"I'm gonna give you fifty off on the flowers considering what you did to get them. Hows that sound?"

Gene smiled as he reached for his wallet. "Yeah, that sounds good, thanks."

The clerk shrugged. "Hey, it's only fair."

The transaction was completed and Gene picked up his candy and flowers. As he turned to leave, the clerk called out, "Hey, I hope she's worth it."

Gene paused and glanced back to the clerk. "Oh, yeah. She sure is, see ya."

The clerk waved and then Gene was forgotten as another customer came up to the counter to buy a pack of cigarettes.

Gene left the store and began walking down the sidewalk, a skip to his step and a smile in his heart. He couldn't wait to see Sandy's face when he gave her the Valentine's gifts. Yes, sir, this was going to be the best Valentine's Day ever.

There was a news stand on the corner, and a crusty old man hiding behind a pile of newspapers and magazines like a W.W.2 solider taking cover behind sandbags. Five people were gathered around the small shack and Gene strolled up to see what was so interesting.

A small man with a balding pate, a pale complexion, and square glasses glanced at Gene as he came up. The man gestured to a small black and white television the owner of the newsstand had on and everyone was watching attentively.

"The whole damn world's goin' ta Hell," he said as he turned and walked away. Gene saw the briefcase in his right hand and figured the guy was one of these Wall Street types or maybe a lawyer.

Turning back to the television, a report was droning on about unsolicited attacks on unwary pedestrians. Gene watched for almost a minute and then turned and moved on, not caring about what was happening.

After all, if it didn't affect him personally then in the end it didn't really matter. He had learned a few years ago that he couldn't save the world. At such a young age, he was proud of knowing that, as many others his same age would take another decade to figure it out.

As he walked down the sidewalk, he grinned widely, thinking what Sandy would say when he gave her the flowers and candy. He imagined she would gush with happiness and give him a big kiss. Then they would eat dinner, the special one she was making just for him and her. Then later, if he was lucky, they would spend the night together. Just thinking about touching her curvaceous form caused his pants to grow tighter.

He turned the corner and headed down 5th Street, knowing he only had three more blocks to go. All around him the city was full of life, cabs honking, people yelling and a few sirens in the distance.

If he had paused for a second, he may have realized there were more sirens than normal, but it would have been a fleeting thought.

As he passed by a line of cabs, the second one in line had the radio blasting, the windows open, despite the fact it was February. The radio announcer was yelling about some kind of tragedy on the west side, some kind of massacre. Police were called in and every person involved had been put down, killed with shots to the head. They were on so much speed or LSD that nothing but a head shot would work.

Then Gene was past the cab and whatever else was being said was lost in the cacophony of the city. With a renewed hop to his step, he reached the next corner and made his way to Sandy's apartment.

But on the next corner, there was something going on. Three squad cars were surrounding a car crash. From the looks of it, a cab had plowed into a Lincoln Town Car. But that wasn't the real problem. The true problem was the fact that the people in the wreck, covered in blood and one with an arm hanging by tatters of flesh, seemed to be up and attacking nearby gawkers. The cops were screaming at them to stop and of course they weren't listening. Gene stood stock still as he watched a policeman put three rounds into the cab driver's chest. The man, Pakistani or from the same region by the looks of his dark complexion and head wrappings, staggered backwards from the blasts, but no sooner did he stumble, then he was moving forward once more. Only now there was a gaping hole in his chest where the rounds had blown through and out his back. Blood and viscera dripped like slime from the edges of the wound and Gene was amazed the guy was still mobile.

A veteran cop by the look of his hard, chiseled face, stepped forward and shot the cabbie from almost point blank range in the left ear. Brain matter shot out of the right ear, blowing half the cabby's head off. Like a sack of potatoes, the guy dropped to the street, stone dead.

More shots echoed in the street and the other victims of the crash were riddled with bullets, their bloody frames twitching as each shot took out a chunk of their bodies. A middle-aged woman with bright red hair, who had been riding in the back seat of the cab before she was ejected through the windshield, came at the police like a banshee, snarling and growling. She absorbed five shots to the chest and lower torso before one cop shot her in the face. Her mascara, already running, was ruined forever when her faced dissolved into a mini-implosion. The back of her red hair flew out like it had been caught in a wind tunnel as her brains splashed the pavement and she fell to the road. Gene could see that no amount of lipstick and blush was going to save that train wreck of a missing face.

He stared in shock and quickly decided this wasn't where he wanted to be, so turning, he got the hell out of there, while the sounds of screams and gunshots followed him.

By the time he reached Sandy's building, he was feeling a little better. The carnage of the accident was a few blocks behind him and he knew in the city what he had witnessed, though visceral, was nothing new.

The doorman nodded politely at him, knowing him from past visits, and in no time he was riding the elevator up to the fifth floor.

Inside the elevator, the flowers smelled even more fragrant. He fiddled with the bouquet a little, fixing any of the flowers that weren't as perfect as the others. He patted himself on the back once more for managing to actually make the bouquet at all. He wouldn't have wanted to try to search another store if he had struck out at the Hallmark store. He checked three other stores before that one and each of them had been cleaned out, picked so clean it looked like a Valentine's Day apocalypse had occurred and people had hoarded every item they could find with a red heart on it.

The elevator pinged and he stepped out onto the fifth floor. As soon as the elevator doors closed, he began to hear a lot more noise than usual. Thanks to the sound deafening doors and walls, it was all muffled, but as he walked to Sandy's apartment, he could hear muffled yells and what appeared to be screams coming from the other apartments.

But once again, he barely gave it much thought. If people wanted to fight and argue, that was their business. All he cared about was himself and his best gal.

At the end of the hallway was apartment 3D. That was Sandy's place.

Looking down to the mat outside her door, he saw a pair of worn loafers sitting like an old incontinent dog forced to stay outside for risk of peeing on the carpet. He recognized the loafers immediately.

They belonged to Sandy's mother, Agnes.

Made sense, he figured, Agnes probably came over to help with the dinner Sandy was making. That bode well for Gene's stomach. Agnes and him got along all right, though Sandy's father was another matter altogether. If he had been visiting, as well, his old black work boots would have been sitting shotgun next to the loafers. He liked Agnes. Despite her name making her sound old and ugly, she was very attractive, and it was obvious where Sandy got her good looks from. There had been times when Gene had admired Agnes when no one was watching him, staring at her curves and shapely butt.

He reached up to knock on the door, careful not to drop the flowers, and as he wrapped the wood with his knuckles, the door creaked inward.

It was unlocked and open.

That was odd. But maybe she knew he was here and had unlocked the door for him.

No, that didn't make sense. As he pushed the door open, his eyes immediately went to the doorjamb and what was splattered on it.

Ketchup?

It had to be. It looked like someone had been trying to open a bottle and had accidentally sprayed some on the jamb. Stepping inside, he saw the jamb had a handprint on it, the palm pressed into the ketchup.

Oh, what a mess, Sandy must be so upset. She must be going to get a cloth to clean it up, he thought as he closed the door with his foot. Both hands were still holding the flowers and candy.

"Sandy? It's me, Gene," he called out. He could smell the delicious aroma of a roast in the oven and his mouth began to water. He walked deeper into the apartment, his eyes playing over the furniture. On the end of the couch was Agnes' coat, the one with the imitation fur on the collar.

"Sandy? Where are you?" he called again. He was anxious to see her, he couldn't wait to see her face when he handed her the candy and flowers.

With both still in his hands, he went to the kitchen, but just as he got to the entrance, Sandy poked her head out.

He expected her to be in an apron, so she wouldn't ruin her clothes while she cooked, but his actual image of her was far different.

Sandy was covered in ketchup, her white teeth peeking out of the scarlet syrup, and her hair was hanging limply over her shoulders, because there was more ketchup in her hair. To Gene, it looked like she had squirted an entire bottle over herself and rubbed it all in.

"Sandy, what the hell is going on? Why are you covered in ketchup?"

Sandy lowered her head and bared her teeth like a wild dog, a growl emanating from deep in her throat.

That was when Gene took a step closer, wanting to go to her. His eyes caught movement behind her, on the kitchen floor, and he spotted two stocking feet twitching like the body they belonged to was being electrocuted. The heels of the feet were beating a steady staccato on the linoleum and Gene figured out almost immediately it was Agnes.

He stepped closer and the legs became the lower half of the woman and he gasped in shock when he saw that Agnes had no abdomen, only a jagged hole where what looked like wild dogs had attacked her, tearing and rending her flesh from her body.

"Holy shit, Sandy, you're mother, what happened?"

Sandy's reply was to lunge at him like a sprinter at the sound of the starting gun. Gene was caught off guard and he was thrown backwards with Sandy on top of him. At first he tried to fend her off, not understanding what was happening, but then some of the ketchup on her chin dripped into his open mouth. Instead of tasting the tangy spices of the confection, he tasted copper, realization flashing through his mind instantly.

It wasn't ketchup on the door jamb or on her body, and he was positive what she was covered in was blood; Agnes' blood.

Then he had no time for thought as Sandy tried to sink her teeth into his throat. He used the flowers like a bat, slapping her on the side of the face, but all that happened was the stems broke, the flower pedals evaporating, loose pedals drifting to the floor like feathers.

As he swiped at her again, one of the thorns on a rose stem caught her open right eye and tore it sideways; opening the orb up like it had been sliced by a tiny knife. Clear ooze dripped out and Sandy roared in either anger or pain.

Gene was still slapping her with the flowers, the pedals falling around him like snow, and when they were nothing but small nubs, he dropped them, the stems falling around him.

Sandy was still trying to eat him, as unbelievable as that seemed, and her teeth clacked on empty air as he fought to keep her at bay. He hit her with the box of chocolates, but the box was weak and it broke open, chocolates falling onto his chest and around his head. All the while Sandy hopped on top of him, desperately trying to sink her bloody teeth into his flesh.

He managed to get his left hand under her chin and try to push her off, but her weight on his was at such a point he couldn't get any leverage. She was about the same size as him, though was curvaceous like a woman should be, and he was evenly matched as long as he was trapped on the floor.

Her teeth clicked shut an inch from his ear and he winced, expecting to feel pain, then he shoved her away again. His free hand reached out; all that was close was the scattered chocolates, so he grabbed some with his hand and brought them up. When she came at him, he shoved the chocolates into her mouth, her teeth clamping down on a pink nougat and apricot swirl.

Now she couldn't bite him; her mouth full of chocolate.

That gave him an idea and he quickly reached out for more stray candies. Finding three, he brought them up and forced them into her mouth. Her cheeks plumped up like she was a squirrel carrying nuts and she groaned and mewled like a wounded animal.

It was obvious she didn't want sweets, she wanted meat...his meat to be exact, and not in a good way.

He forced the candy deep into her mouth, a peanut brittle and a chocolate nougat becoming squished, her cheeks stretched so thin it looked like they were going to blow out.

As she fought him, she shifted her body, and he took the opportunity to throw her off. She rolled to the side and he got on top of her, now having the upper hand. Not knowing what to do next, he continued doing what he'd been doing, and that was force-feeding her candies.

With his legs on both sides of her chest, and his butt on her breasts, he reached out with both hands and grabbed more candy. Then, with a rueful look, he shoved them into her mouth and down her throat. Peach nougat, dark chocolate and the dreaded lemon crèmes, were squished and pressed into her mouth. Some of the chocolaty clump began to work its way down her throat and it looked like there was an apple in there.

The entire time he shoved candy into her mouth, tears fell down his cheeks. He knew she was suffocating, her airway clogged with chocolate and nougat. As he shoved more and more candy into her mouth, he didn't hear the soft footsteps coming up behind him.

But he did feel the strong white teeth of Agnes when she sank them an inch deep into the back of his neck.

He cried out in pain and surprise and punched back with his free hand. He caught Agnes in the nose and it fractured, now looking like she had run into a glass door and smashed her face like putty. But she barely felt the blow and an instant later was jumping on Gene's back, her teeth tearing off his right ear and woofing it down like taffy.

Gene roared with pain and terror as he tried to get her off him, but she was like a gymnast, her wiry body moving about. As he fell off Sandy, she got up, soon coming for him, too.

As the two women began to tear into him, sharp, manicured fingernails like small razor blades, he thought back to a wet dream he'd had a few months ago. Back then he had dreamt of a mother daughter tag-team, with him in the middle, but this wasn't what he had dreamed about.

Agnes came around to face him, and Gene got a good look at her torn-out torso, her insides dripping and sagging like a rotting pumpkin. Her lungs glistened in the light of the living room, her rib cage cracked open like a spent turkey carcass on Thanksgiving.

Gene managed one last look as both mother and daughter growled at him, then Agnes sank her fingers into his eyes as Sandy brought her mouth down over his in a perverse French kiss. As she sank her teeth onto his lips, melted chocolate seeped from her mouth, soon to mix with his blood. When she lifted her head and sat up, his lips stretched like taffy, until like an elastic at its limit, the flesh parted, leaving him forever grinning with no lips. He screamed in pain as blood mixed with chocolate flooded into his mouth, the world forever dark thanks to Agnes plucking out his eyes.

Agnes shoved both morsels into her mouth, the orbs popping like grapes. She chewed merrily as viscous ooze dribbled down her chin. Agnes had once been a polite eater, but now she was just shameless.

Gene screamed again, his tongue protruding from his mouth and flapping past his lipless mouth, and was rewarded with Sandy leaning down and clamping her chocolate-covered teeth on his tongue. Bleached enamel sliced the tongue in half, and she wolfed it down, the lump in her throat growing ever larger. It appeared the candy hadn't made it through her esophagus and now all the flesh she consumed was becoming impacted, like rush hour grid-lock in Boston.

Of course, Gene didn't know any of this.

His torn throat was still pumping blood, and as each squirt bathed the carpeting, a little more of his life's fluid seeped out.

Agnes and Sandy went in for more, again and again, teeth and fingers finding flesh. It was Agnes who bit off his dick, chewing on it like it was the best summer sausage she'd ever had. By then, thankfully, Gene was past feeling anything.

His heels were tapping a steady drum roll on the floor and his blood had ceased to pour from him.

Agnes leaned over and pulled Gene's right hand to her mouth, biting off the first three digits. Finger food at its truest form, the mature woman chewed happily, crunching on bones like they were pretzels dipped in blood.

The mother-daughter team ate heartily for the next hour, and when Gene was all but consumed, they stood up. Agnes' belly was distended from all the human meat she'd consumed and Sandy's throat had indeed blown out, chocolate and partially eaten flesh now dripping out of the open wound. No matter how much she tried to eat, it would only fall out of her neck hole, and there was no way for the mindless woman to realize her dilemma. But still she would try, until the end of time if she was allowed.

Mother and daughter moved to the front door of the apartment, which was still partially open from Gene entering, and both stepped out into the hallway.

Other doors were opening now as tenants, once dead and then revived, joined Sandy and Agnes in the hallway.

As one crowd, similar to a high school band, all the people turned to their right and marched towards the stairwell door.

Upon reaching it, one pushed it open, by luck or design, and each of them filed down the staircase to the street below.

By the time they reached the street and the light of day, more screams of chaos filled the air. Sirens wailed, people screamed, and humans dying was the status quo, and with barely a nod to one another, the tenants joined the fray, feeding, killing, and eating.

For this would be a Valentine's Day to remember, where the tagline should be, *You always hurt the one you love*....or was that *eat* them?

THE SELECTED

TOM HAMILTON

1

Once I had the dough kneaded out into a circle, Isaac strolled over and draped a cheese stick onto the bottom half. This created a mouth for our head. There I promptly supplanted two pepperonis for the eyes and even gave it some brows by carefully placing two banana peppers over the slices. We looked at our Frankenstein and then at each other before bursting out laughing. Big Barry came back from the register. For the last several minutes, he'd been kissing the ass of some old woman who was complaining about something alien found in her ham and cheese sandwich. He'd ended up coughing up a refund, and if this didn't put him in a sour enough mood, now he heard us snickering.

"Knock it off, assholes!" he growled through his grimace. "It's almost time for the buffet crowd."

Isaac turned back towards the ovens, and when he was sure that they shielded him from Big Barry, gave the fat man a mock drill sergeant's salute. I disassembled the food face and quickly went about the business of properly placing the raw ingredients, which we were going to meld into a sausage pizza, onto the cool dough. Isaac went back to prepping the ovens.

What else could we do? The fat prick was still our boss and I needed the money for the university. Unless I wanted to languish in the kitchens of Pizza Gut for the rest of my career, that is.

With us checked back into line, Big Barry hurried out towards the register, his corpulent belly hidden underneath a black apron. Isaac made his hands into a cross bar, and using my index finger, I kicked a field goal with the last round sausage left on the chopping board. With the back of his throat, Isaac breathed out the roar of an imaginary crowd.

After that however, we knocked off most of the bullshit and prepared to shuffle out the pies for the lunch crowd. Yet surprisingly, few customers rotated through those usually hectic doors.

Plus, all the delivery drivers had gone out but none seemed to be returning. After a couple of hours of this, Big Barry came into the back and said, "Where and the hell have all those slackers driven off to?"

2

I guess that I've always been in love with Theresa. Hell, every boy at our school was enchanted with her. You'd have to be a faggot not to be. I even knew a couple of girls who thought that they were in love with her and they weren't lesbians.

She caught me looking at her while she was taking some simpleton's order, the slashed splashes of her blonde hair framing her docile Cancun blue eyes. But she only smiled innocently; a carefree smile full of idealistic teenaged happiness and hope. My heart tilted like the old, sometimes broken, pinball machine which sat half lit in one cluttered corner of the restaurant.

But I knew there was a lot of competition in those 12th grade hallways and that most of these predators were only sniffing around for the keys to Theresa's chastity belt; meat headed ivory-smiling jocks or droop-jeaned rappers all spitting their repulsive, street lingo filled, spiels at her. And the prettiest ones always seemed to believe them. I'd known a few womanizers in my day and I was always struck by their sheer heartlessness; at the quickness with which they'd disposed of their conquests. Like a two of clubs being placed onto the discard pile, or a sudsy prophylactic wrapped in tissue being socked into a trash pail.

I didn't want to see this happen to Theresa, but there wasn't anything I could do about it. I didn't have any claim to her and some of these pricks looked like movie stars for God's sake. Sure, she knew that I was alive, but she also knew that the night crawlers at the bait shop across the street were alive, and that didn't mean she was going to French kiss one of them.

3

So most of the time Isaac and I just goofed off by the big black ovens. At least as much as Big Barry would allow us to. During lax moments, I would try and spy Theresa refilling customer's drinks or setting out the silverware. But the dining room was dark and we still weren't a smoke free establishment. So trying to catch a glimpse of her was like searching for a bright star through early morning fog or passing clouds.

Isaac was from Westin, which was the proverbial and literal, *other side of the tracks*. All I'd ever heard about the black kids from over there was how much they hated us lily-white preppies who were being primed for the university. But Isaac wasn't about anything like that.

He was a tall, muscular kid with a face that still hadn't lost its baby fat. It was a very soft face. One day I told him he looked like 'Fat Albert' and it was no joke, there was a fierce likeness. But he only laughed and barked, "Hey, Hey, Hey!" with a perfect 'Cosby' growl. Evidently, he'd heard that comparison a hundred times before.

Joking around with Isaac made the monotonous workday pass by a lot faster, and looking back on the whole thing now, I'd have to say I loved Isaac, too. No, not like no faggots or anything, but like one friend loves another, like brothers. It's just like John Cougar Mellencamp lamented from the tabletop jukeboxes which still worked in most of the booths; "Can't tell your best buddy that you love him."

4

Sure it was pretty damn slow, but it was a Monday. Yet when no one, and I mean no one, showed up for the six p.m. supper rush, it became obvious something was amiss.

Finally at seven-fifteen, Isaac said, "I don't believe it, here comes a live one." All the Pizza Guts stores in our area, including mine, had a sort of thin, red contact paper baked onto all of the entrance doors. So all we could see was the outline of a stumbling form approaching the threshold. The form bounced off of the door and then staggered over to the first window. We didn't really get a clear look at its face; it just looked like someone with a five gallon bucket of red paint poured over their head. But when the arm came up, and with a motion like a windshield wiper, started smearing blood all over the tinted glass, Theresa screamed and staggered backwards. Whoever or whatever it was then wandered away.

Big Barry had seen enough. He hastily spun the bolt lock and said, "Call 9-1-1." I obliged, but some strange message played back out of the receiver; something about all emergency frequencies currently being disabled or some such bullshit. I repeated the recording to my portly boss but he still seemed hopeful.

"No," he said. "When you dial 9-1-1 they...the cops, they have to call you back." He paused, one grimy paw wiping white powder onto his apron, his eyes darting around nervously.

I had my doubts but I only shrugged. I didn't feel like arguing with him, besides, I didn't want to alarm Theresa any further. She was already sitting ghost-eyed in one of the booths, her blank order pad resting on her delicate, blue jean-covered knees.

Voices of violence rose from the incoming night outside. Hearing those gruesome calls prompted us to turn off the lights, save for the store room bulb back behind the ovens. We drew all the curtains closed as Isaac took the long pilot lighter and went around to each table, firing up those trademark 'Pizza Gut' candles so we wouldn't be in total darkness; you know those ones which look like the bottom of a pirate's wine bottle covered in maroon fishnet. We tried the phone lines incessantly but were rebuffed by the same monotone, taped recital. We heard a boom that sounded like a car backfiring somewhere out on the road. And then later some scuffling noises, maybe the stampede of running feet. We were afraid to put our faces in the windows to find out, but it seemed as if some sort of war was going on outside.

We had no access to any media outlets. We weren't allowed to have a radio on the job. Big Barry had made sure of that; he said the music took our minds off of the work at hand and also that it discouraged the customers from plugging quarters into the juke boxes. The television had been broken ever since I had started working there; it sat high in one shrouded corner like a detached retina.

Of course we continued to try and call the police until I thought the rotary was going to break off of the phone. After this proved futile, we all took turns trying to call home; Isaac buzzed his mom but received no reply. When Theresa called home, she was extremely worried about her little sister, her picturesque face fraught with worry, as it rang incessantly. Big Barry called God knows who in vane and I may as well have been dialing the number of an old phone booth outside an abandoned, deserted gas station.

We sat for several hours in the cozy glow of the candles, all of us speculating in our minds about what in the hell could be going on outside, but no one voiced his or her opinion. I chivalrously offered to give Theresa a ride home, but she only shook her head no with a near catatonic stare, and despite my bravado, I was silently relieved.

"I don't care about my mom," she said out of nowhere. "But my little sister's out there."

"You shouldn't say that," I said, not really knowing why I was daring to correct her. "I'm sure your mom's not that bad, and she and your little sister are both going to be okay."

"Hmm, she doesn't even keep food in the house," she countered.

At our regular closing time, things seemed to have quieted down a bit outside and Big Barry announced he was going to try and make it home. I thought this was a bad idea but I didn't convey my concern; if the overbearing fat bastard wanted to get himself killed that was his business. He told us we could have the rest of the night off--which was damn sporting of him, since it was already past time to clock out and there seemed to be some sort of apocalypse going on outside--and that he was sure the authorities would have order restored soon, certainly by tomorrow. Henceforth we would all be expected to be there at nine a.m. the next morning as usual.

Hiding my disdain, I told him that I'd be there. Theresa said nothing. Isaac wisecracked that he'd probably still be here if and when Big Barry returned for the regularly scheduled opening. The fat man uncharacteristically ignored the clever comment, for he was not his usual rude self. He looked shaken and disheveled.

"Nine o' clock... sharp," he repeated before exiting through the rear kitchen door. Which wasn't far from where he always parked his 1979, Lincoln Continental; it was the Bill Blass. He looked both ways fearfully before going, like a man about to cross a busy intersection, and I *almost* felt sorry for him.

I swiveled the bolt locked behind him before dropping the long, wooden reinforcement bar into the steel support arms.

We never saw him again.

5

At five a.m. the streets were empty. After Big Barry had departed, the pace of the melee outside quickened. Shambling subjects skulked across the parking lot as Isaac and I peeked out the tinted windows. After a large chunk of something hit the side of the building with a loud bang, Isaac was startled into action.

He almost tripped over one of the tables.

"Help me with this damn thing, man!" he barked out in frustration. I quickly got to my feet and we reinforced the entrance by turning the tables over and covering the door. Miraculously, Isaac found a still charged, electric framing nail gun in the store room and we shot them into place with the long, four inch nails. After we were satisfied with our work, we plopped down in one of the remaining booths, panting like street dogs in the summer.

Outside, the carnage continued. A huge pack of individuals, all their arms and legs entangled within, danced across the asphalt in a flailing circle, feral dogs snapping at their calves and unwanted cats digging angry claws into the backs of their tattered clothes.

Nearby, a man was standing on the roof of a car brandishing a handgun. He fired repeatedly into the spinning gang with zero effect. The mad people punched and kicked at each other senselessly until they were out of view. The man skipped across the trunk of the car and jogged away.

We had jumped up to peek around the edges of the curtains to watch him. Now we simultaneously sat back down. "What the hell, man?" Isaac said. "What the hell's going on?"

6

As the days past by, I grew tired and the air inside the restaurant seemed to grow stale from inactivity. We sure as hell didn't have to worry about food; we had enough pizza ingredients to feed a battalion. Plus, salads, sandwiches, lasagna and so forth. Though

I must admit my appetite was lacking. There were no showers of course, but the restrooms were sufficient for cat baths. A lack of deodorant, toothpaste and a laundered change of clothes, however, prevented us from ever feeling really clean.

We were worried that perhaps some flipped-out shadow would kill the electricity, but the lights just continued to glow. What few bulbs, that is, we allowed ourselves to switch on. During the day, we made a conscience effort not to use any lights at all, save for perhaps the store room bulb, which we were confident couldn't be seen from the outside. At night we'd just use the candles and placed them on the floor or underneath the booths. We wanted to give off the appearance, to anyone or anything that may be searching from the street, that the restaurant was closed or ideally that the franchise was even bankrupt, with all employees let go and the equipment long removed.

We didn't really feel all that secure, of course, but the number one criteria which we had to bank on, our one baseless hope, was that no phantom, fiend or freak had attempted to breech or break into the establishment.

Being in this close a proximity to Theresa for such a prolonged period, you would have thought that some of her luster would have worn off by now, or at least that she would have been relegated to the status of a mere human being. But the opposite happened; I was helplessly smitten and overwhelmingly star struck by her, and, even though she ate little, slept less and wept almost every waking moment, her electrifying beauty hadn't lost any of the sharpness of its pristine edge.

Watching her walk by was like a thrilling punch to the chest. Even the mere twist of her artful feminine body inside of her modest clothes gave off the effect of a shot of adrenaline to me. That attire never seemed to wrinkle or stain even after being worn for days. One night she washed her feet, lavender nail polish still glowing on her alluring toenails, in a lasagna pan. I had to pour a pitcher of ice water over my balls in the black rimmed sink, then I hated myself for lusting after her in such a callous and impure fashion. Suddenly I felt no better than the womanizers, except that they could get girls like Theresa and I couldn't.

Still I valiantly tried to keep her calm, often standing guard over the makeshift bed which I had made for her underneath the center booth at the front of the restaurant.

When I encouraged her to eat, she asked, "Why are you being so nice to me?" *Aren't all the boys nice to you?* I thought and wanted to say but I held that one back. "Because we're co-workers," I said instead.

"Well, thank you," she said kindly.

"You're welcome." I said, smiling and lifting my eyebrows, like me falling all over her wasn't any big deal.

A little while later I came back with my special; an Alfredo and Mostaccoli mix. It was great but it wasn't like I had cooked it from scratch. I mean, the Pizza Gut food is pretty good anyway, though processed. Even though I had no choice but to scarf it down hour after hour, I still hadn't gotten sick of it.

"This is my special recipe," I quipped. "All the way from the boot of Italy." This made me wonder what in the world a real Italian chef would say in the wake of this processed, tomato sauce-laced pulp.

She smiled a little, but it was a pain-wracked grin and she could only nibble a couple of bites down.

"Do you think Barry made it?" she asked naively.

Christ, I sure as fuckin' well hope not! Anyway, no fuckin' way. "Yeah." Was what I really said, "I'm sure he told the cops we're in here. They're probably pretty busy with what's goin' on and all. But I'm sure they'll get to us pretty soon." This false view would have to be classified as optimistic in the extreme.

"What do you think is going on out there?" she asked, her bright face tight with worry.

"I don't know," I shook my head. "But, you know, with the army and everything, they'll get to us soon."

She stared at the floor and seemed to grow sad. "You know," she began, "what I said about my mother the other day, I didn't mean it...I mean...I hope she's okay."

I shrugged. "We're all tired," I said simply.

Suddenly she seemed to crumple up, like a flower in a fast-forwarded video frame curdling in the cold. She leaned forward and wept into my chest. And although her closeness felt exciting to me, I could feel her sadness soaking into me as the tears saturated my shirt. The cadence of her heartbeat throbbed like my will to live. And it suddenly occurred to me that this disaster, or whatever it was, was almost like a lucky break for me.

All my competition was now dead, or at the very least running for their lives. I would have stayed in that lifeless restaurant with her forever. It's like I had always known; if only she would get to know me I could make her fall in love with me, and, as it turned out, that's exactly what happened.

7

After that, the whole romance sort of came off like a miracle. Everything I said somehow came out just right. Or at least that's the way it seemed to strike her. My tongue, which had always been thick and clumsy in the presence of the worldwide sorority of the softer sex, had suddenly turned as silver as a rare nickel. I was as competent and astute as the womanizers, only the words which came from me were genuine, while their false phrases were practiced and counterfeit. I felt like she knew this and was refreshed by it even. Perhaps I hadn't given her enough credit when it came to protecting herself from such monsters.

I realized, of course, that she had no choice but to talk to me, but I could see something different in her gaze, a recognition of a goodness *within me* that she would never have known about otherwise; a longing glare usually reserved for the most popular and athletic heartthrobs at our school. Sure, a trillion bastards had always hit on her, but she had no official boyfriend. So, in lieu of the absence of our classmates, I confidently stepped into those comfortable shoes. We were thrown together in a haphazard yet somehow spectacular fashion. Like two Indians in an arranged arrowhead marriage or two Celtic gypsies jumping over a matrimonial broom.

I admit, in the normal nuances of our high school home rooms, this might have felt strained or strange. But here, in the greenhouse atmosphere of our incarceration, our love grew like some bizarre and brilliant new species of flower. And then, as a speeding August rain slammed against the red roof of the restaurant, her irises shifting down, cascading within their own pools, smitten with permission, we kissed serenely, the struggling dance of the candles painting their pale beige ballet underneath our chins.

And a joy poured out of us as honest as a shooting star, a comet which we were too afraid to search the night sky for.

8

"What's that?" Isaac asked, and I saw that he was straining to look a great distance out beyond the parking lot. I followed his gaze past the bait shop and several scarred foundries, then over into the bleak prairies beyond the edge of town. We shaded our eyes from the rippling effects of the sun.

Of course we didn't have any binoculars or anything like that, we had gotten lucky with the nail gun, but you could forget about firearms or anything else that might be of some practical use. Unless you wanted to consider a butter knife or a pizza cutter a deadly weapon.

"What?" I asked. "Where?"

"There!" he exclaimed, and pointed between two deceased factories near a far off field. On the very last rim of the horizon, right before the land disappeared on the cusp of the firmament; I could barely see what looked like an endless herd of cattle or buffalo. A great mass on the tip of the plains.

I shook my head. "I don't know." I pulled my Pizza Gut cap down tight over my eyes and refocused. No, these forms were taller than cattle, like bears in a mosh pit, but that just couldn't be, you'd need two hundred thousand creatures to create a mass that large. It was like the awesome rows of an endless army and yet... some smaller dots moved above the crowd, like animalistic bodies being passed from one figure to the next or giant wolverines walking on each other's shoulders. No way, it just couldn't be, and it was still more than five football fields away, making it impossible to tell what we were looking at from this distance. Then I thought I heard a scream and it was like a thousand arms had come from the crowd and reached for the sun. Like eighty thousand Muslims rising from their rugs in a prayer. I stole a sideways glance at Isaac, and ascertained that, he too, had heard the scream.

"I don't know?" I said again.

9

I got into the habit of waking up about five a.m., although I hadn't really been sleeping in any kind of traditional sense. It was more like a fear-fueled, nightmare-riddled trance, full of colorless, steeped towers which were only trumped by the bleak reality of the actual situation whenever I moaned awake.

Wiping the blackness off of my face, I stumbled towards the restroom. One of the fishnet candles sat on the sink and it had died down to a barely visible waver. I knew where the urinal was, however, and I'd long been broke of the ritual of snapping on the light. As my piss hit the depreciating mint, my thoughts traveled back to the mass on the horizon which Isaac had noticed earlier that day. After the sun had dipped, we were no longer able to follow its progress, if indeed it had made any progression or regression, and we had gotten nowhere as far as trying to figure out what it might be.

I zipped up and sleepily scratched the back of my head. That's when I realized I had gone to sleep with my cap still on. The sun would be up in forty-five minutes or so and at that point I would be able to see if the mass was still out there. After leaving the bathroom, I kneed my way into the booth and pulled back the curtain.

I thought I had known moments of fear before in my life; when my Indian motorcycle went air born and I knew I was going to come down hard, when I had shared my mother's darkened house with a burglar, my sweaty palm clutching a pocket knife as I knelt in a clothes packed closet. When three gang bangers surrounded me and threatened to beat out the brains I needed for the university. But the sight I beheld now gave me a far more morbid start. There was a white face washed with streaks of gray not five centimeters from the glass. The eyes glowed dirtily, like two grimy pennies recovered from a mud puddle. They didn't appear to focus on me, but rather they were muddled, like the stare of a sleepwalker spying a dread-tainted dream instead of what was actually in front of him. It was as if this looker had seen something so scarring that he could never use those seared irises again. As if his vision just couldn't reconnect to the hard surfaces of the real world, and this reaper, this phantom wasn't alone, for there were thousands, what seemed like millions, of his kind right behind him. They were packed shoulder to shoulder throughout the parking lot and beyond, as far as my yellowed eyes could see. They were packed as tight as cattle in a stockade or those poor people the Nazis had shuffled into those boxcars. They didn't attempt to break in. For they really didn't appear to be conscious at all as they swayed softly back and forth in the early morning drizzle like worshippers of some pseudo-Kentucky hillbilly, snake religion, the slime from their grimy bodies and the acid rain mingled to drip off of their brindled chins.

I retreated in a stumble back from the window. I thought my chest would cave in or that my chin would crack right off from the terror, as it ripped through my arms and legs with the force and effect of a heart attack. I heard a sound like a cannonball as I defecated into my drawers and fell into a heap with my back to the iron-colored salad bar. Then, another thought ravaged my brain and I scurried to the opposite side of the restaurant, almost stumbling over Isaac's sleeping form. I slid into a new booth and slowly reached for the curtain, as if I could change what was behind it depending on which angle I approached it from.

I saw the back of a woman or maybe a girl's head, her black mane smashed against the window like a squashed spider's web. I couldn't really see behind her, but I could just sense from her body's odd angle that there was a thousand of her kind pressing against her, and now I could see them, all tangled in each other's limbs like some septic vision of the pits of Hades. Satisfied there was no chance of escape, I was just about to drop the curtain, when the girl's head whirled around suddenly, like a sleeper coming up from a nightmare. She bared her brittle, orange teeth and barked at me as wild as a wolf. I stumbled backwards as the curtain fell across her ghastly face and rode one of the tables to the floor. I bit back a scream like someone trying to hold in a wave of vomit. But the noise from my tumble woke Isaac anyway. He danced around, throwing punches at his own imaginary enemies like Mohammed Ali.

"What...what the hell is it, man?" he stammered, still half asleep.

"Nothin'," I explained. "I just had a nightmare, man, everything's fine. Go on back to sleep."

"Shit, man." He ran his fingers through his short hair. "You really had me scared. I thought that somethin' was goin' on outside." He made a move towards the window.

"No, no, don't," I implored while making my palm into a stop sign. "I just looked out man, everything's cool, it's all right. I got this. I got it."

Even though I surmised that none of us would last the forty-five minutes until dawn, I was still desperate to save my friend and my beautiful sweetheart from the misery of knowing what was in store for them behind the red curtains until the absolute last instant. Why inject any more trepidation into their lungs than they'd already been living with? Why cause them to suffer as I was suffering?

"I got it, man, I'm on guard duty. Go on back to bed." Like there was anything the 'guard' could have done about it when thousands of walking ghouls tried to gain access to the restaurant.

"All right, man," Isaac said. "That's cool. I'll relieve you in a couple of hours." With that he pulled a table cloth over himself and laid his head on some piled up 'Pizza Gut *pizza to go*' t-shirts.

"Fair enough," I said as he quickly retreated into a world of dreams; a world we were all far better off visiting nowadays. I dumped myself down by the salad bar, a shiver overtaking my entire skeleton as if I were sitting outside, naked, in subzero temperatures.

Thank God the hubbub hadn't awoken Theresa. She lay as peaceful as a princess in a fairy tale, her closed eyelids flushed with purple, even though her make-up had long faded. Some girls needed cosmetics, even the very pretty ones. It was as if their stripped down faces were deflated somehow, discolored or shrunken without this protection. But Theresa didn't fall into that category, even here in the vicious raw of a savage morning, perhaps our last ever; she glowed like a pageant queen.

I was afraid to look out the window anymore. So I just sat with my back to the salad bar, shaking and looking around the restaurant, expecting to hear glass break at any second. I thought about the panels which made up the pizza joint. They would fold back like cardboard when a mob that size pressed their weight against it. Especially since they were probably not worried about the ones in front getting trampled and so forth.

So this was it, the end of my life. Jesus, I hadn't even gotten to have sex with Theresa. There was still so much I wanted to do. I had been looking so forward to the university. I wanted to learn, but I also wanted to party in the frat-houses. I wanted to get hammered at the football games. I wanted to pinch the cheerleaders' asses. This was the United States, for Christ's sake. I had dreams. I wanted to write the great American novel.

Sometime after six, the climbing sunlight began to slant through the curtains. I could hear nothing outside and the only noise in the dining room was Isaac's heaving and Theresa's delicate breath. When nothing else happened for another twenty minutes, I dragged myself towards the curtain. After another five minutes of cowering in the booth, I somehow mustered the courage to brave a peek. What I saw next was a miracle in its own right. There was no one outside, only an empty parking lot with stained papers and crap-colored wrappers flushing through an empty wind. The streets and thoroughfares adjacent to the restaurant were also deserted. Not one Godless form in sight.

Had it all been some horrid, twisted nightmare? No, I'd had some bad dreams before but...

10

After that we had some sort of peace for a while. I kept expecting the ghastly figures to reposition themselves outside. I must have looked out the window every forty-five seconds, but they didn't return, at least not so far.

Theresa talked about her little sister a lot and about what we would do once we got out. She said she had seen a TV special about the country of Iceland. According to the program, it wasn't cold there at all. Turns out the first Viking explorers had only christened it Iceland to discourage various other squatters from coming ashore. Imploring other plunderers to bypass it for neighboring Greenland, which actually *was* as frigid as hell.

She thought maybe we could rescue her little sister and then head there. I agreed with this wholeheartedly, even though I knew that it wasn't the least bit feasible. We'd be lucky to get outside and get a car started, let alone drive halfway across the country to a dock. And once there, how would we get to a boat or a plane? How would we know how to operate either one? How did we know that Iceland wasn't affected by the crises? I didn't even know where Iceland was on the globe for Christ's sake. But I let her have her dream; why spoil it?

If she wanted to go to Iceland, Iceland it was.

Isaac meanwhile was boxing his own demons. As Theresa and I slow danced to the scratchy ballads on the old jukes--after not seeing a soul out the window for a couple of weeks, we'd gotten confident enough to let the slower songs play on a very low volume--Isaac glanced up from his mop. He was still performing his daily tasks, either out of unbreakable force of habit or a desperate attempt at normalcy. His face looked troubled and drawn which, given this instance, wasn't really a revelation, and yet, I sensed that something else was bothering him. When Theresa went to do her girly thing in the restroom, I walked across the freshly mopped tiles.

"What's wrong man?" I asked him.

"Oh, nothing," he smiled weakly. "I'm fine, I'm real glad for you and Theresa. I know that's what you wanted."

I nodded and grabbed a couple of tinted-red, plastic glasses from the drink bar. I shot us a couple of Pepsi's and said, "C'mon, let's take a break, bro'."

He nodded and we slid into a booth.

"Talk to me, man," I implored.

He slunk out from what had been a dumpy posture and sat up straight. "Did I ever tell you I have a girlfriend, man? Or maybe I should say...had."

I was shocked. "No," I answered, taken aback.

He nodded. "Yeah, she's pretty cool." He reached for his wallet and took out a tattered photograph of a likeness of a light-skinned black girl. She was standing with some children and a rotund clown.

"Jesus," I said, staring into her coffee-colored irises. She's a fuckin'… She's beautiful, man."

"Yeah," he nodded, looking sadder yet. "She's pregnant, man." I took a deep breath, tried to put on a fake brave face, decided I couldn't, and whistled a sigh.

"Jesus," I said.

"Yeah," he countered.

"When's she due?" I inquired, trying to find a silver lining. If she were due at a later date, maybe I could make him feel better by convincing him that we would all be free by then. Free of the Pizza Gut, anyway.

"She's due today." He looked as if he might cry when he said it.

"Oh." I handed him back the dog-eared picture. I was out of answers. Not that I'd had very many in the first place.

"You know, I never even knew my old man," he said. I nodded my head yes. That much I had known.

"Well," I tried again. "I mean, this circumstance… it sure as hell isn't your fault.

"Shut up, man!" he snapped suddenly, the fear, depression and repression had drove him to a breaking point. "What do you know about it, man? You ever been poor, man? I bet you never even been to Westin? Shit… assholes like you be walkin' around in a polo shirt out to the university."

"Isaac," I said calmly, for I realized it was his hopeless plight which was fueling his angry words. "There is no more university."

He seemed to slump, as if defeated by the slow and constant pressure we were all under. "I'm sorry, bro," he said teary-eyed. "You know I ain't 'bout nothin' like that."

"I know that, bro," I said earnestly. "Don't worry 'bout it." Then after a few seconds I added. "Look, maybe it's time we tried to get the hell out of here?"

He nodded in concurrence, still looking dejected and ill. Theresa returned from the bathroom and searched our faces.

"What are you guys talking about?" she asked.

"Iceland," I answered.

11

And we actually thought we were going to get out of there, too. The next morning we even began mapping out routes in our minds such as what might be the fastest way to pick up Theresa's little sister. Then the shortest shortcut over to Isaac's girlfriend's apartment, all the way up to the time that we crossed the city limits What none of us mentioned of course, was that there was little incentive to believe that any of these people were still alive.

We even took one of the tablecloths and spread it out on the hard carpet near the register and began throwing supplies on it. Theresa dug out her backpack, which she sometimes took to school and then to work. Isaac seemed to cheer up; there was some extra pep in his step. We were all very encouraged at the prospect of escape. And then we heard the most startling noise, louder than lightning striking a tin roof; like the sound of a hammer pounding on a ringside bell.

We all jumped and followed the noise to its source, looking in the direction of the ringing telephone.

12

We had forgotten that the phone was even there, conceding it was as dead as the rest of the city. It rang three times, as clumsy as a clunking engine before any of us could move.

"Finally," Theresa said. "Maybe it's the police? 9-1-1 always calls back, right? Just like Barry said." But her eyes were wide with doubt, and she was shuffling her feet like someone trying to keep warm in a bitterly cold wind.

I nodded, although I knew her theory was bogus. Isaac's eyes darted around, like someone looking at a crime being committed, yet helpless to stop it. The phone continued to ring like a jackhammer down a morning street.

I walked over and picked it up.

"Hello?" I asked tentatively.

"Hello, yourself," a smarmy voice returned my greeting.

"Who's this?"

"Look," the voice said. "I'm not going to waste your time answering questions which will ultimately be rendered meaningless. I'm simply going to say that I need for you to send the girl out."

"What girl?" The moment I asked this I regretted using the word girl. For a new fear filled Theresa's eyes and they got even wider, which I hadn't thought possible.

"Why, Theresa, of course," the voice said.

I paused perplexed. Then I said, "I can't do that."

But the voice didn't grow angry or flustered, it only continued in a tone so cold it was almost bureaucratic.

"Have you been paying attention to what's going on outside?"

"Some of it." I replied, trying to hide the horror in my voice.

"Well, I'm in control of that rabble. And I'll unleash that fury upon you if you make me. But it would be easier on all parties involved if you'd just send the girl out."

Now it was time for me to shuffle my feet. "Look," I said through a frown. "I don't know who you think you are. But you couldn't possibly control them."

"Control who, man?" Isaac broke in suddenly. "Who the hell is it?" I put up my hand, indicating that I couldn't talk to him yet.

"Oh, you don't think so?" the voice spoke over Isaac.

"If you had that kind of power, why would you ask me? Why wouldn't you just have them level this whole building?"

Isaac held up his hands and asked no one, "Who's them?"

I covered the speaker and said, *"Please, man, quiet!"* I didn't mean to snap at him but it was far too important that I hear the speaker.

"Given the power of my position," the executive voice began, "that would be grandstanding. Besides, I don't care about you or the southern Baptist. But the girl's been selected, she has to come out. Or else I'll impose a will which isn't mine but yours, since you have the power of choice."

As helpless as I was, I resented the insinuation that I had a choice about anything. "I don't believe you," I snapped.

"All right," the voice said. "If you wouldn't mind going to the front of the restaurant; the north side, I shall provide for you an example."

I thought this over for a second. "All right," I said. "I'm going to put the phone down for a second."

"By all means."

I put the receiver down and zigzagged through the remaining tables towards the front window.

"What is it, man? Where ya goin'?" Isaac pleaded, but I waved him off again. I pulled back a tiny fraction of the curtain, half expecting to see the army of menacing white faces once again. But the front parking lot was abandoned and there wasn't a car on the road. For a second, I really wanted to believe that the voice was bluffing, or better yet, the cruelest of crank callers. But that's when I noticed a large shadow, like a passing cloud only it was utterly still, its huge body of shade holding in place on the ground.

This prompted me to look to the sky. And when I did, I saw the most amazing and terrifying sight perhaps ever beheld by a humans being.

At first I thought I was looking at a bird, albeit a much larger avian anomaly than was native to the modern skies. Then I thought it was a cross, although the design itself was not as consequential as the sum of its parts. For up there in that magnesium hued sky, some two hundred and fifty feet or eighty three yards from where I stared dumbfounded, were those people, those dead people. Their bodies, scaly broken arms and decaying crooked legs all locked together in a solid yet writhing mass. The limbs wrapped tight around each other like acrobats on a trapeze, only with no visible means to support their weight. Defying the laws of gravity and flight, they were making the form of the cross, taking on the shape of the thunderbird. They even cooperated to work the mammoth wings. Yet as they exerted themselves to perform this, each member of the macabre team seemed to be looking directly into my eyes, their eyes like the gaze inside a bull's head as its neck is locked in the stocks of the abattoir stall.

I slowly backed away from the window, stifling a scream for the benefit of the others, though they would have had to see me blanch down to the color of the raw dough in the freezer.

"What is it?" Isaac asked with a fear so sharp it was filled with pain. Theresa ran up to me and searched my eyes. She felt my brow like one does a child for a fever. "It's okay," I managed, nearly stumbling. Isaac clambered into the booth, but the monster must have been gone by now. Or maybe I was the only one who could see it, because he said, "I don't see anything?"

"It's okay," I repeated, putting my hand over Theresa's, before suddenly releasing it and walking back to the phone.

"Do you see?" the voice asked, as if it knew I'd be convinced.

"Yes," I said, but I didn't know where I was. I felt like a revived boxer discovering he'd just been knocked out.

"Then I expect you'll be sending the girl out?" The voice tested its most confident tone yet, almost presidential.

From somewhere deep inside me, the last sliver of my courage rose up.

"Never," I whispered.

"I'm so sorry to hear that. Is that your final answer?" the voice asked.

"I'm afraid so," I replied, not wanting to anger the man, yet realizing that anything short of the answer he desired would anger him.

"Don't be a fool," the voice's composure seemed to crack for the first time. "Send the girl out and you and your friend can eat pizza until you burst." I hung up.

"Who was that?" my fellow prisoners asked in unison, but I could only shake my head.

13

We went through an odd, three day stretch where the sun didn't rise, never mind blaze, but by now we were beyond being surprised by anything. This made me remember a prophecy which my grandmother had laid on me years before. She said that when God is finally disenchanted with his Earth, with its breakdowns of the family unit; immorality, adultery, perversion of youth, faggots, lesbos, sodomites, transsexuals, blow job queens and kings, racy fashions, lack of charity, heartlessness, indifference, contentions, godlessness, lawlessness, and pride in human knowledge, that he would exact a final judgment against his fools.

At this point a cross shall appear in the sky and I was pretty sure that I'd already seen the cross, as a warning to all to repent.

Then demons and evil spirits would be released from their bondage in Hades and permitted to roam the Earth to do as they wish. Gruesome apparitions will dance across the sky and people will fold up and wither from sheer fright. Meteors will rain down onto the fields, cities will be swallowed up and digested by the center of the planet. Poisonous gasses will take the place of oxygen, and the shrieking lamentations of the sinners will be heard before their bodies burn out in the withered grass. And of course, the corpses would be ejected from their cracked and mud caked caskets, to visit each abode like some lethal census bureau.

There were several precautions one could take against this retribution of course. I think it involved not looking or going outside, lighting blessed candles, sprinkling holy water around the windows and entrances, and not answering to any visitors no matter how dear they were to your heart, etc.

Of course we had no holy water, though I doubt I would have had the initiative left to douse it around the thresholds in any case. We did have all the candles we needed, though I doubt they were blessed, however, by any authority higher than the Pizza Gut corporate office. We had looked out the windows until I thought our eyes would pop out and be reduced to cinders by the light of God. Though at times, that ending would have probably sounded all right to us.

I was so tired my eyes burned. You wouldn't think someone could ever sleep again after seeing what I saw, knowing what I now knew. But exhaustion takes its toll and even the fear itself turns to some type of sleeping tonic. But your nerves are so on edge it's like trying to snooze on the top of a telephone pole. And that's how it got, I didn't know when I was asleep or when I was awake. I would be outside the restaurant, even though that was the one place where I was the most terrified to venture. I was being passed above the mob, silver hands, yellow nails. Then I was below the streets in the ankle deep bile; the run off of the sewers, where sketchy creatures, part human, part vermin, part death, rubbed against me with sharp, bristly hairs before scuttling off with a splash through the stinking waters.

Then I was in an abandoned lot. For some reason, I turned over an old piece of siding which was laying on the ground, where the balding grass had bleached down yellow from lack of sun, and snakes with the faces of people slithered out. They screamed like startled women and side-winded off through the orange grass. Then I was inside a burned-out building. There was a body lying on a filthy, ruined rug, the corpse having been cooked until it no longer had any relation to humanity. Yet somehow it was still writhing among the charcoaled sticks and stalks of the collapsed furniture. Its black hands seemed to be reaching for my ankle, driven by a perverse and mysterious notion to get me. Then I was climbing the highest tree in the forest, I could almost feel the wetness of the moist leaves, hear the moans of the crowd on the ground, all after me like a trapped raccoon. Then I was up again, back inside the restaurant. Theresa asking me when we were leaving, gesturing to the trivial objects we had placed on the table-cloth to take with us. But when I opened my mouth to answer, tears came out instead of words and I cried like a child in front of my true love. And then she cried, slapping me in the face, over and over, seeing my true helplessness; seeing my weakness. Then my head hurt, like I had smashed it against concrete, and I was in the air, I was part of the bird, my face hot and tortured as it pointed to the sun. And I answered to the angel, his face sharp and beautiful. And he told me the world was evil and that it was ending. And that only a few hundred thousand had been selected. And I thanked him for saving me. But he only shook his head no. And his voice was so cold, like a bill collector on the telephone and he said, "No my son, you do not understand, *YOU... HAVE... NOT... BEEN... SELECTED...*"

And now I really was awake. Isaac was crying roughly like a man does when he can't hold back the tears. "Shit, shit, shit," he kept saying over and over. Theresa was surprisingly calm. She sat in the last table, mouthing silent prayers while keeping time on a purple, little girl's rosary.

Before I even pulled the curtain back, I knew what it was going to look like outside. An orgy of writhing bodies, squirming like worms in a box of dirt. Just as I looked out, they all stopped gyrat-ing and got up off the ground. Now they stood silently, looking at my position with eyes as bright as marbles. Some of them were nude, and others were literally decomposing, naked of flesh. There was no mistaking what this grim army's mission was to be.

A ways behind this throng there was a cherry picker, one of those trucks with the bucket for a man to stand in for working on power lines or cutting tree limbs high up near the tree tops. There was a man standing inside the bucket. He had no shirt on, revealing a marvelous physique. His hair was blonde and his face was exceedingly handsome. He also seemed to be looking right at me. From somewhere, he produced a cell phone. As he pointed at me, our phone began its horrific jangling. No one even thought about moving to answer it. I felt my face shrivel up from terror.

There was something on the man's back; something crawling above his shoulders like a little white animal. But no... it wasn't separate from his being and now I realized they was furry wings rising above his head; huge wings, though I couldn't judge the scale or the span since they were still partially folded.

I began to laugh. Isaac and Theresa couldn't even hear me from inside their own terror trances, but still I laughed.

"Jesus Christ," I spat out loud. "It's an angel with a goddamn cell phone?"

Epilogue

The ham and cheese tasted pretty good. I really like to dip mine into ranch dressing and chase it down with a mouthful of Pepsi. There was still some pop left in the machine, believe it or not. Barry, that fat bastard, must have filled the damned thing up right before he left. There was plenty of dough for pizza left too for that matter, but Isaac had always been the main pizza chef around here, so with him gone, I really didn't feel like putting in the effort. Besides, I couldn't eat a whole pizza by myself and it just seemed like such a waste. Hell, nowadays I couldn't even eat half a sandwich by myself. Isaac had assisted me in what had to be done. After that, he said he just couldn't stay around here and that we should never talk about it again. He also said because, "It had all gone down so bad," That he now needed to see his girlfriend and the assumed new baby all the more. I didn't say very much back. I mumbled something about not blaming him and all that. He didn't ask me to come along, but even before then I knew there was now a permanent rift between us. He resented my cowardice, and what was even worse, he resented the cowardice he had shown to a lesser degree in going along with me.

Anyway, we wrapped him up some food inside Theresa's backpack. I knew he wasn't going to find what he was looking for, that in all likelihood his girlfriend and his offspring were as dead as zombies, that is, dead but still trucking around. I didn't bother to say this however. It wouldn't exactly be like wishing someone good luck to tell them something like that. So we just shook hands at the door, even though we both knew our friendship was destroyed forever. My old, beat-up Nova would've been lucky to start under normal conditions and Isaac had ridden the bus to work back before it all began. So he just strode across the abandoned parking lot without turning back, heading in the general direction of Westin.

When I was alone, there were no reasons left to hold back the tears, and they came like rain from a cloud too dark to do anything else except release the storm. I didn't think or say to myself, "What have I done?" or anything that dramatic. I had known what had to be done, and left with no choice, I did it.

Oh, sure I could still see Theresa's face. Who could ever forget a face that beautiful; so big and innocent, like a baby fawn in a Disney cartoon. She looked so happy and peaceful when I kissed her awake, and for the first time in I don't know how long.

"Are we getting out of here?" she asked, a smile beaming through her fading sleepiness.

"Sort of?" I said with a sick grin pasted onto my red faced exhaustion.

"What do you mean?" she asked, her face as trusting as an infant's.

"Well," I answered. "You are anyway."

She almost bit the duct tape as I lifted it up to her mouth, as if I had playfully offered her a snack. She must not have realized what was truly going down until the tape sealed her lips shut and Isaac simultaneously roped her feet together with some box cord we had found in the store room. Once he tied her hands behind her back, I think the reality of what was happening to her finally started to sink in. Although I'm not sure she ever understood the reasoning behind it.

Hell, I'm not sure I do.

She began to buck and kick as we lifted her up and her eyes filled with a purple panic of wetness and sadness. We carried her to the door where we removed the long nails securing the door and sat at the table.

"It's all right, Theresa," I pleaded. "The angel, he gave me his word, you've been selected." This didn't seem to calm her. I don't think it would have been much consolation to me either, had I been in her situation. As we got her through the door, where the crowd of cadavers had dispersed after my second and final phone conversation with the angel, we saw that the parking lot was clear once again. We sat her next to a pot hole which a gypsy had repaired for Barry the previous spring. But whatever the gypsy had repaired it with was long gone and the hole gaped open once again. After we sat her down, we quickly retreated back towards the restaurant. She tried to roll towards us and black soot from the pavement stained her jeans and purple shirt. A closed mouth scream rose as loud as her vocal cords could pitch it from behind the duct tape. I closed the door and twisted the deadbolt. Isaac punched the pinball machine and it made its digital/free game sound and almost toppled before banging back down onto its worn spot. "This is bad, man," he lamented. "This is so fuckin' bad."

I had to concur.

"*I know, man!*" I shouted loudly before plopping down in the booth and rubbing the stubble on my face. My explosion seemed to satisfy Isaac into a temporary silence.

I tried to rationalize our actions in my butchered thoughts. If we hadn't given up Theresa, we all would have died or became part of the heinous Catholic prophecy which we were being forced to act out. At least now, the memory of our love would live on in my surviving mind. Otherwise, it would have just floated off into the sky like a lost balloon. I hated myself, of course, but even the hate itself was still something; you had to be alive in order to hate. And let's be honest, I wanted to live. I was only eighteen years old and Isaac, despite all his dirty looks and tearful posturing, wanted to live, too. Otherwise he would have never played his callous role in the tragedy. And tragedy is what it was. We didn't invent this Armageddon, we only had to live by its rules. We were innocent bystanders forced to react to each instance or die. Or worse yet, perish only to perform again as possessed puppets strutting across the spare stage of the empty streets in the hot beige dawn.

After a few hours, Isaac self-righteously came up to me and put his palms flat on the table, his back arced like a cat on a thin branch.

"She's still out there, man!" he said through clenched teeth.

I refused to look, even when the rain pounded the roof as it had at our happiest moment, when we first kissed, as softly as a red rose touching a bed of grass.

I couldn't look, because she was gone now. Vanished, like the comfortable benefits of our society. Vanished like my bravery and pride.

You may think me spineless or yellow. And I might even agree with that assessment. But I will say that I know of no one who wouldn't have been worn down by the passing weeks of relentless horror and constant worry. No one who could have honestly looked at themselves in the wash room mirror and said in all certainly, without one cold beer coursing through their brain, that they could have done any better, or any different than I.

No one would have had the mental fortitude to follow the right path, a path which led to an unimaginable horror which it wasn't necessary to have to imagine.

Epilogue 2

After I nodded off, my eyelids as heavy as my guilt, still sitting up with my chin on my chest, they were inside the restaurant. They weren't shoulder to shoulder as they'd been on the asphalt, and they no longer seemed mindless or in some fog. They were simply sitting at the tables like ordinary patrons or partygoers; garrulously chatting. Their faces were as white as the blasted rocks inside the salt shakers. I was as helpless as a paraplegic; any one of them could have taken me out at any time. Then the door opened for the final time and the angel walked in. His wings were as big as the trunk of a car before he neatly folded them onto his back. He wore a smart gray suit with a white tie and his face was even more beautiful than Theresa's.

Theresa.

He spied me sitting in the corner booth and coldly nodded. It was like seeing a hated acquaintance on the street, yet, you nod anyway. That was how he seemed to me; like his hands were full of packages preventing him from waving. Only the angel didn't have any parcels.

I was part of an evil culture, that's what he told me on the phone, and therefore unsalvageable. But looking at him now, I didn't sense a great deal of goodness within him, or certainly not the divine elegance mandatory to cast a stone.

I knew right then that it had all been for nothing, that they had simply killed, raped, or eaten Theresa. That only Jesus himself was qualified to judge and this fraud before me, this charlatan, was as evil as he claimed I was, and I was damned.

He zigzagged through the milling dead and sat down across from me, the wings folding in neatly behind him. They were as much a part of his body as his arms and legs. Now that I could see his evil exposed, some of his beauty had spoiled and his cheeks looked sunken, his eyes more sullen.

I wasn't sad or afraid and I realized at that instant I felt good for no reason at all, like someone who was invigorated even though they hadn't slept in two or three days.

He took a sheet of paper out of his breast pocket and placed it on the table. It wasn't really a contract in the Beelzebub tradition, it was more like a waiver, as if he couldn't be responsible for what the dead were about to do to me.

He offered me a very nice pen, like it came from the desk of a corporate office somewhere. He made a little wiggly motion with his wrist, indicating he expected me to sign.

Once again, I felt I was left with no choice, so I snapped the pen in half and offered him a cheese stick.

FOOD FOR A VALENTINE

SPENCER WENDLETON

1

Debra Wilkinson didn't have an opportunity to correct the barricade job once the shambling dead man approached from the back room of *Precious Seasons Greeting Cards*. She was caught reading this year's stock of Valentine's cards unawares, her club for a flashlight too far away to help her. She shuffled backwards and crashed into the tower display of greeting cards, showered in red hearts with the messages: **I LUV YOU, BE MINE FOREVER**, and **U R MY ONE AND ONLY**. Crying out for mercy, on her back defenseless, she closed her eyes and cursed herself for believing she was safe. The dead man bent down, dripping maggots and turpentine blood onto her neck, and instead of puncturing her flesh with its butter-colored teeth, it plucked the card from her chest and those cataract-crusted eyes lit up, expressing a sentiment she couldn't place. She lay there as the zombie left her alone, returning to the ruined barricade, taking the card instead of her flesh.

2

That night, Debra prayed even though she wasn't a religious person; she promised to limit her cussing if the world ever returned to normal; it was an easy promise considering she was probably the only one left alive in the city.

The patch in the back storeroom window was the ultimate cause of the break-in; the boards were too thin, and the nails weren't driven deep enough to stay intact. That was the last time she'd make that mistake, she vowed.

She had worked at *Precious Seasons Greeting Cards* for eight months before the outbreak occurred, and presently trapped, she stayed inside living off of the meager supplies in the **Employee's Only** fridge, mostly her co-workers' barely edible leftovers. She ate

Martha's re-heated tuna casserole and Cindy's vegetable lasagna without complaint once the hunger pangs raged. She had been holed up for four days now, and already, the fridge was empty except for ice. She resorted to eating the chocolate treats in the Valentine's Day boxes; the special day had passed three days ago, the holiday pre-empted by undead cannibals.

Debra sorted through the smashed chocolate boxes to retrieve what could be saved after the intruder's attack. The dead man was bare-footed, hunks of green flesh stuck onto the outer packages and stinking of gangrene and maggot death. She caught a broken toenail wedged onto the corner of one of the boxes. She winced, breathing deep to overcome the thought that it could be her one day, a walking, rotting killer.

But why had the zombie picked up the Valentine's card? She knew they were blood-thirsty, so why not chew up her neck instead? One time she had caught a police officer pulled through the grates of a gutter, and the fingers and mouths wouldn't stop reaching and gnashing until every ounce of the man was accounted for.

Debra hugged a red teddy bear against her chest at the dreadful thought and squeezed it tight, imagining this ordeal was over and that she wouldn't have to worry about her next meal or when the electricity would finally go out or when running water would cease to be available. She could return to her apartment, her computer, and her calico cat, Minx, who was probably foraging the apartment for food and wondering why the hell nobody had changed the litter box.

Her life had been on the upswing before the dead returned to life, mostly because she had a new boyfriend named Charlie Wray who she'd met on Valentine's Day during a blind date. Several hours later, that outbreak occurred, and right after he hugged her goodnight, Charlie saved her by slamming closed her apartment door and telling her to run like hell. She fled down her fire escape only to be chased out of the alley by the cannibals, and then after running through four city blocks, she finally hunkered down at her place of work, minus her new boyfriend who was more-than-likely eaten to death.

She wept, stuffing chocolates into her mouth, imagining Charlie being attacked, and how he had potential. He enjoyed golf, video games, staying at home instead of going out, and chick flicks; the guy honest-to-God loved Patrick Swayze films, especially *Dirty Dancing*. Alone, there was nobody to wipe away the tears or console her loss. It wasn't until after the next radio broadcast that she found a disturbing clue about the identity of the dead man who'd broken into the store and possibly why he didn't eat her.

3

Nine o'clock meant the W-RAD FM station would broadcast the latest news, though it was from one guy named Lester Birmingham who spoke briefly, giving what information he could, though whatever he said could've been read on the Internet, she supposed, but the broadcast was vital since she had no access to the information superhighway. The reasons for the dead coming to life changed nightly, sometimes bi-nightly, by the end of Lester's program: *"Traces of an unknown chemical in treated water from local waste management companies has proven to have an adverse affect on the recently dead... "Clean Glacier" bottled water contains Neurogen-B, a super steroid that has proven to turn living flesh into decaying flesh...sewer smog, as the Chicago board of health director has stated, is a chemical so potent it can turn the living into crazed lunatics...gasoline fumes from a tanker from Crude Inc. have proven to turn the human brain into a primitive vessel of violence..."* Whatever the causes, many of the reasons had to do with water being contaminated. That's why she believed Lester didn't know what he was talking about; she'd had gallons of the stuff, and she was healthy.

She listened despite her reservations about Lester's level of being in-the-know and sat on her swivel chair keeping her ears open to the broadcast. *"This is Lester Birmingham, and I say this with much regret, that this will be my final broadcast. Stay in your homes. Lock yourself up tight. Ration your food. If you have no food, send the healthiest and smartest in your group to seek out the nearest rescue station, though I'll warn you, many are out-of-commission. Your safest bet is to stay local; hit the grocery stores and pantries for supplies. Now my reason for leaving, I've been bitten while on one of these missions for food. I wish the world well. Whatever is coursing through me, I feel like I have the flu, and my blood is slowing in my veins. I'll be dead soon, so my legacy to you, to whoever's listening, stay with your loved ones, anybody you'd want to spend your last moments with, because that's what I'm doing right now. May God be with you."*

"What, that's it?" She clutched the radio perched on the edge of the check-out counter and shook it, screaming at it. "May God be with you, what about the rest of the world? How many of us are still alive, you bastard? What about tomorrow, and the next day, and the next day?"

Out of breath, forcing her emotions down for the sake of the dead in the streets not overhearing her, she curled up into a ball on the floor and kept breathing, what many victims in the Chicago area—and the rest of the world—had recently ceased to accomplish.

4

Clearing the tears from her eyes, she was about to stand up again, finished with the self-pity session, when she noticed the wallet on the floor. The leather was covered in red gel. Congealed blood. It belonged to the man who had attacked her. The question posed itself again in her head; why didn't the dead man eat her? Another question; why did he enjoy the greeting card so much?

Wiping the leather clean with gift-wrap paper, she opened it, and learned it belonged to Mr. Adamson. Roy Adamson. He was a frequent greeting card customer. The man was in his mid-fifties who'd retired early from *Best Occasion Greeting Cards Inc.* to become a self-employed "idea man" for hire, a wingman for greeting card companies across the United States. Mr. Adamson had penned over a thousand concepts for greeting cards—a thousand and one. The last time he visited Debra's store was nine days ago. Proud of his genius accomplishment, he claimed, "I was the idea man behind the sucker through the Valentine card. That changed the industry forever." He had frowned at Debra then, ruffling his feather-white brows. "But I was gypped out of the royalties through contractual mumbo-jumbo."

Debra eyed Mr. Adamson's driver's license, and she darted for the back room, the cogs of her mind spinning, a question burning in her mind. She used a crowbar to peel back the topmost wooden board from the window and peered outside. She was shocked, but also impressed, by her intuition.

5

Lester Birmingham did have one thing right, something he mentioned in a previous broadcast, about how the undead were still human on a primal level, *"I've seen baseball umpires in local parks stand on home base acting like they're officiating a game. Dead police officers are directing traffic. Teachers return to their schools. Dead hookers walk the alleys expecting someone to hit them up for business. Bookstores are plagued by the dead thumbing through the shelves, piecing together torn books and magazine pages. They're doddering idiots, but traces of their former selves do manage to break free from time-to-time."*

And now Debra was forming the same observations. Mr. Adamson was standing guard in his blood-stained, gray overcoat and business pants, limping back and forth from the alley back to the front of the store again and again. A woman with a tank top trudged towards the building, naked from the waist down—missing an arm, the stump serrated and uneven as if shot off—and pale as talcum powder, and Mr. Adamson squabbled through a gargle-heavy throat, intercepting her, *"Baaaaaaaaggghh!"*

He pursued her in his limp gait with a broken broomstick raised in his hand. It was a slow-motion event, both stricken with rigor mortis, but the woman took immediate action, turning the opposite way, and finding some other building to investigate. Satisfied the fort was safe, Mr. Adamson waited for anybody else who challenged his authority, a liquid smile spreading across his blackened lips.

6

Mr. Adamson protected her from outside harm, but inside, she had eaten up most of the chocolates and was rationing them along with the worthless heart-shaped suckers, though she'd be reduced to consuming anything if it meant living that much longer. Three days had passed, and Debra was growing weak, delirious from lack of food, and she drank water to keep her stomach full, but it wasn't enough to survive long-term. Outside help wasn't coming, and without Lester Birmingham's broadcasts—or anyone's broad-casts—she was responsible for her own survival.

She kept peeking out at Mr. Adamson through the window to check her level of safety. The dead man had jammed the broken broomstick through a traffic cop's eyeball moments ago, and then Mr. Adamson leaned the dead corpse against the wall to create what she believed was a scarecrow for other zombies. Six dead victims were posed against the wall of the store, their heads bashed in by his new weapon, a loose chunk of the curb.

Bored after the area was clear, she re-checked the fridge and was delighted to find a package of croutons wedged in the back of one of the food drawers. Crunching on them with fervor, her joy quickly became a joke. *You're going to die here and you know it.*

Despite the dread attaching itself to her body, she did her best to enjoy the taste of salt as opposed to the sugar diet she'd been subjected. Eating contently, she stared at the trashcan next to the fridge and experienced an epiphany. She tipped over the waste receptacle, sorting through the trash, as she got to work on her idea.

7

Cindy Hawkins, the general manager of the store, often ate bean burritos to save money. She didn't recycle despite Debra's efforts, which entailed setting out a box for recyclables that she promised she'd deliver to a facility, but Cindy threw away the bean cans anyway, and there were two cans presently in the trash. The idea was random, but the way Mr. Adamson was thinking, she had to try it. She took two Valentine cards from the shelf and taped them to the bean cans. After tearing open a board from the win-dow, she dropped the cans down to Mr. Adamson.

The living corpse was disturbed from his duty, stumbling after the cans that were strewn on the sidewalk. He picked one up, sniffed it, shook it, and then craned his neck up at her, his features sliding down his waxen face. She wasn't sure what drove her to shout at him, the demands erupting from her throat unconsciously, "You bring me food, I give you Valentine cards! Food for a Valentine, you got that, Mr. Adamson?"

Mr. Adamson turned his head to the side, and out his ear, a stream of tobacco juice splattered the walkway. Disgusted and feeling foolish for believing her plan could actually work, she grunted, "*Ugggh*, happy Valentine's Day, you dead schmuck!"

She missed her apartment and her boyfriend, a guy she could have had sex with; she hadn't been laid in nine months. She was angry she was denied the season finale of her favorite sitcom, *Padres*, and how she'd never see Minx again, the poor cat starved or dehydrated by now, and she began wondering how much worse things could get.

Done with the holiday and Mr. Adamson, the man who invented the sucker through the Valentine card, she nailed shut the wooden hole where she'd dropped the bean can's outside, and dipped into the fifth of vodka Cindy kept hidden in the back storeroom. She drank until the bottle was empty.

8

Two more days had passed, and Debra hadn't given up on her in-store search for food. Finishing off the chocolates, she checked Cindy's desk. She had to pick the lock—what took four hours of guesswork and a modified paper-clip—and was rewarded by a back-issue of *Cosmo*. She read about thirty ways she could keep her sex-drive alive.

Great, now I find out how to have a vaginal orgasm!

The better surprise was underneath the magazine, a bag of Doritos, unopened. She devoured them, and the moment she was finished, she was startled by the clatter of wooden boards in the back room.

She waited for the intruder to enter, but after watching the store for fifteen minutes without hearing anything new, Debra skulked to the backroom with a crowbar in her hand. Mr. Adamson had crawled through the back window again, but first he'd claimed an entire box of overstocked Valentine cards.

Forgetting the ruined blockade or Mr. Adamson's visit, Debra focused on what he'd left behind.

9

A large pile of food was placed on an empty wood pallet. A dozen cans of refried beans. Tortilla chips. Canned fruit and vegetables. Spam. Pasta. Beef jerky. Soda. Bottled water. Debra dug in, peeling back the key for the Spam and delving her fingers into the salty meat until the can was empty.

Moving on now that her stomach was full, she looked out at Mr. Adamson and her mouth fell open. Along the storefront, the Valentine cards were stuck to the glass and brick by pieces of dead flesh used as sticky tape. Victims of the dead were posed, standing or sitting clutching onto teddy bears or heart-shaped boxes with smiles smeared on their faces in rust-colored blood. Turning over the scene and how Mr. Adamson stood guard, she thought, *This is what he enjoyed the most, bringing happiness to people, and now he's at it again.*

Shaking her head, she sighed, "As long as he keeps me fed and safe, I guess I don't give a shit what floats his boat."

10

The next week, she located another batch of overstock Valentine's cards, and she used them immediately to barter with Mr. Adamson. For this trade, he brought her a wrapped honey-glazed ham, unexpired. She ate a portion of it and then kept it in the fridge for safe keeping. The zombie brought milk that had expired, but most of the other items that were perishable were still edible. The best items were raw cookie dough, eggs, steak, bacon, and bread.

With Mr. Adamson enjoying his next batch of cards outside and her enjoying her acquired supplies; she could focus on the rest of the world by listening for radio broadcasts on an hourly basis. She received faint signals, mostly gospel radio stations with rogue preachers giving cockamamie sermons about how Heaven was open to the deserving while another she supposed was a joke. It was a guy playing rap and techno music and dedicating each new song to the end of the world. And as funny as it was hearing Cypress Hill over the airwaves, she couldn't shrug the overall sense of doom. Everybody she knew was dead or inaccessible. Even Mr. Adamson was baking in the sun; he'd lost most of his skin, now wrapped in desiccated muscle tissue; a walking hunk of teriyaki beef jerky.

She had to look on the bright side or else plunge into the abyss, she kept telling herself. The outside of the store was decorated in Valentine cards; that had to flag the attention of rescuers, if they ever arrived. And she did have food and water to last quite a while. All she had to do was wait it out and hope the conclusion it could potentially turn into an apocalypse was false.

11

Mr. Adamson came and went on his food missions during the next few weeks and suffered various forms of punishment. Debra noted the bullet holes in his torso, and she couldn't help but picture another survivor's shock as they battled a zombie for the same food rations at the grocery store. And depending on the connotation of the Valentine card, Debra learned she would receive differing kinds of food. The more presumptions and romantic, she'd receive comfort foods like chips, sodas, chocolate, licorice, and one time, a bottle of Malbec wine, but the utilitarian, friendly cards, granted her Banquet frozen dinners by the arm-load.

Alongside Mr. Adamson's damage, the threat of the encroaching dead was a continuing problem throughout the passing days, but her zombie dispatched them with extreme prejudice. It wasn't until he located a fire axe within a dilapidated building that he'd scared them away permanently upon braining five of them in one evening. Not a single zombie dared to walk within eyeshot of *Precious Seasons Greeting Cards* after the impressive show of dominance.

Comforted, Debra would spend afternoons sunbathing on the roof and eating her acquired goods, wondering if things would ever change. There was no indication of being saved or the military or government swooping in to reclaim world order, and that disturbed her as much as Mr. Adamson's worsening condition.

He was now stooped over at all times, the weight of the axe threatening to rip his arms from their sockets, and his eyes were so deep in his head, buried in orbital goop, that any second he could go blind. Deciding the zombie wouldn't last forever, she began working on a contingency plan. But before she could brainstorm successfully, she encountered new problems altogether.

12

When she ran out of Valentine cards, she panicked, but then decided to create her own by cutting up old ones from other holidays and using a red magic marker to write out Valentine greetings. She had a batch of thirty now, but when she dumped them out onto the street, Mr. Adamson wasn't there. She called out to him, but he wasn't roused by her summons.

Where the hell is he?

She called out five more times, begging him to return, and bragging about how colorful and sweet the new batch of Valentines had turned out.

Forced to make a hard decision, knowing she'd starve without his help, Debra clutched a crowbar and decided she had to look for him. Moving silently and swift out the window, she edged down the front walk, working around the piles of dead bodies whose flesh had been pecked by birds and writhed with fresh fat maggots. She growled at the woman who clutched a small Valentine card in her hands that said "**BE MINE FOREVER.**"

Be dead forever, more like it.

Edging across the storefront, she questioned if Mr. Adamson had gone out for more food again, but he never worked without being given his greeting cards first. Or had he moved on after putting it together that her supply of cards had gone dry?

He's a dead man. He wouldn't know the difference between the real cards and mine.

Worried, she moved faster, shocked she hadn't found any new zombies nearby; they had a way of honing in on the living, she had learned.

Maybe they were all gone too, she thought. *What if I'm the last person still alive, period?*

Stepping into the side alley of the store, her search for Mr. Adamson suddenly came to an end after finding another survivor like herself.

And he was pointing a rifle at Mr. Adamson's head.

13

Debra begged the man to stop, to not pull the trigger, but the thunder clap served as the indicator that her final lifeline was stolen. Mr. Adamson's head caved-in as if from a high-speed fist. She stared at the mess in horror, knowing the zombie wouldn't have survived that much longer anyway, but that wasn't the point. This was her meal ticket, her protector, and this man, this fuck-up, couldn't protect her like Mr. Adamson had.

The bearded man in a bomber jacket and jeans reloaded his 30-.06 and stepped up to her, proud of his accomplishment, but she wiped the smirk off his face when she berated him.

"You asshole, do you realize what you've done? By the look on your face, you think you've impressed me; you've saved the princess holed up in a castle, right? Well, you can go to Hell! You ain't getting anything from me. Do you see these Valentines on the wall? Do you notice how I'm not skinny and emaciated like you? This zombie was keeping me safe and fed, you idiot, which is something you'd never be able to accomplish."

The man shifted into criminal mode, training the bolt-action rifle at her. "Then you're saying you have food?"

"I had all the food I could ever want," Debra said, lowering her tone and raising her hands. She hung her head low, defeated. "Whatever you want, just take it."

"That was the plan, lady," he said, winking at her. "I've hit so many places, and they're like you, people alone and desperate, and most of all, trusting." He spat on the ground. "And they're usually nicer to me." He smiled again, spelling out his treachery. "There're no rescue stations. No police. No one left but the few and far between, so you could've been nice to me, and I would've shared with you what you got, but now, I'm taking it all."

He raised the gun to her head. "I need a distraction while I carry the shit out. I'm sure the dead have heard us, and they're already heading this way. Your body will keep them occupied long enough for me to—*aaaaaaaaaaaaaagggggghhhhh!*"

The dead had heard them, hidden in the buildings close-by, crawling out of gutters, broken windows, fire escapes, and abandoned rooms in alarming numbers. They stared at Mr. Adamson's half-empty head, and confident they wouldn't be harassed, charged in at them, fearless and hungry as ever.

The rifle went off, the barrel aimed at the sky, and the man was tugged backwards off of his feet. Debra sprinted from the scene, horrified after catching a set of pale fingers plunge into the man's eyes. The blood and clear ooze mushroomed from the sockets as hands tore into the body, soon turning it into bloody chunks of meat.

Debra crawled back through the window of the store, the soundtrack of flesh tearing and rib bones breaking her motivation to nail and barricade the window with speedy resolve. Before she could finalize the barrier, screaming in horror, she was outflanked by the throng pouring in, crawling and limping towards her. Soon tackled, her head struck the floor and she was rendered unconscious.

14

Shortly after feasting upon Debra in a collective buffet line, one of the zombies who happened to be Charlie Wray, Debra's boyfriend, discovered a heart-shaped Valentine wedged under a nearby desk.

The zombie cradled the card against his bared sternum, temporarily claiming a thread of his former self, before rejoining the others and delving into the gut pile for another handful of juicy intestines.

THE PULL

ROB ROSEN

I woke up feeling truly strange, and knew in an instant that something bad was going on. First off, wherever I was, it was dark, and cold, and wet; which meant that I was no longer in my cozy bedroom, where I should have been. There was also an unusual enveloping aroma. Like a garden; no, scratch that, like a bed of soil, minus the flowers. And I was being weighed down by something, something really heavy, so that I couldn't move my arms or my legs. Clearly, I was trapped. I thought that maybe I was dreaming, but knew instinctively I wasn't. It was all too frighteningly real. I also had an inkling that something awful had recently occurred, but couldn't for the life of me remember what it was.

So I stayed put and racked my brain to try and figure out what had happened. And that's when it hit me. That is to say, I realized why I felt so strange.

If I was being weighed down by something, something that was completely covering me up, then how was I breathing? The answer to this, unfortunately, was I wasn't. The life of me that I was trying to remember had obviously been snuffed out. Okay, I suppose I should have been scared, terrified even, but I wasn't. I guess when you die, the one thing you're not scared of anymore is death itself, right? Well, death and taxes, but I had serious doubts it was the IRS that had dumped me wherever it was I now found myself.

In any case, the strangeness I was feeling I now took to be the negation of my living self. Death, to be quite honest, felt weird. Not like life at all. But then again, what was I expecting? And it wasn't just the obvious stuff that threw me, like not breathing or not being able to hear my heartbeat in my ears. No, it was more of an internal thing, really. Spiritually speaking, well, to be frank, I felt spiritless. My being, though not my physical being of course, had left me. I was all shell. Well, mostly, anyhow. I mean, I still felt things; just not as deeply as I once had. I don't know; it's hard to explain.

Guess you have to be dead to understand. Since you're probably not, you'll just have to take my word on it.

And the heavy thing that was weighing down on me and smelled like a garden, I figured out right quick, was a lot of dirt. I was in a makeshift grave. I say makeshift because I wasn't in a coffin, and I sensed I wasn't buried all that deep. It took some heavy-duty pushing and shoving and digging, but eventually I proved myself correct. I had been under about three feet of soil.

"Well," I said, glad that I still had a voice since I seemed to have little of anything else. "My first shallow grave, and wouldn't you know it, it's my own." I laughed at my newly acquired morbid sense of humor, and then wiped the excess dirt off my tattered clothes. The earthy smell lingered. I hoped it was just the dirt and not me. "When does flesh start to rot?" I asked, aloud. "Better yet, am I rotting already?" It didn't feel like I was. Then again, it didn't feel like much of anything, actually, as I've already said. Yes, considering the situation I was in, I figure it bears repeating.

Anyway, once I'd gotten as clean as I possibly could, I had myself a look around. I was in a thick forest. It was nighttime. I could see the twinkling stars through the overhead branches, and I could feel the warm breeze flowing around the trees and over my otherwise cold body. Except for the whole death thing, it was rather a lovely evening.

"So, Geoff, how'd you end up here? And like this?" I asked myself, as I started to walk through the thicket I now found myself in. There were no answers to these questions. For whatever reason, I had no recent memory. I knew who I was, where I lived - had lived, that is to say - and what I was; which was, obviously, for lack of a better or more agreeable term, a zombie of some sort. Creepy, yes, but it could have been worse. Well, maybe not worse, but I'd always considered myself an optimist in life, so why not in death?

In any case, the woods, like my grave, were not all that deep. It only took about fifteen minutes to make it to the highway; and once reached it, I knew in an instant where I had been unceremoniously buried. I was, perhaps, a mere five miles from my home. I'd driven this exact stretch of road countless times before and knew it like the back of my hand. Then again, the last time I looked at the back of my hand, it wasn't hardening with rigor mortis, nor was it covered in thick, nasty, blue veins. I quickly looked back up the road and watched as the cars drove on by.

I wished, at that moment, that I had my own car, but, seeing as I didn't and I certainly couldn't stop and ask for a ride, I started the long walk home. Strangely, that being the optimal word for the night, it wasn't the least bit tiring. Then again, I supposed, when you're dead you don't need to rest. Let me rephrase that, when you're dead and you're not already at rest – such as *in peace* - you don't need to rest; which was the situation I now found I was in; undead and mighty ticked off.

I arrived at my home soon enough. It was wrapped in the tell-tale yellow police tape that meant something bad had happened but no one was around, the house empty of life. Suddenly, I felt a twinge of panic run up my spine. I reached in my pocket for my house keys. They were still there. And my wallet was tucked safely in my back pocket.

"Left for dead, but not robbed. Hmm?" I wondered, more than a little bewildered. I went inside.

My living room, it seemed, was fairing about as well as I was. It was a wreck. But upon closer inspection, it too wasn't burgled. Actually, it looked like there had been a scuffle, not a robbery. If the police had been inside, they left no calling card; and I seriously doubted they were the cause of so much destruction. I hoped they were out looking for me, or at least for the person or persons that did this. Boy, wouldn't they be surprised if they found me like this? Then again, they couldn't be half as surprised as I was.

Then, at that very moment, as I stood there pondering all this, I spotted it; the picture on the wall. It was hanging crooked now, and part of the gilt frame had been chipped off. A speck of memory came seeping back at that point, and quickly turned into a torrent. The picture was of Jennifer and me. Jen is my fiancée. Today, as far as I can recall, was to be my wedding day. Now I felt something. Deeply, finally. An overwhelming sadness swept through my body. My heart, though still not beating, was nevertheless aching.

I ran up the stairs to our bedroom. Like the downstairs, it was a disaster; only now there was blood—on the wall, on the floor, on the banister. Mine? Jen's? I hadn't a clue. And Jen was nowhere to be found. Had she met the same fate as I did? Should I have looked for another shallow grave next to my own?

Please, God, no, I said to myself in a silent prayer. Though if the Lord was listening, he had a funny way of showing it.

I searched the other rooms upstairs. There was still no sign of Jen. Then, the last place I looked was the bathroom. This was the one room I dreaded entering more than any of the others. It was, after all, the only room with a mirror. If my house looked this bad, what must I look like? Oh, let me tell you, as it turned out, considerably worse–as the saying goes, *like death warmed over.*

First off, the blood in the bedroom and in the hallway was, most probably, at least partly my own. I was covered in it. From head to toe. Well, mostly from head. There was a giant, gaping wound in the back of my cracked skull that had already clotted in a big, blackish, gooey mess, dirt encrusted in it, too. I was also dinged up and bruised pretty badly. There must have been a fight. But why? And with whom? The last memory I had was waking up next to Jen.

Jen and her glorious smile and long, blond hair. We were both nervous and excited about our wedding day, but mostly the latter. Everything else beyond that was a total blank. There was Jen's smile, her hand in mine, and then nothing until I woke up enveloped in soil.

Speaking of which, I was still covered in it. Between the blood and the dirt, there was little of me left to see. I decided on a quick shower. If I had to go searching for Jen, which is all I could think about doing, I knew I couldn't do it looking like I did. I decided to do this in the dark, though. I'd had enough shocks and surprises for one day–for one lifetime, as it were–and the thought of seeing what I now looked like naked was more than I could bear. Even the dead, it would seem, have their limits.

So, with the lights off, I got undressed and hopped in. The water was cold. I kept turning the knob farther to the left, but nothing worked though what looked like steam swirled around me. It felt like ice was raining down on me.

"Oops," I said, once I realized what was happening. "It's not the water. It's me." And I'd always so enjoyed a hot shower. Oh, well, I figured, it was just the start of a long list of things I'd miss. I prayed that Jen wasn't going to be on it. She was my whole life; my reason for living, really.

"Hey," I said, with a snap of my fingers. "Maybe that explains it. If she was the reason for my living, then maybe she's the reason I'm not dead yet; well, not totally and completely dead, anyway. Maybe I can't leave this world with something so unresolved. Makes sense. As much as anything does, anymore."

And it felt right. Besides that odd feeling I've described, there was also something else. Something was drawing me. Pulling me forward. Beckoning me. Until then, I'd attributed it to the whole death thing, but now it seemed to have some separate significance. If I was to ever get any peace, I reasoned, then I needed to find Jen; and hopefully still alive.

With a newly found determination, I hopped out of the shower and, out of sheer habit, flicked the lights back on.

"Eew, gross," I said, and winced at my grotesque reflection. As suspected, I looked like a giant, bruised blueberry; blue from cracked skull to water-shriveled little toes. The only white left was in my teeth, of which I was now missing several, and my eyes, which were badly bloodshot. I was a big, dead, hideous mess. Not at all the handsome groom I expected to be that day. But where was my bride? That thought kept me going. Kept me moving ever forward. I had to find my love. And I had to do it, I figured, before there was nothing left of me but bone. The skin, I felt, was fast deteriorating. I probably shouldn't have scrubbed so hard in the shower.

And then a new thought popped into my head; a new memory that is. It was a sound. A crash. First there was Jen's smile, and then there was a crash. And a new piece to the puzzle was added to the rest. I ran back downstairs to the kitchen, well, staggered anyhow. Pretty much every joint and muscle in my body was hardening by the second. What I discovered when I got to the kitchen was that there was indeed a hole punched through the rear door, and there were glass shards on the floor. With all the rest of the mess around the house, I had missed this on my first look-through.

"Well, someone broke in. That much is clear now. And they did it sometime between last night and this morning. Now all I need is the who and the why."

Directly to the left of the kitchen door was our answering machine. The light was blinking.

I hit the button and listened to my mom wail on the tape.

"Geoff, are you there? I was in the shower, and when I got out there was a message on my machine, and the police said that there was a break-in at your house, and that Jen is at County General, and they don't know where you are, and if I know where you are." She said this all in one breath before she paused, and in a teary voice, asked, "Geoff, where are you? Why are the police asking where you are?" And then the tape, like my heart, had stopped.

Oh, man, that was a lot to take in. Had any of my bodily fluids still been flowing, I'm sure I would have been a sobbing wreck. Instead, I was just angry that I'd left my mother like I did, and Jen, too. And the rest of the world. Did the police think I had anything to do with all this? They couldn't find me, so they just started assuming stuff. But there was a shining ray of hope. Jen was still alive, or at least had been alive earlier in the day. And I knew where she was. But how does a dead man saunter into a hospital after hours?

"I guess I'll figure that out when I get there," I said, as I left my house, for the very last time. I waved a final farewell, and than ran as fast as was possible down to the hospital. Taking my car was out of the question. There was now no way for me to turn the steering wheel or shift the gears. Too bad my run was more like a wobbly hobble by that point, though. I was getting all creaky. Picture the Frankenstein monster being chased by the angry villagers. It couldn't have been a pretty sight. But that was the least of my worries. And Jen was the most. Though something told me she was still alive. It was that pull I mentioned.

The draw of life, I assumed. I prayed as much.

Before I knew it, I was at the well-lit hospital emergency entrance, and light was no longer my friend. It pointed to the obvious; namely that a rotting dead guy was about to enter. Granted, it was the middle of the night, and there weren't many people about, but still, I'm sure I would have caused quite a scene. Then I'd never make it to Jen. I felt that ache in my stilled heart yet again, which was followed by the now familiar pull forward.

"I'm coming, Jen," I whispered. "Somehow."

Luckily for me, my one and only option lay waiting just off to the side of the emergency room entrance, in a semi-shaded sitting area. The gurney must have been left there after a drop off, or something along those lines. In any case, it was vacant, but not for long. I lumbered over, making sure to stay hidden in the shadows, and then laboriously hopped on. I then covered myself with the sheet and waited for the inevitable.

"What the hell?" came a voice a few seconds later. I heard the scampering of feet approaching, and then a gasp as the sheet was lifted up. I must have looked truly horrific by that point.

"How on earth did you get out here?" the man asked as he started to push me inside. "Someone's in trouble," he added, and I thought that clearly that someone was me; though I was reluctant to voice my opinion, for obvious reasons. In any case, the gurney came to a stop a few minutes later, once I'd been wheeled into a silent, darkened room. "Stay here, I'll be right back," the man said to me. I almost started to laugh, but caught myself. Boy, I thought, won't he be surprised when he returns and the dead guy that suddenly appeared then suddenly vanished. I didn't wait around too long to find out, though.

I scanned the room and found a doctor's jacket, surgical booties, a cap, and a facemask. There was also a tape recorder sitting on a nearby desk. I grabbed that as well, knowing exactly what I'd need it for. Now, if no one noticed my sickly complexion and nauseatingly bloodshot eyes, I might make it, I figured. To be on the safe side, though, I'd just keep my head down. Way down.

Then, as fate would have it, I noticed the computer monitor just before I exited the room; the room, which was, by the way, the morgue. No surprises there, right? I mean, where else was the guy going to drop me off, the cafeteria?

The computer was already on, and it only took a second or two to find Jen's room in the system.

"You guys really should be more careful," I said. "No telling who, or what, might be lurking around the morgue in the middle of the night. Sometimes the dead do tell tales." And then I was off and, for lack of a better term, running again.

As one would expect, the hospital at that late hour was about as lifeless as I was. There were only a scant few people milling about, and nobody paid the slightest bit of attention to me. A scant few minutes later, I found myself standing before Jen's door. I paused and looked up to the ceiling.

"Please, Lord, let her be okay," I whispered, and then gently pushed the door open. The room was dark, save for the lights of the machines she was hooked up to. She looked bad, but of course, not nearly as bad as I did. Of that I was thankful. At least she was still alive. At least one of us was.

Silently as I could, I tiptoed over to her side, though silence was no longer my forte. Every joint in my body creaked and groaned and locked with each troubling step. I sounded like my car when it was low on oil. Jen's eyes opened in a flash upon hearing my bodily racket. With my doctor paraphernalia on, and in the relative darkness, she couldn't have known who I was. And yet, the first words out of her mouth were, "Geoff, is that you?" Her pull towards me must have been as strong as my pull towards her.

"Yes, Jen, it's me. I'm here. I'll always be here for you." I had little hope of that, but it was something I nonetheless felt was the truth. It was pretty much the only feeling I had left by that point. The ominous specter of death was quickly overcoming me.

"But I thought you were...you were," she couldn't say it. I sat in a chair by her bed and wiped a tear off her cheek. I didn't finish her sentence.

"It's okay, Jen, I'm here now. Do you know how this all happened?" I knew it would be painful for her, for us both, but I had to know before time ran out. I was, I figured, down to the last few grains of sand in my hourglass.

She nodded and looked over at me. I took my mask off, knowing she could only see the whites of my teeth in the dark room.

"You don't know?" she asked.

I said I couldn't remember.

She shut her eyes and paused for a moment, sucking in her breath with a raspy inhale. "I can't remember much myself," she finally said, with a sigh and a wince of pain. "There was a crash downstairs. You put your clothes on and went to check it out. Then I heard a scuffle and called the police, but before I could say anything into the phone you and a man came running up the stairs. I guess you were chasing after him. Trying to chase him out, but he went up instead. You two started fighting, and I tried to help, but he was big. And crazy. On drugs, I figured, by the looks of him. I don't know. Anyway, there was lots of punching, and there was blood everywhere. He beat us both up pretty badly. Then he ran downstairs. We both followed after him. It was like a bad movie, Geoff. So bad."

I caressed her cheek while she collected herself. I stared intently down at her, trying to forever etch her features into my memory. The pull I was feeling had started to abate. I'd obviously reached my goal. I knew what would be coming next for me, and soon, too soon.

"Then what happened?" I asked, in a gentle whisper.

She stared up into my eyes. "Then you had him down on the ground, somehow. And I tried to help, but he punched me in the face. I fell over backwards and landed hard against the wall. Then it was all just a blur. But I can remember hearing a vase crashing down on something. I managed to open my eyes and I saw you...saw blood...you weren't moving. It was awful, just awful. And then I woke up here." She shut her eyes and breathed heavily.

"Yes, Jen. You're here, and safe. I remember now. Thanks. And the guy's gloves got ripped off during the fight. His fingerprints should be all over the house. The police will find him and he'll never hurt us again."

"But the police were here. They said they couldn't find you. I was too doped up to tell them anything. I think they believe you might have done it. They heard me screaming, 'Geoff, no', on the 9-1-1 tape. But I blacked out before I could tell them anything else. You gotta tell them what happened, Geoff. You gotta."

I nodded and managed a comforting smile. "I will, Jen. Don't worry. Now go back to sleep. You need your rest." And so do I, I thought. I was waning fast. "Goodnight, Jen. I love you. I'll always love you. And I'll see you soon." I kissed her on the lips one last time before she finally fell asleep. It was the last touch of warmth

I'd ever feel again. And it will stay with me for all eternity. Then I wobbled out and slowly made my way back down to the morgue.

So whoever finds this tape, please make sure that the police know what happened. Though you might want to leave out the whole zombie thing. They probably won't believe you. Hell, I barely believe it all myself. And don't tell Jen this is how it all ended. Poor thing's been through enough already. And please tell her that the last words I said were that I love her, and that I will see her again. Of that I'm certain. Death isn't so strong and final a thing as I used to think it was.

There's one thing much, much stronger.

Love.

MILK RUN

MARC WIGGINS & ANTHONY GIANGREGORIO

"Come on, go, goddammit!" Linda roared while accelerating her Honda Civic to ride the rear bumper of the car in front of her. The left turn signal just ahead was still green but the guy in the other car was taking his sweet assed time. She just knew she was going to miss it.

"Come on...!" she tensed. The light was still green and had been for a long time at that. It taunted her, growing pregnant with promised delay.

"Let's go..." she shrilled. The light turned yellow, mocking her.

"You bastard!" she screamed, watching the driver in front of her leisurely pass into the intersection without worry. The light blared red and she slammed on her brakes. The red light camera pointing at her seemed to smirk on its pole.

"Damn it," she muttered in defeat. The last thing she needed was another ticket. She wouldn't hear the end of it from her husband.

Her favorite CD played on, a Christian tune about loving thy brother and praising God. She otherwise loved that song.

Linda released her tight grip from the steering wheel and sighed while leaning back deeper in her seat. She knew from dreadful experience that this was a bastard of a long light. It seemed each one grew longer the closer she got home and this was the last major one before she reached sanctuary.

Sanctuary. That was an interesting and loaded term. Just a few weeks ago, she left her husband when she'd had enough of him. Everything was so unbearable. But that wasn't the first time she left and again, after talking with him, she was back and fully committed to their marriage.

She knew she was a good person. She was a Christian. She was a good mother. And, once again, she strove to be a good wife. After all, she loved her husband, even if he could be an ass.

Life was complicated. She had desires and those desires had always nagged at her at every turn of their routine problems. However, she had made a commitment long ago. So long ago, it seemed she was bound by the choices made from a very different person.

Now, yet again, she was back and she was determined to make it work. It had all made sense to her just hours before. She knew her course. However, now, while coming home from work after an unusually bad day of traffic, she had too much time to consider her old and familiar themes. They stewed within her.

"No!" she exclaimed refusing to let those rambling thoughts derail her plan of action. She had to focus on the moment and just get home. Thoughts were dangerous.

She scanned the familiar intersection. At first, nothing out of the ordinary popped out at her. She looked on with bored and routine interest. To her left was the path to her destination, an uninteresting road with concrete walls lining the backyards of housing tracks on either side. To the right, was a convenience store. That was the place they would go to in a pinch when they didn't feel like going to the supermarket a few more miles down the road. It was a little more expensive but it saved them time.

"Oh, shit!" she said as she remembered her husband had asked her to pick up some milk on the way home. Not just any kind of milk, he wanted all natural whole milk. The same they had gotten for years but he always specified exactly that; all natural whole milk, every damned time. As if she didn't already know after all these long years together. That and a thousand other things he wanted just perfectly so.

She sighed. She was already in the left turn lane and would have to back up so she could switch lanes and go the other way. She was tired and torn. He might still be on his best behavior given their reunion just a few days ago and not give her an hour of grief for forgetting. More likely, he'd get pissed and go out and get the milk himself. That would be followed by him spending the rest of the night waving the carton around while he pursued her and ranted about how thoughtless and irresponsible she was. She knew if it didn't happen today, it would happen sometime down the road.

She sighed again and looked into the bay windows of the convenience store across the street. At first, she gazed in with thoughtless meandering. However, it was the red in the teenage clerk's uniform that caught her eye. The kid was running towards the door but he was pushed down by someone before he could reach the exit. The clerk squirmed about while his attacker hunched on top of him. Another person came to him and knelt down. The clerk thrashed in his red uniform while the other two figures leaned into him. She was too far away to really see what was happening. But she knew this had to be a robbery.

"What the..." She grabbed her cell phone to call 9-1-1. Before she could press the first button, a horrendous slap sounded and something struck the driver's side window of her car. She jumped from the surprise and turned to look.

The first thing she saw was smeared blood on her window, followed by a hand sliding across to make another streak. Then a fist began to pound on the glass but the window held. She looked out past the blood to see her attacker only had half a face. He was a homeless man she had seen working this corner countless times. He would always be holding a piece of cardboard with the words, "Will Work For Food" scribbled in messy handwriting. She recognized him by the right side of his face but the other side was a bloody skull with strings of ligament swaying against his violent motions, the eye missing to leave a gaping socket.

The bum punched her window again and again the glass shook slightly and then spidered her view. She screamed and stepped on the gas.

Screw the red light, she thought. *This man's trying to kill me.*

Her car shot forward passing a Buick in the next lane, the face of its driver also filled with shock and terror. For there was someone at his car window, too, but he didn't have air conditioning and his window had been down. A man who once sold crack on the corner five blocks down had wandered into the better part of town, the reason obvious to anyone who got a good look at him.

For the man wasn't himself any longer. Perhaps because of the large tear in his throat, right where his carotid artery was. His shirt and pants were covered in red and his jaw was crooked, as if the tendons were taut and wouldn't release. The crack dealer reached into the car and yanked the screaming driver out, the man shrieking for help. Linda had already passed them while the driver pleaded for mercy. The crack dealer sank his teeth into the man's nose, tearing it off and leaving a gaping wound that shot blood like a fountain. As the man began to drown in his own blood, Linda turned the corner and was gone from view. She did glance one last time in her rearview mirror to see the teenage clerk from the convenience store now on the street. He was missing an arm and his throat was torn out, much like the crack dealer. Both of them set their teeth into the driver of the Buick and soon internal organs weren't so internal anymore.

Linda didn't see this part, though, as she quickly drove away.

By luck, she avoided hitting another car while making her fast turn to escape the violent scene. She drove on for a few blocks and then stopped on the side of the road, her hands shaking as her body filled with adrenalin. Still breathing heavily, she switched from her CD to the radio.

"... violence throughout the city. In just the last half hour we have reports of the same phenomenon in four other states. Whatever's going on, it's spreading fast. There's no official word as to the cause but authorities advise you stay off the streets and barricade your homes. I don't know what is happening for sure at this..."

She stared at her car radio in disbelief and didn't notice the woman coming her way on the sidewalk until she jumped onto the hood of her car. Linda didn't scream until she saw the caked blood in the woman's hair, the glazed eyes filled with hunger, the missing left ear and hunk of scalp torn free to leave a glistening piece of exposed scalp.

Linda screamed and hit her horn, as if the woman would act like a wild animal and scurry away. But she didn't. Instead, the woman stood up on the hood, the metal creasing from her weight, and Linda put her car back into drive and punched the gas with her foot. The woman fell forward and rolled over the hood and then off the back of the car like a stuntwoman in an action movie.

Even over the roar of the car's engine, Linda heard the crack of the woman's neck as she landed on her head. The body slumped over and then fell to the road where it twitched for a few seconds to remain still.

As the body crumpled to the road, more people arrived, rounding the corner twenty feet away, all with a disheveled look about them. They acted like they were drunk, shambling and lurching, and they fell onto the corpse of the dead woman. Hands tore into flesh and began ripping and tearing, stringy ropes of intestines quickly yanked out of the stomach like some bizarre magician's trick. The rib cage was cracked to expose the juicy organs within and the crowd wasted no time in delving hands into the quagmire of meat. One of the crowd secured the heart and sank his teeth into the meaty organ, squirting blood in all directions, as if he had taken a bite of a blood-soaked sponge. Two more of the crowd had a leg in each of their grasps, and with strength that bellied their mass; they tore the dead woman asunder, spilling blood onto the street where one of the crowd dropped down to all fours to lap it up like a stray dog.

But Linda didn't see any of this, her eyes only for the road ahead.

"Oh my God! Oh my God!" Linda screamed as she drove on. By instinct, she made the turn that led to the street her house was on. She slowed, comforted by the normalcy. Things appeared normal. Whatever was happening didn't seem to be affecting her neighborhood; at least not yet.

By the time she parked in her driveway next to her husband's Bronco, she had mostly regained herself. She cut the ignition and took another moment to completely calm down. Linda looked around; the neighborhood seemed quiet. But from what she'd seen so far, she knew it was an illusion and just a matter of time.

She concentrated to gain complete control of herself. She knew she wasn't a very strong person. She always gave in. Her husband was waiting for her, expecting the milk. The kids were home schooled by him while she worked. Television or radio wasn't entertained in the house since her husband had always said they only provided Godless distractions. She doubted anyone in her home knew what was going on.

Linda got out of the car and straightened her outfit. With a deep, calming breath, she strode up the stone walkway.

Unlocking the front door, she entered her home.

Her husband was in the kitchen cooking dinner. "Hi, honey, did you get the milk?"

"Oh, sweetheart. I totally forgot. I'm sorry," Linda said.

Her husband bit his lip with disappointment, his expression was laced with the disgust he was so expert in conveying, subtle or otherwise.

Linda pushed it further, ensuring his rage, "Oh, I've had such a long day, sweetheart. Would you mind going out and getting it? Why not just hit the convenience store to make it fast? In fact, I think they're having a sale."

Though annoyed she hadn't gotten it, he nodded. "Fine, it's not like I have a choice," he clipped. He turned down the flames on the stove and stirred a few pots. "I'll be right back," he promised as he grabbed his keys and stiffly left.

She was looking for a promise, all right, but it was in God's hands now.

THE LOVER

SHERI GAMBINO

Misty wept as she stood and watched Brian's casket lowered into the ground. His friends and family were in shock over his sudden death. All Misty could think about is when she could hear his voice again and feel the touch of his hands. She felt that life wasn't fair. You find someone you're compatible with, fall in love, and then the world shits on you and takes him away.

But Misty had learned she didn't need to follow the rules.

Death was not the end.

She looked around at Brian's family and could hear their muffled whispers. Most people didn't know that she and Brian had been an item. In such a small town, gossip is what everyone thrived on. But they had kept their romance a secret.

Brian had separated from his wife, Lucy, of ten years about three months ago, and was finished with the relationship but his wife didn't want to give him up so easily. He had rejected Lucy and told her that it was over after catching her in a third infidelity. She still persisted on not giving up on their marriage.

Misty's mind wandered to when she first met Brian. She had closed out the priest's voice because she wouldn't accept his death.

Misty had met Brian two months ago when she moved to Orrick and opened up a small nutrition store. He had walked in one day to check out the store and was immediately smitten with her. Over the next month and a half they had a passionate love affair. Brian found Misty appealing. She was not a normal small town girl like he had grown up with and married. She had traveled the world and was very educated.

Misty was also an expert on voodoo. Brian was intrigued about learning more about her beliefs. Misty let him know that her voodoo practice was something she really didn't want to discuss. At least not yet; it was private and Brian respected her wishes. He thought it was strange she was so secretive, but didn't let her beliefs get in the way of their relationship.

Misty respected Brian for that. What she did was dark magic, and once you submitted to the powers, there was no quitting.

She stood silently and was patient until the priest finished with his service. She was waiting to place something in the coffin with Brian. When the priest was done, and he let everyone say their last goodbyes, she slipped an amulet into his breast pocket, close to his heart.

After the funeral, Misty endured the typical small town gathering. She wasn't hungry nor did she want to be glared at by Brian's wife.

Maybe Lucy knew about them, Misty thought. She had never gotten a good look at Lucy before, but she did look like a bleach blonde bimbo. She wondered if Brian had married her for her big tits and tight body. Misty didn't feel threatened by her at all. She did sense that Lucy hated her.

At that moment Lucy started to walk over to Misty.

"So, how do you know my husband?" Lucy inquired.

"Brian came into my store a few times," Misty smiled

"Oh, yes, you're the lady that owns the granola store. Never would have figured Brian for having an interest in that kind of thing."

"Actually, it is a nutrition store. And I do sell granola there," Misty replied in an irritated tone.

"Hmm," Lucy murmured.

Misty looked at Lucy directly in the eyes. "Guess there's a lot you didn't know about Brian, huh."

Lucy's Botox lips puckered up and she turned around and stomped away. As Misty was leaving the gathering, she could hear Lucy's big mouth going. She was babbling something about who does Misty think she is and blah, blah, blah. Then she was discussing life insurance with some woman, perhaps her mother.

Misty wanted to say to Lucy, "Just *who do you think you are, whore?*" but held her composure.

After all, there were easier ways to get her vengeance.

* * *

Brian had died suddenly and strangely to Misty.

His car had run off of the road and hit a tree head on. He was killed instantly. Misty thought it was an accident until she picked up strange vibes from Lucy today. Could Lucy have had something to do with his death? She had to find out. If Lucy was responsible for killing Brian, Misty would make sure she suffered a horrible death.

Misty contemplated if she should do the ritual again. Last time it was a disaster when she brought her sister, Beth, back from the other side. She was too far gone and came back evil. When Beth was alive, she was a loving, sweet girl, and meant more to Misty then anything.

But when she returned, Beth became uncontrollable; her thirst for blood and flesh now overwhelming. After killing several people, Misty had to put Beth down, and it tore her up. But that was years ago and since then she'd perfected her voodoo powers. The question in her head was: should I bring him back?

"Yes!" she said out loud.

Misty had to move quickly now that her mind was made up. In three days Brian would come back. She would start the ritual and he would be reborn as a zombie that she could control, but most important, love again. She was ready and knew she could control him this time. The problem was, once he came back she would need to adhere to his specific diet of human flesh and blood. But her love was so strong she would find a way.

For the next three days, Misty closed her store and remained in seclusion while preparing the spell that would bring back her lover. Light illuminated from the back room of her store. She removed her clothing and tied her long brown hair back. Reaching into the wire cage, she grabbed the first squawking chicken by its neck and cut slowly, slipping the blade deeper into its throat like butter. The chicken's blood squirted into her face and mouth, now lying limp in her hand. She began chanting and covering her body in the blood of the first sacrifice.

She stared in a trance-like state at the flickering candles, her eyes turning black as coal. She called upon the god of Death holding a matching amulet in hand and asked for Brian to be awakened. Once the ritual was finished, she would wait. Brian would come to her on the third night.

The time went by quickly and finally it was the night Brian would awaken. She laid in bed waiting. When the clock hit 12:30 a.m., Misty heard wet sucking noises. She smiled and listened as he clambered closer, anxiously waiting for his touch. The dark figure walked over to her and climbed into the bed. His smell was sweet like rotting flowers. Brian climbed on top of her. She could feel his skin was leathery in areas and mushy in others. His hand caressed her naked breasts and she gasped in delight.

Brian leaned down to kiss her with his soft squishy lips, and stuck his tongue into her mouth. She could feel something wiggling on her tongue. Small maggots coated her lips and were inside her mouth, and she gently swallowed them. His touch set her on fire. She wrapped her arms around his decomposing torso and waited in anticipation for him to enter her once again.

He slowly slid inside of her and she could feel the wetness of decay and desire explode within her as they made passionate love. Brian moaned in delight as he sank deeper into her body. She wondered how long it would be before certain parts of his body decayed so much they fell off. Hopefully nothing would come off inside her. She giggled at the thought.

Nothing mattered now except that she had him back again, and they would be happy forever. They lay in bed together and embraced. Brian looked into Misty's eyes, his own boney and sunken into their sockets.

In a gargled voice, Brian muttered, "I love you more than anything, Misty."

"I know, my feelings are the same for you," Misty replied.

Brian's face had been reconstructed for the funeral. It had been crushed in the wreck. Pieces of putty the mortician had used was melting away, leaving him with practically no eyelids at this point. His eyes were wide as he looked down at her.

"Do I disgust you?" he asked.

"No!" she whispered. "I'll love you forever."

Brian smiled at her and she melted back into his arms. A stray maggot inched across his face and Misty flicked it off. She leaned back up to Brian and asked him a question.

"What happened, why did your car crash?"

Brian looked at her and replied, "My brakes stopped working and I lost control of the car and crashed into a tree. That's really all I remember. Then I heard your voice calling me and I woke up, forced open my casket and crawled out of the ground."

Misty's face turned red, realizing what Lucy tried to hide. "I think Lucy did something to your car."

"Why do you think she would do that?" Brian rasped as he ran his leathery hand across her face.

Misty looked into his eyes. "Because I know she did. I heard her talking about life insurance at your funeral."

"That bitch killed me for my life insurance? How could she do that to me?" Brian exclaimed.

He paused for a second then doubled over in pain.

"I'm so hungry it hurts. Why does it hurt so bad?" he moaned as he grasped his stomach.

"You need to eat, my dear, and you'll feel much better afterward. Fresh flesh and blood will become your new diet and I know just who to get it from. Let's go pay Lucy a visit."

He only nodded, his face creased in pain.

Misty just smiled as she stroked his face.

* * *

Misty led Brian to her car and had him sit in the back seat so no one would see him. She had to check on something she suspected and find food for Brian. She drove through town and everything was silent as it was two in the morning. It would be perfect, everyone was asleep.

She had only seen the house one other time when Brian had driven by and pointed it out. He'd worked so many years to provide Lucy with a beautiful place to live. Brian worked long hours as a top notch programmer while Lucy was a homemaker. They never had children because Lucy didn't want to ruin her body and in fact, she hated children.

But Brian had always wanted children and felt cheated by her. As Misty drove to Brian's home, now Lucy's, she could hear his moans coming from the back seat.

"I'm hungry, please stop, the pain," he moaned.

"Soon, lover, it'll be time for you to eat *and* get your and revenge," she replied. Her face was a mask of determination. She kept playing the same thought through her head that *Lucy will pay.*

She slowed the car down and passed by the house once, looking for any signs of life within. She saw an unknown car in the driveway and only one light on in the house. She was positive the other car was Nathan Tucker's car, the man Brian had caught Lucy sleeping with.

She parked down the street and sat in the car. She turned around and looked at Brian.

"I think Nathan's at your house with Lucy," she told him.

Brian's jaw dropped and pus dribbled down his chin "That bitch!" he rasped. "I'm hungry, I need to eat!" he roared from the backseat.

Misty knew that zombies were always very unstable when they were hungry. The first feeding was very important in sustaining his life or unlife. But with two hosts to feed on, she wondered what the results would be. Each life a zombie consumes holds healing properties. She smiled. She believed the more human sacrifices a zombie took, the more they rejuvenated. Brian could possibly look human again after tonight was over.

She got out of the car and opened the door for him. He was beginning to become stiffer, and as he climbed out of his seat, she could now hear a crackling noise. After a few hours being exposed to the air, it was drying his body up. No longer did he have the secretions of his body to keep himself limber. He was beginning to look more leathery. She bent down and helped him up.

Looking into his dry, sunken eyes she muttered, "Let's go, it's time for justice."

She walked down the sidewalk and approached the front door with Brian clambering behind her. Misty reached out and rang the door bell. They waited. She could feel someone was looking through the peep hole and had made sure Brian was out of sight.

The door opened and Lucy poked her head out.

"What the hell are you doing ringing my door at this hour, you crazy bitch!"

Misty smiled, ignoring the insult. "I'm sorry to bother you, do you have a second or are you busy?"

"What do you want?" Lucy huffed impatiently.

Misty looked around, making sure no one heard Lucy's outburst. Everything was still quiet and dark around them, the windows of the neighboring homes vacant of curious faces.

Misty pushed the door open and grabbed Lucy around the neck. "I've got someone that wants to see you again. You both have some unfinished business."

Lucy's eyes grew big as she looked past Misty's shoulder to see a dark figure getting closer. The figure moved slow and crackled, and as it got closer, the face became clear.

Lucy began to panic, not believing her eyes. She tried to scream but Misty's hold on her throat was tight. She could barely whimper, "Brian?"

She screamed in terror as Misty pushed her back into the house. Brian followed and shut the door once everyone was inside.

Misty looked at Brian and whispered, "Let's go to the bedroom."

Brian walked ahead and went down a long hallway until they both could see a light on in the bedroom to the left. The door was ajar and the light shined on Brian's deformed face as he walked closer.

"Hurry up, baby, Daddy's not finished with you yet," a male voice called from the bedroom.

Misty walked quickly past Brian and seemed to glide down the hall with Lucy still in her grasp. She pushed open the bedroom door and threw Lucy onto the bed with Nathan. Lucy let out a blood-curdling scream.

"He's alive, Nate! Brian's alive!" Lucy shouted.

Misty stood in the bedroom and looked at them both. Brian came around the corner and looked at Lucy with his cold dead eyes.

"I gave you everything, Lucy. Why would you do this to me?" Brian asked and paused as he winced in pain.

Nate got out of bed and stood before them naked. "What the hell's going on here? Is this some kind of a joke? I saw your body. How can you be here, you're dead!"

Misty stared at them with disgust. "What did you do to his car? I know you guys did something to cause him to crash."

Lucy was hysterical, "Nate did it. He cut the brake lines. It was all his idea. We needed the money, and he decided to kill Brian to collect on the life insurance. You left me, Brian, with only this house! How was I supposed to survive?"

Nate gave Lucy a hard glare and then looked back at Misty and Brian; Nate smiled malevolently as he started to walk towards them.

"Well, little lady, you look easy to handle, and Brian their looks a little crispy. I think it's safe to say that you're both good as dead."

* * *

Misty spun into action. She charged at Nate, grabbing him by the arm, and throwing him onto the ground next to Brian, using the man's leverage against him. Nate was dazed as he lay on the floor out of breath. He slowly opened his eyes and saw Brian's rotting face looking down on him, the dead man's mouth open wide. Nate screamed as Brian tore into his throat.

Brian started to eat Nate alive. No screams could be heard since Nate's throat had been ripped out. Gargled noises came from Nate's mouth as he lay dying in a pool of his own blood. Pieces of flesh were being ripped from his body. Brian's hunger was intense as he continued to feed on Nate's twitching body. Soon, only small pieces of flesh were still attached to his bones. Brian continued to suck on them, leaving nothing.

Misty watched as he consumed the body. She felt turned on as she watched her lover seek his revenge. She looked over at Lucy who had passed out from terror. She was still sprawled across the bed. Misty walked over and looked down at her.

"How do you feel, Brian?" Misty asked.

When Brian looked up at her, she noticed he appeared to have regained some of his vitality. He no longer looked like a giant raisin. He rose from the floor, a chunk of Nate's flesh hanging from his teeth.

"Much better but I am still hungry," Brian replied.

Misty looked again at Lucy. "What do you want to do with her, dear?"

"Eat her," he smiled. "What else?"

Brian walked over to the bed and sat down beside Lucy. Her robe had come open, exposing one of her fake breasts that he'd bought her last year. He looked at her and no longer saw beauty, now she was just food.

Brian leaned down and grinned at Lucy. He shook her a little, wanting her to wake up so he could relish all of her terror.

Lucy opened her eyes and screamed.

"I'm so sorry, please forgive me. It was Nate's idea," Lucy begged.

Brian looked into her eyes and whispered, "I'm going to eat your tits I bought you first, then I'm going to consume every bit of your body. Then I'm going to suck the meat off your bones."

Before Lucy could respond, Brian's teeth clamped down on her right nipple and he ripped it off along with a chuck of her flesh. He put his hand over her mouth so her screams were muffled. She could smell the putrid stench from his body and gagged. Lucy tried to scream but he held her mouth shut. Brian ate her slowly, making sure she suffered with every bite that he took. The bed was soon soaked with blood, looking like a crimson pool.

Lucy finally died as she lay upon the blood-soaked sheets. Her eyes were still wide open in pain and agony. Brian had his face in her stomach, tearing out her guts, eating her like a wild animal. He felt stronger with each bite he took.

Misty watched as he finished eating Lucy. Her bones were visible and glistening under the overhead light when he was finished. He stood up and stretched and he looked like the old Brian Misty knew. His hair and eyes had turned black. His skin was an alabaster white. He looked like someone who had been out of the sun for far too long but was still healthy.

Brian smiled at Misty. She walked over to him and placed her hands on his face, ignoring the blood covering him from head to toe. She started to lean into him for a kiss but he pushed her back a little,

"How long will it last?"

Misty smiled "I don't know, dear. Not too many people have successfully brought back the dead, you know."

He looked in a mirror set on the dresser in the corner of the room. "And you have control over me."

"Yes, dear, with this amulet I'm wearing," she responded.

Brian looked at her and gestured to the corner of the room on the floor. "You mean the one that's over there on the floor?"

Misty looked where he pointed and saw the amulet had fallen off in her tussle with Nate.

He approached her slowly. "I feel so different and alive. I never felt like this when I was alive."

He moved up close to Misty and began to kiss her passionately. He wrapped his arms around her and held her tight. She was so in love, and knew that as long as they found fresh meat for him, he would remain the same. He was a zombie but one that could think, talk and love her.

Misty leaned into him more as her lust for Brian began to kick in. But then she felt a sharp pinch and then blood dribbled down her lip. Brian pushed her onto the floor and climbed on top of her.

"Ouch, hey, why so rough Brian?" she exclaimed.

"It's okay, I just wanted a little taste," he whispered.

He gently kissed her neck and was massaging her breasts as she writhed in pleasure.

"Take me now," she moaned, her eyes closed in passion.

Brian did take her, but not in the way Misty expected. He bit into the side of her neck, opening an artery. Warm blood shot out of the wound and into his mouth and she started to feel dizzy.

Brian was chewing her flesh he'd ripped from her neck. "I'm still so damn hungry," he moaned.

Misty drifted off from loss of blood and shock. She felt nothing as Brian consumed her body. When he was done, he cleaned up and put on a fresh pair of Nate's clothes. He picked up the amulet off the floor and placed it in his pocket to join with the other one he'd received when Misty had set it in his pocket at his funeral. He figured they were keeping him alive so better to have them.

He looked down at Misty's eviscerated corpse, "Sorry, baby, but I've changed. All you are now to me is meat."

Brian smiled as he walked out of the house.

He took Misty's car and drove off. He figured now he would start his life over, maybe learn more about voodoo, and pick up a few snacks along the way.

TEENAGE ZOMBIE PARTY

DAVID BERNSTEIN

The Valentine's Day party was a hit. Almost every teen from town was at Holbrook's Farm, partying and dancing as if the world was about to end. The barn was secluded, half a mile from the nearest road. Jebediah Holbrook's parents were away at a farmers' convention in Albany, New York. It was the perfect time to throw a party.

Jeb, Debbie--Jeb's girlfriend-- John, Alice--John's girlfriend-- and Keith, all partook in the party's construction. Christmas lights, fitted with red bulbs, ran throughout the barn and along the nearby fence. The barns walls and posts were littered with hearts, cupids, and romantic words cut from red and pink construction paper. Disco balls were hung from the rafters, and most of the barn's lights were replaced with red and pink bulbs. Strobe lights, two on each side of the makeshift dance floor, hung on the walls. Hay bales acted as seats, placed inside and outside of the barn. Jeb and his friends had pooled their money together and purchased five kegs of beer and numerous bottles of rum and tequila. They were going to make a killing and make a name for themselves as the best party throwers around.

Jeb and Debbie watched over the crowd of teens from the loft area of the barn. John was behind his crude saw-horse D.J. table, making sure the music flowed continuously. Keith, all six-two, two-hundred and five pounds, patrolled the floor, checking in the barn's nooks and crannies, making sure no problems arose. Alice was in charge of the outside, patrolling the grounds and keeping an eye out for the police, though it was unlikely that cops would show up with the barn being numerous acres away from the nearest residence. All five friends had agreed to remain sober and make sure, with all the hay about, that the barn stayed smoke free.

Jeb signaled John from above, putting two fingers to his mouth before pointing to a particular area of the barn. Someone was lighting up. John in turn relayed the signal to Keith who found the smokers and made them head outside to finish their cigarettes.

With the barn doors wide open, Jeb could see who came and went, and the newest arrivals had made his stomach queasy. It was the Mahoney brothers.

Alice confronted them as they neared the entrance. Jeb had been hoping they wouldn't show, but word spread fast in the small town of Oneonta. He watched as Alice spoke to them. It was her job to keep track of everyone that paid, keeping a written log. Her body motions were becoming animated, clearly indicating her level of annoyance. Jeb told Debbie to wait in the loft and keep an eye on the crowd. He climbed down to the barn floor, took a deep breath, and headed toward Alice.

The Mahoney brothers were notorious for causing trouble. The oldest, Jim, was serving time in jail for attempted robbery. All the younger ones, two arriving at the party, had all had run-ins with the law.

"Hey, Tyler," Jeb said as he approached Alice and the brothers.

"This bitch won't let us in," Tyler said.

"Ten bucks gets you all you can drink," Jeb said.

Tyler came over, putting his arm around Jeb. "Jeb, you see, I left my wallet at home thinking this was a free party. But I'm willing to help you out." Tyler motioned to his brother Teddy, who reached into his jacket and pulled out a clear baggy full of red pills. "We'll sell these at your party, giving you a cut. Fair?"

"No," Jeb said, vehemently, pulling himself away from Tyler.

"You don't think that's fair?" Tyler asked, sounding astonished.

"I don't want you selling drugs here." Jeb had a twinge of anxiety in his stomach, a butterfly or two. Standing up to the Mahoney's was asking for trouble.

"You heard him, boys," Alice said, holding out her hand. "Ten bucks each." Tyler placed a finger against one of his nostrils and launched a slimy yellow booger at Alice. She retracted her arm quickly, barely getting out of the snot's way. Fuming, her face scrunched up in an angry snarl, she raised her hand to hit Tyler, but Jeb held her back. The Mahoney brothers began laughing.

"You're a disgusting dirt-bag, you know that?" Alice told Tyler.

"That wasn't called for, Tyler," Jeb said.

"The bitch started it," Tyler said, an evil grin on his face.

"Listen," Jeb began. "If I let you in without paying then every-one will want their money back. I think you should just leave."

Keith, who had been walking the dance floor, came over. "Prob-lem?" he asked. Jeb worked hard to restrain a smirk. Keith was a formable foe. Even the Mahoney brothers wouldn't want to start a fight with him around.

"No," Tyler said, flatly. "We were just leaving." He turned, about to leave, adding, "Besides, we already sold a shit load of the pills. Why do you think everyone is having such a good time at this lame-ass party?" His brothers laughed, before following him into the night. From the shadows Tyler yelled, "You'll be seeing me, Jebediah."

"Better not be tonight," Keith warned back.

"Assholes," Alice said.

"Come on, guys, forget them," Jeb said. "Let's get back to our posts and keep this place from burning down."

Keith took out his cell-phone, holding it to his ear after punch-ing in numbers. "Can't get a line." He tried again. "Strange, all circuits are busy." Alice took her phone out.

"I don't even get a signal out here," she said.

On their way into the barn, a gut-wrenching scream broke out. All three turned to each other before running inside. No one was dancing; instead everyone was standing around and staring at Jill Hickcox and Aaron Bluehorn lying on the floor. The music ceased, leaving the air eerily still.

"What happened?" Jeb asked.

"I don't know," a freckled blonde said. "We were just dancing and they both started seizing before dropping to the floor. I think they're dead." Some of the people had phones to their ears, but everyone had confused looks on their faces. Murmurings of circuits being busy buzzed the crowd.

Keith came over, bending down next to the two bodies. He felt for a pulse on the female then the male. He shook his head. "They're both dead."

Everyone looked at the bodies with horrid expressions. Some of the onlookers began crying. The strobe lights continued to flash until John pulled the plug. The barn was cast in a fleshy red-pink hue, making the macabre scene hellish in appearance.

"Call 9-1-1!" Jeb yelled.

People already had phones to their ears. Tim McCormick, newspaper editor for the school paper, had his cell phone out, but was taking pictures of the bodies.

"Can't get through," one of the bystanders said.

"Me either," another echoed.

Soon the crowd of thirty became a jumbled muddle of confusion.

"What the hell is going on, Jeb?" Debbie asked, having climbed down from the loft. Before he could answer, a scream broke out, followed by another from the rear of the barn.

Jeb pushed his way through the packed crowd, Keith behind, followed by Debbie and Alice.

At the rear of the barn to the left side, behind a couple bales of hay lay the body of the team captain of the football team, Damon Kile. He was naked, his penis erect and glistening. His girlfriend, Barbara Giles, stood next to him, also naked except for the letterman's jacket she held in front of her.

"What the...?" Jeb began.

"We were," the girl swallowed, tears falling down her cheeks, "going at it and he just started convulsing. I had to shove him off of me. He hit the ground and stopped moving."

Keith came over and felt for a pulse. He looked back at Jeb. "Dead, like the others."

"What the hell is happening around here?" Alice asked. "No phones, people dying..."

Barbara Giles, shaking, said through tears. "He took some pills a while ago." Alice went to stand by her, putting a hand on her back. "He must have OD'd."

"What kind of pills?" Jeb asked.

"I don't know, they were red," Barbara said.

Jeb and Keith looked at each other saying the name "Mahoney" in unison. Brett Daniels, another kid from school, stepped forward. "I took some red pills, too. I bought them from Tyler Mahoney. Am I gonna die?"

"Me, too," another voice from the crowd said.

"And me," said another.

"I don't feel so good," someone else added. A hush broke out over the crowd.

"Everyone!" Jeb shouted. "Calm down. Everything's going to be all right. Alice took Barbara behind a pile of stacked hay bails to help the girl put her clothes back on. More screams broke out from the crowd. Jeb could feel the group's anxiety level growing like a giant ball of static electricity.

"We've got to get these people out of here and to a doctor," Keith said.

"Everyone who took the pills should get to a hospital. Make sure the person driving hasn't taken anything. I'll take a bunch in my..." Jeb stopped talking; he was watching the barn doors close. The crowd which had been facing him turned as the doors boomed shut.

"What the hell?" Debbie asked.

"Hey, who closed the doors?" someone yelled.

Jeb and Keith ran to the doors, trying to open them. Others joined, but the sturdy barn doors wouldn't budge. People began banging and demanding to be let out as laughing erupted from the other side.

"Who's out there?" Jeb asked.

"Awe, Jebby Webby afraid of the dark?" It was Tyler's voice. He'd locked them in.

"It's not dark in here, you moron. Now let us out," Jeb demanded.

"No way. You should've let us stay."

"Tyler!" Keith yelled. "People are sick from the pills you gave them. They're dying. We need to get them to a hospital." More laughter erupted from outside.

"Yeah, right," Tyler said. "Have a nice night in there, assholes."

"Let us out!" Jeb yelled, pounding on the heavy wooden door.

Alice came running up to the group. "What's happening?" she asked, breathing heavy and appearing jumpy. "Why are the doors shut?"

"Tyler Mahoney happened," Jeb said disgustedly. "He locked us in."

Debbie approached Jeb. "Some of the people aren't looking so good," she said. "We really need to get them to a doctor."

More screams erupted from the crowd. Then someone said, "They're getting up." People backed away, forming a circle around Jill and Aaron, the two teens that had just died. The two teens struggled as they rose. They had blank expressions on their pale faces and were moaning as if in pain.

"Impossible," Keith said. "They were dead."

"Check Damon," Jeb told him. "Maybe he's alive, too. The drugs must have only slowed their pulse down or something; it made them appear dead."

"I'm telling you, they were dead," Keith reiterated, his eyes fierce, voice certain.

"They're not now," Jeb said. More kids began collapsing, as people jumped and screamed in horror. "Damn, how many people took those pills?"

Keith ran over to one of the fallen, leaving Jeb, Alice and Debbie standing together. Some of the kids started helping Jill and Aaron to their feet.

Mark Grunger had Aaron by the arm, aiding him when Aaron turned and took a chunk out of Mark's bicep. Bloody flesh dangled from Aaron's lips while Mark screamed. He reared back his good arm and punched Aaron in the face, knocking him to the floor.

Jeb stared in disbelief, thinking how badly the drugs must've screwed up Aaron's brain. Then Jill Hickcox sunk her teeth into another kid's neck, tearing a huge piece of flesh free. Arterial blood shot out like a burst water-main. Four nearby party-goers were doused with crimson, making them glisten under the red and pink lighting. Alice began screaming at the site.

"Something's wrong with them!" a red-headed girl yelled. Other screams broke out from around the barn as more kids collapsed.

Aaron was already working his way back to his feet, face smeared with blood like a lion after a fresh kill. He grabbed a nearby girl, Karen Rose, and chomped down on her face. The girl wailed as blood poured from where Aaron was biting her. Two boys, both on the varsity football team, pulled Aaron off of her. The girl's right eye was gone, now a pulpy, bleeding socket. Her eyebrow was missing, too, a shiny piece of skull showing. Aaron chewed as he was held in place.

The two football players began punching and kicking Aaron, other teammates joining in. They took Jill down, too, stomping them both viciously on the ground like a gang initiation. Jeb and Keith jumped in, breaking up the melee.

"Stop, you're killing them!" Keith yelled.

Aaron and Jill lay in a heap, bloodied, broken and almost unrecognizable; as if they had been run over by a semi-truck. Jill's left leg was bent in the wrong direction at the knee, her right hand a mangled pulp. Aaron's head was fractured and caved in, his jaw completely dislocated. The place had gone quiet for a brief moment. Twelve people had fallen dead.

"We need to bust down the doors!" someone yelled.

"Yeah," another said. "Find something to bash them with."

Jeb didn't want to break the doors down, his parents would be pissed, but what choice did he have? People were dying. He was about to speak up when his voice caught in his throat.

Aaron and Jill began moving again, struggling to rise once more. No one had been watching them, the scene too gruesome for most. Jill had crawled a short ways and grabbed a girl's ankle. The girl screeched in horror as Jill pulled the leg to her mouth and bit down, piercing the jeans. At the same time, Aaron rose to his feet, his face sagging from the dislocated and broken jaw. He began hobbling forward, arms out as everyone screamed and began backing away.

"Look out!" Jeb yelled, finding his voice.

Aaron was about to grab hold of someone when one of the varsity members rammed him into a support post. A normal person would've been knocked unconscious, but Aaron tried getting up immediately. The huge jock roared, and charged the thing that was Aaron, trapping him against the post with bone crunching sound. The jock began punching him with tremendous blows to the gut. Aaron's face remained stoic. He craned his neck forward and began digging with his upper teeth into the varsity member's neck. The jock pulled away, stunned, holding his hand feebly over the gushing wound.

Brett Rogers, another football player, came forth wielding a pitchfork. He rammed it into Aaron's stomach, pinning him to the post. Aaron continued to struggle, trying to walk forward, completely unfazed by the large prongs sticking through him.

"What the...?" Brett said, eyes wide with shock. "Why isn't he dead?"

Three people were holding Jill down, staying away from her snapping jaws. The crowd was stunned into silence, watching two of their peers refusing to die. Another scream quickly broke out, putting the crowd into motion like bees crawling over each other in a nest. Everyone turned in the direction of the shriek.

Damon Kile stood naked, arms wrapped around Bobby Striker, a kid Jeb knew from one of his classes. Damon's jaws were clenched over Bobby's ear, gnawing away as blood and flesh mixed.

More screams rang out from within the crowd and people began losing it, panicking. Two more dead teens were up and attacking people. The air was filled with cries and grunts, the barn turning frantic as people scurried about, most getting as far from the undead as possible. A few stood their ground, punching and kicking their undead mates.

"Find a weapon!" Jeb hollered into the crowd. People began grabbing tools from the walls. Jeb grabbed a machete, Keith a sledgehammer, and Debbie a sickle. Alice was crying. John was trying to calm her down when he was grabbed from behind. Two undead classmates began tearing at his flesh. One sunk its fingers under the skin on his forehead and began pulling backward, removing John's scalp. The other had John's right arm, its teeth clamped down into his flesh, blood oozing from the wound like crimson maple syrup.

Keith ran over and smashed the undead teen peeling John's scalp off in the head, demolishing it. The damage was awesome, caving the zombie's head in like a watermelon. He did the same to the other undead member as Jeb pulled a blood-drenched John out of the way. Both undead teens lay on the floor, unmoving, dead this time for good.

With John on the ground, Keith knelt next to him. John's scalp had fallen back down on his head, but was slanted to the side, like a misplaced hairpiece. Keith pushed the flap of scalp back in place before checking his pulse. "He's still alive," he said, turning hope-fully to the gang.

"Everyone," Jeb said to his friends. "Follow me. Keith, can you carry John?"

"No problem," he said, bending down and picking up his un-conscious buddy, fireman style.

Jeb led his friends to a corner in the back of the barn. The area was somewhat secluded, blocked from view from the rest of the barn. He'd hoped no one saw them head off, wanting the space for themselves. It was cramped enough. Most of the people were busy, either fighting the undead or pounding on the barn doors.

Keith laid John down on the hay-covered floor, his arms stained with blood.

"I'm staying here with him," Alice said.

"Good idea," Jeb acknowledged. "Deb, stay with Alice and John. Me and Keith are going back out there."

Deb nodded, kissing him on the lips. "Be careful," she whis-pered.

"Don't hesitate to use the sickle. Hack any zombies that come your way."

"Zombies?" Alice asked, seeming a bit out of it.

"Yeah, what else would you call what's happened to everyone?"

"I think destroying the head...uhm brain, will kill them. At least it's worked so far," Keith told the group. "Remember to aim for the head, guys."

"I think you're right," Jeb echoed. "Based on the damage to the bodies, it was your sledgehammer to the skulls that stopped them." Everyone looked at each other before Jeb and Keith departed, the two boys heading back to the area of carnage.

As the two friends entered the barn's main area, a room of chaos appeared before them. Fellow classmates, now members of the living dead, crouched over bodies, feeding upon them, ripping entrails and other parts free. Zombies roamed free, attacking anyone that wasn't undead, maiming and killing. More people were fighting back, swinging everything from barn tools to fists. Zombie Aaron was still pinned to the post, trying to break free. The inside of the barn had become a vision of Hell, the golden hay stained crimson with blood. Body parts scattered about as if an explosion had occurred.

A zombie, Ken Peters, lunged from the shadows, catching Jeb off-guard. The zombie's rotting, death-filled breath assaulted his nostrils, making him want to vomit. The animated corpse's mouth opened wide, an inch from Jeb's face, the stench overbearing. A cool breeze brushed Jeb's cheek as Keith's hammer sailed past it, colliding with the zombie's head. Its left eye popped out, plunking Jeb in the forehead. The zombie flew sideways crashing to the ground, its head resembling a destroyed cherry pie.

Jeb turned to Keith, breathing hard. "Thanks."

More dead teens, many having been mutilated by the zombies, were rising. Jeb saw a kid, Jared Milstrum, come to life while two zombies were feasting on his intestines.

"People!" Jeb yelled over the crowd. "Smash the zombies' skulls in! You need to destroy the brain!" Jeb's yelling seemed to attract a couple of nearby undead. He swung his machete at a neck, the blade cutting through, separating the head from the body. Dark red, almost black, fluid spurted from the stump as the headless corpse tumbled to the ground. Keith took care of the other zombie with a crack to the head. Both weapons were caked with zombie sludge.

"We need to find a way out," Keith said. "There's too many of them. We'll tire before we can kill them all." Keith motioned to the loft. "Let's climb up and see what we can find up there."

"What about the others? And John?" Jeb asked. "He can't walk, let alone climb a ladder."

"We'll have to leave him, come back for him later."

"We can't. He'll be defenseless."

"We don't have a choice."

They fought their way back to Alice and the others. Both girls lay huddled next to an unconscious and bloody John. Deb got to her feet, and rushed to Jeb. "What the hell's going on out there?" she asked. "Sounds like a battle."

"It is," Jeb answered. "We're going to try a window in the loft. It might be boarded over or locked, but we've got to try."

"Look out!" Deb yelled as a zombie came around the bend. It was the big jock who had rammed Aaron earlier, his neck now having a raw fleshy hole in it. The zombie reached for Keith who had his back to it. Keith spun quickly, bringing the hammer up, knocking the zombie in the head. It didn't do any damage as the walking corpse kept coming. Keith slipped, dropping his weapon as he tried regaining his balance. The zombie took hold of his neck and began pulling him toward its gaping mouth.

Jeb charged, thrusting his machete ahead like a fencer and impaled the zombie in the throat. The blade went all the way in. The zombie twitched as if short-circuiting. Jeb yanked the weapon backward, severing the undead's spinal cord. The head teetered before Keith gave it an upper cut with his fist, sending it flying through the air.

"Damn, that was close," Keith said, picking up his sledgehammer. "I'm not going with you," he told Jeb. "Someone's gotta stay and keep the others safe."

"And I'm not leaving John," Alice said, caressing his cheek.

"I'll go," Deb said.

"No, I don't want you going back out there," Jeb said. "I'll be fine. Stay here and keep Alice safe."

"You just make sure you get that damn door open," Keith told him, grabbing his shoulder. "It's your barn, if anyone can find a way out, you can."

Jeb took a deep breath. "If I'm not back in thirty minutes, I'm probably dead. Then one of you will have to find a way out." He went to leave when Deb grabbed him. He embraced her warmly, giving her a passionate kiss before pushing her off and walking away.

He left his friends behind, creeping around the barn's outer edges, staying in shadow, hoping to avoid an encounter. A group of five survivors were huddled together near the barn's doors. They used rakes, sickles and pieces of cut lumber to keep back the wave of undead. More and more zombies joined the throng, pushing forward like crazed paparazzi, as if the people were famous celebrities. Jeb could tell the kids were tiring. They wouldn't last much longer. He needed to find a way to open the doors.

He reached the ladder leading to the loft, scaling it quickly. He wasn't sure if zombies could climb, but didn't want to find out. He reached the top to discover two female members of the undead roaming about. They spotted him immediately. They were at opposite ends of the loft. One wore a short, tight red dress and had blonde hair. Jeb didn't recognize her, but imagined at one time she was attractive. The other girl had dark hair, stood at least six feet and had on one high heel that made her walk with an exaggerated limp. They both had oatmeal-like puke covering their chests. Jeb figured they'd climbed up when no one was watching the ladder and took the infamous red pills before overdosing and dying.

The blonde was closer, Jeb attacking her first. He swung the machete, removing the zombie's outstretched arms. The second swing took the head off, dropping the corpse dead, the way it should have been. He heard the moan of the six-footer from behind and spun around. Her hands gripped his shoulders, the fingers curling into his shirt and pinching his skin. Using two hands, he shoved the machete upward, striking the zombie under the chin, thrusting the blade deep into her head. The body collapsed forward, Jeb scrambling out of the way to avoid being crushed. He flipped the zombie on its back and pulled the machete free before heading to the window.

The window was more like a mini-door, solid and heavy with no glass. He felt foolish for not thinking about the exit earlier. He couldn't blame himself; the night had been complete and utter chaos. There was no lock on the window. He unlatched the lever and pushed outward. The cool night breeze struck his sweaty face, rejuvenating him with hope.

Screams sounded from below the loft and he knew he had to hurry.

Looking out the window at the ground, he saw the drop was at least twenty feet. Attempting a straight fall might result in a broken ankle or worse. He glanced around, looking for a rope. In the left corner, hanging on the wall was a chain looped around a large railroad spike protruding from the wall. He ran over and pulled the chain from the wall. It was rusty and heavy, but would do. Upon laying it out, he saw it was about eight feet in length.

There was nothing around the window for him to attach the chain to. Using his machete, he ran over to the spike and began hammering down on it. The spike came free with a piece of barn wall attached to it. He went back to the window and began pounding the large spike into the sill, using the back end of the machete. The plastic handle cracked, but he kept hammering away until the spike was embedded deep enough. Sticking one of the chain links over the spike, he tugged hard to make sure it would hold. Next he lowered the chain as far as it would go.

He climbed onto the window sill and sucked in a deep breath. He dropped the machete to the ground before gripping the chain and shimmying down. Its thickness made gripping easier. He moved hand over hand, the rust leaving his palms orange. When he reached the chain's end, he dangled a good twelve feet from the ground. With no choice and time running out, he let go.

He landed on his feet, letting his legs collapse under him, before tucking his head and somersaulting into an impact-lessening roll. Flopping onto his back, he lay still for a second, making sure he had no pain. Relieved and grinning, he got to his feet, ready to run to the barn doors, when he was grabbed from behind. He began flailing and kicking when the person who held him started laughing. Then from out of the gloom, he saw Tyler.

"Was wondering if one of you assholes would try the window," Tyler said with a grin.

"Let me go," Jeb demanded.

"Hold him, Teddy," Tyler commanded his younger, but much stronger, brother.

"People are dead and dying inside. You have to open the door," Jeb said.

"I'll open it when I damn well feel like it." Tyler walked to where Jeb had dropped the machete and picked it up. "And what were you planning on doing with this?"

"I've been killing zombies with it," Jeb spat, not caring how ridiculous he sounded. Tyler and Teddy began laughing. "I'm not joking."

Tyler's face faltered and the laughing ceased. "You're serious," he said. "What'd you flip out and kill someone with this thing?" He looked at the blade covered in gore then tossed it to the ground with a look of revulsion. "What the hell?"

"I told you the truth," Jeb said vehemently.

"You're a sick bastard," Tyler said, a look of hatred on his face. "Hold him, Teddy." He walked up to Jeb. "I'm going to teach this punk a lesson before we hand him over to the cops."

"We'll be heroes," Teddy said giddily.

"Yeah, heroes," Tyler agreed, clearly liking the idea. "And get the cops off our backs for once. Change our image with them."

Tyler stepped up to within an inch of Jeb's face. "Look at this guy. He's covered in blood. The police are gonna have a fun time with you and I doubt they'll care that we kicked your ass."

Jeb brought his leg up, kneeing Tyler in the balls. The kid bellowed a sigh before crumbling to the ground, holding his groin. Feeling Teddy's grip loosen, Jeb threw his head back, head-butting the big oaf in the nose and breaking it. He was free in seconds, Teddy holding his nose as blood poured between his fingers.

Jeb bent low, plucked the machete from the grass and took off toward the barn's front doors. He arrived quickly, removing the wooden plank that held the doors shut. When the doors didn't burst open, he grew worried and cracked one open, peeking inside.

Zombies were everywhere, more in number than before. Some of the teens that had been holding the zombies off were up in the loft. Jeb saw none of the undead up there with them, guessing zombies couldn't climb. The group of survivors must have spotted him earlier and made their way over to the ladder. Not knowing what else to do, Jeb swung both doors wide open and took off, hiding in the nearby bushes.

Tyler and his brother rounded the barn, heads down and running hard. They entered the barn, smacking into a horde of living dead. The zombies encompassed them quickly, dragging them into the fray. Jeb watched as mouths closed over the two brothers' bodies, tearing clothing and flesh. Screams erupted from the pack of undead as Tyler and his brother disappeared from view. Jeb didn't like Tyler, but the kid didn't deserve to die and in such a horrible manner.

He sat for what seemed like hours, watching the zombies pour out of the barn and head off into the fields and down the driveway.

Finally, with the coast clear, he ran into the barn. A lone zombie remained. It was Aaron, still stuck to the post with the pitch fork.

Jeb walked up to him. "Sorry, buddy," he said before slicing Zombie Aaron's head from his shoulders.

As Jeb ran to where he left his friends, he called out, "Deb? Keith?" He rounded the corner to find them all huddled together. Deb ran over and wrapped her arms around him.

"I knew you'd do it," she said.

Keith high-fived him. "Good job, man."

Alice sat weary-eyed next to John. His face looked pale, his eyes sunken around the sockets. Jeb noticed his chest wasn't moving.

Keith shook his head, whispering to Jeb, "I think she's in shock."

Jeb walked over to Alice. "I'm sorry," he said.

"Why did this happen?" she asked through tears. "Why John? He was such a good guy."

"I know," Jeb said, softly. "And he loved you very much, but we have to go." He held out a hand for her.

"Okay," she said flatly, as if in a daze.

Upon Alice rising, John reached out, grabbing her ankle. She fell backward, slipping from Jeb's hand, and landed on top of her zombie ex-boyfriend. She screamed, her eyes widening in terror, as the Zombie John sunk his teeth into the back of her neck, tearing away a large chunk of vertebrae and flesh. She looked up at Jeb, the life already fading in her blue eyes. Jeb reached out, pulling her off the undead John, but it was too late. She was dead.

The zombie chewed its food, and the sound of sloshing meat and crunching bone seemed to echo in the confined area. Keith raised the sledgehammer, then brought it down, obliterating the zombie's face.

Jeb held a lifeless rag doll-like Alice in his arms. He placed her down gently, blood covering his fingers from her wound.

"She's dead, man," Keith said, putting a hand on Jeb's shoulder.

Deb was crying hysterically.

"Time to go," Jeb muttered. As he turned around, Keith raised the sledgehammer and crushed Alice's head.

"No!" Jeb screamed, grabbing Keith and pushing him against the wall.

"It needed to be done," Keith told him, his eyes cold. "I wasn't going to let her become one of those *things*."

Realizing he was right, Jeb slowly released his friend. "Let's go," he said.

Together, with a few other survivors, the group walked to Jeb's house and called the police using a landline, their cell-phones still informing them that all circuits were busy. Jeb listened in horror, hardly believing what he heard.

"What?" Deb asked.

Jeb put the phone on speaker.

The recording kept repeating itself.

"You've reached the Orange County Sheriff's Office. All personnel are out responding to the current epidemic. Stay inside your homes, lock the windows and doors and stay away from any walking dead."

WILL YOU DIE FOR HER?

MARK M. JOHNSON

The stairwell door creaked open into the gloom of the underground parking structure, three levels below the ground floor of the up-scale Riverwalk Luxury Condominiums. The lights in the stairwell were dead, a wall of inky black dividing it from the dim illumination in the parking garage. Only the battery powered emergency lights lit the shadowy, car-lined corridors from high up in the corners. Out amongst the many expensive vehicles parked in the garage, the figures moved beneath the weak lights. Attracted by the door's creak, several of the shambling figures paused and gazed with an empty craving at the darkness within the stairwell, but upon seeing nothing emerge, they gradually lost interest and resumed their shiftless shuffling.

"There's too many of them," a female voice whispered from the darkness inside the stairwell.

"We can't go back," a male voice, answered.

"We'll never make it to the car," the female voice hissed.

"Mommy?" a little boy's voice asked.

"Ssssh!" both adult voices hissed.

"Jeremy," the male voice whispered. "We have to be quiet, buddy, so no more talking."

"Okay, Daddy," the little boy answered in his best conspiratorial whisper.

"We can still go back," the female voice insisted. "We were safe upstairs."

"Damn it, Susan, we can't have this argument again, especially here and now!"

"I'm scared, Justin."

Justin sighed gently, "So am I, let me think for a minute." He scooted forward as quietly as he could and peered out from the darkened doorway. Spotting something to the left, he slowly withdrew back into the stairwell. "There's a big SUV parked just a few yards away, the driver's door is open."

"Jesus," Susan whimpered, "I think one of them saw you."

"Hold on," Justin said and peered out again. "No, he's moving on." In the darkness, Justin reached out and found his wife's hand still clutching the pistol he'd given her. Fumbling past her right hand, he found her empty left and gathered it into his. "I'm going to sneak out to that SUV and see if the keys are still in it."

"This is crazy," Susan protested.

Justin took a breath and let it out slowly, "If the keys are in it, I'll start it and back it up to the door."

Beside him in the dark, Susan whimpered softly.

"We're going to make it out of here!" Justin insisted quietly, "We have to."

"Okay," Susan agreed. "So what next? I grab Jeremy, jump in the SUV, and we drive off into the sunset?"

Justin nodded his head, but suddenly realizing that Susan couldn't see him, he smiled and said, "Something like that."

In the darkness beside him, Susan wasn't smiling. "What if the keys aren't in the truck? What if it's out of gas? Even if the keys are there, where are we going?"

Justin sighed long and hard. "We're between a rock and a hard place, Suzy, I'm making this up as I go."

"You're playing with our lives!" she said.

Justin fell silent and carefully considered his next words. "We've been down this road before. We're already weak from lack of food, and if we don't try to leave now we won't be able to later, we'll starve to death."

"I'd rather starve than be eaten'."

"I don't wanna get eatin," Jeremy said.

Justin growled softly in frustration then said, "I love you, baby." He squeezed her hand once more and let go. "If something goes wrong, close this door and go back up without me." Without another word, he settled down onto the floor and slowly crawled out of the stairwell. He crept across the concrete with his only weapon, an aluminum baseball bat, cradled in his arms. After several agonizingly slow minutes, he made it to the SUV. Taking a deep breath, he pushed himself up on his knees and peered through the Escalade's tinted windows, the vehicle was empty.

Blowing out the breath he was holding, he continued alongside the vehicle until he made it to the open driver's side door.

"Thank you, God," he whispered when he saw the glint of a ring of keys on the driver's side floorboard . Moving as quietly as he could, he dragged himself into a prone position inside the SUV and squinted at the darkened dashboard. Without the engine running, he couldn't tell how much gas was still in the gas tank. He felt something wet soaking through the arm of his jacket and put his hand down to the driver's seat to find it was wet, sticky, and stank of coppery death.

"Damn it," he hissed, realizing what he was laying in. He swallowed and started to gag. Biting down hard, he drove his revulsion back and regained control. Reaching up to search for the keys, his hand brushed against them and they clattered to the floor of the SUV with a loud jangle that echoed through the silent garage. A loud groan, very close to Justin, followed the jangle of the keys, then another moaning call answered the first, and then the garage came alive with hungry, shambling death.

"Oh, shit," Justin mumbled as he drew his feet into the vehicle, sat up in the bloody mess in the driver's seat, and slammed the door closed. He tossed his bat onto the passenger seat and fumbled with the keys. Something banged against the hood of the SUV but Justin resisted the urge to look up. Finding the key for the Escalade lost in the jumble of keys on the ring, he jammed it into the ignition and then paused for a second when his eyes glanced over the little Nassau Bahamas surfboard key chain. He'd taken Susan there for their honeymoon; they had stayed in one of the best rooms at Paradise Island's Atlantis resort. Shaking off the distraction, he clicked the key forward, a dinging alarm immediately accompanied the lights on the dash as he turned the key the rest of the way and the engine rumbled to life.

Something slumped against the passenger door, and when he glanced over, he saw a heavyset woman with no lower jaw gaping at him as she pounded her fleshy fist on the blood-smeared window. "Sorry, lady," he said and shifted into reverse. The SUV tore away from the walking dead woman, catching her legs beneath the front tire and crushing them. With a screech of tires, Justin stopped in front of the stairwell door, blocking it with the vehicle.

Susan exploded out of the darkness with little Jeremy in her arms. She pulled up on the rear driver's side door handle, and found it still locked. "The door's locked!" she screamed franticly, smacking her hand on the window.

"Shit!" Justin cried and searched for the lock button.

"Jesus fucking Christ!" Susan screamed, and then the lock popped up. She threw the door open, leapt into the truck with Jeremy, and slammed the door shut. "Go!" she shouted.

Justin relocked the doors, put the Escalade in drive and floored it. "Get your seatbelts on!" he shouted over his shoulder. The SUV screamed through the garage as dead bodies stumbled out of the shadows and bounced off the vehicle as it rounded the corners, seeking the surface and the daylight world.

"We never should've left the safe room!" Susan screamed, and Jeremy started crying as she shifted him over and pulled a seat belt around him. Justin grinded his teeth together painfully, struggling not to shout back. He knew she was scared, he was too, and Jeremy screaming from the back seat didn't help matters. The SUV careened around the last level, leaving rubber on the pavement as it almost came up on two wheels, and Justin spotted daylight streaming through the chain-link gate blocking the exit.

"Hold on!" he shouted.

The Escalade crashed through the gate, grinding metal and shattering glass. The windshield sprayed into Justin's face, peppering his cheeks and forehead with shattered shards of glass. The SUV burst out of the garage exit with sparks and shattered glass flying. Catching a few feet of air as it crested over the end of the ramp, it bounced back to the pavement, spinning the steering wheel from Justin's hands. The SUV veered hard to the right and tumbled end over end onto the street.

The centrifugal force of the rolling Escalade ejected Justin from the vehicle, violently tossing his flailing body through the air. The street of Main Street rose up and slammed into his body, knocking the wind from him even as his head bounced off the pavement.

Then his world went black.

* * *

The wind tousled his blond hair as he gazed wondrously down over the side of the mountain, the valley below bustled with the activity of hundreds of little ant people and tiny toy cars. "It's beautiful," he said.

"Justin!" A voice floated on the wind from somewhere far away. He turned towards the distant voice and found himself back in the shadowed parking garage as shambling dead things surrounded him. "Justin!" the voice screamed again, and he opened his eyes. Thick gray clouds hurried across the overcast sky and a wind driven empty pop can clattered by. His head snapped to the left following the can, and then his eyes focused on the Escalade. It lay crumpled and overturned on the sidewalk; white smoke billowed up from its undercarriage, and through the white smoke, he saw Susan standing beside it.

Susan held her son in one arm, her long blond hair blowing across her face and nearly covering Jeremy's, and in the other hand, she held the .45 Pistol Justin had given her. She was pointing it at him.

"Justin!" she screamed franticly! "Behind you!" She shifted her aim slightly up and to his right, and then the gun did its dance. He heard a wet smack followed by a grunt just behind him and he spun around. An old and decrepit aristocrat in a black Armani suit, gore-soaked and tattered, reached out and grasped him by his hair. Justin screamed as the man yanked hard and fell forward onto him. He felt the sharp sting of teeth raking across the crown of his head and twisted away from the zombie with a shriek. He left hair, scalp, and flesh behind as he tried to scramble away. A sallow, bloodied police officer caught him by his jacket as he struggled to escape, and the walking dead cop lunged in and bit down hard, taking a chunk of Justin's neck away in his groaning mouth.

Justin screamed as blood jetted through his fingers and he tried to cover the wound on his neck. He staggered and fell. He heard Susan screaming his name and looked up. She was coming around the wrecked SUV, approaching him with her gun blazing.

"No!" he screamed, stopping her in her tracks. He spied the aluminum bat a few feet away and scrambled towards it. Grasping the bat in one hand, he staggered to his feet again and swung at the zombies gathering around him. The bat bounced ineffectually off the dead cop's shoulder. Justin fell to his knees again as consciousness wavered and threatened to leave him.

"Run!" he screamed with a wheeze. "Run!" he sighed and then fell over as hungry dead things reached for him.

"Daddy!" Jeremy cried.

Susan sobbed in disbelief, "Oh God, oh God," she chanted. She turned in a circle, searching for a way to safety as tears ran down her face. She wanted to run back to the safety of their split-level seventh floor condominium, and the impenetrable safe room therein, but there were too many dead people between her and the lobby doorway. She spun on her heal and ran in the opposite direction; away from the riverfront and deeper into the downtown area. Dodging away from reaching hands curved like claws, she ran around the hundreds of crashed or abandoned cars, city busses and a few empty National Guard trucks scattered throughout the city center. She ran for her life and the little life in her arms.

Spotting an alley that looked deserted, she darted into the trash-strewn passage. In normal times, the alley would have been in sharp contrast to the outer streets of the downtown area, but now, the trashy dark alleyway looked almost inviting. The alley ended at a T-junction, and seeing nothing threatening either way, she went right, but that pass quickly ended in a dead end. She turned back, went left, and stopped after running a few more yards. The alley opened onto Main Street, and if she followed it, she'd be right back where she started.

Jeremy unburied his tear-streaked face from her shoulder and followed her gaze to the end of the alley, and the things staggering down Main Street. They could see the zombies, but none turned their way.

"Their coming, Mommy," Jeremy whispered into her ear as he looked back over her shoulder. "I hear them coming."

"I know, baby," she whimpered. She turned, went back to the junction, and peered around the corner. The alley was loaded wall to wall with the walking dead. They were coming for them.

"Shit!" she hissed.

"Shit," Jeremy mimicked.

Abandoning the junction, she ran back towards Main Street. The street at the end of the alley ran thick with the dead, but she had no choice-- or did she? Susan turned and looked back at the many garbage dumpsters lining the alleyway. "We're going to hide, sweetie," she said and approached one of the dumpsters.

Warily lifting the lid, she held the gun ready, but nothing leapt out.

"This one looks good," she said, and hefted Jeremy up and lowered him into the trash bags littering the inside of the dumpster. Without hesitation, she followed her son into the container and carefully lowered the lid. Hesitating at the last moment, she held the lid partway open and peered through the crack. When she was convinced nothing had seen them climb in, or at least hoped, she lowered the lid. She settled back into the trash bags and began to pull them around and over their bodies.

"They stink, Mommy," Jeremy whispered.

"It's a good stink, baby, and maybe it'll hide our smell," Susan whispered.

"Can the dead people smell us?"

"I don't know, honey, maybe."

She pulled one more bag over them, covering everything but a space to breathe through, then held a finger to her mouth. "Shhh, very quiet now."

"Very quiet," Jeremy whispered. They could hear them coming now. Hear the groaning and shuffling footsteps, hands banging against the dumpsters as they passed by in search of the pair they had seen running down the alleyway. Closer now, so close. Something banged against the dumpster and Jeremy almost yelped. What sounded like hundreds of the undead were shuffling past the dumpster now, in a never-ending procession of living death that seemed to go on for hours. She clutched Jeremy to her, his heart thundering in tune with her own. As the sounds of living dead dwindled, their eyes grew heavy, and in spite of their communal terror, they both gradually slipped into a deep yet fitful sleep full of dark lumbering shapes. Around them, the darkness of the coming night rose up from its grave in the east and leisurely consumed the dead city block by block, as the sun lay down to die below the western horizon.

* * *

Susan awoke with a start when someone lifted the dumpster's lid. Sunlight shimmered in around the head and shoulders of the invader, rendering him in black silhouette. She shielded her eyes from the blazing sun and Justin's face came into focus.

"I'm so hungry," he groaned as he reached for her.

She screamed and almost fired a round through the still closed dumpster lid as her eyes snapped open.

"Shit," she hissed quietly.

She squinted at the real sun as its rays seeped in around the corners of the heavy steel lid of their hideaway. She realized it was daytime outside but had no idea what time it was. *Did we sleep through the whole night?* she wondered silently.

"That's a bad word, Mommy," Jeremy yawned. He sat up and a few bags of rotting garbage slid from his shoulders.

Susan almost laughed, "Yes it is, and I'm sorry, honey."

"'S okay," the little boy whispered, turning on his *cute* as he gazed up at her.

She pulled her little boy close and hugged him tightly, "It's the end of the world and you can still make me laugh," she said. He hugged her back, squeezing a tear from her tired eyes.

Jeremy relaxed his tight hug and sought out his mother's eyes. "Is it really the end, Mommy?"

"I don't know, honey. It sure seems like it, though."

"But we're still here."

"Yes, we are."

"I'm so hungry, Mommy."

Susan brushed a piece of grimy something from his dirty cheek and sighed. "Me, too honey, me, too." She shifted around herself, scattering trash bags as she climbed to her knees and pulled the pistol from her waistband. "Let's see what's going on, okay?" she whispered. She checked the safety on the weapon before disengaging it and then reached up towards the lid. It creaked ever so slightly as she raised it an inch or so, just enough to scan the alley. To her left, she could still see the distant Avenue of Main Street.

A lone zombie shambled into her view of the street, followed by a large grouping of at least ten or more. She panned her gaze to the right. The alley appeared to be empty and she sighed in relief. Then something caught her eye.

Just a few yards away on the opposite side, a heavy steel door at the back of one of the stores that lined the opposing street hung partially open. The faded lettering on the door read, The Health Nut, cleverly written inside the shape of a horizontal peanut.

"I know that place," she whispered. Her mouth watered as her memory strolled her down the aisles of the health food and organic goods marketplace. She carefully lowered the lid, and then found Jeremy's anxious eyes as she settled back into their bed of trash. "I think I know where we can find some food," she whispered.

"Oh, good," Jeremy said. "I'm really hungry." To punctuate his statement, Jeremy's stomach growled. "See? My tummy's talking."

Susan smiled, "Mine, too, honey. Okay, listen," she said gravely, "it's just like before, you stay close to me, and if we have to run, you have to help by holding on to my shirt so my hands are free."

"Okay, Mommy," Jeremy whispered.

Susan could see the excitement in his young, innocent eyes, and hoped he couldn't see the gut-wrenching fear in hers. She lifted the lid once more and checked the alley.

It was still clear.

She lifted the lid just high enough to climb out of the dumpster. Keeping the container between her and the zombies inundating Main Street, she reached back into it and helped Jeremy out.

"Stay low," she whispered. With Jeremy at her hip, they crouched down and crawled across the filthy alley to the partially open steel door. Susan locked eyes with her son, held a finger to her lips, then motioned for him to stay put. Reaching out, she grasped the edge of the door and gently pulled it open, testing it for noise, the door swung open silently on well-oiled hinges and she breathed a sigh of relief. With the door now open enough for her to crawl through, she hesitantly slipped her head around the threshold and peeked into the store.

Bright, late-day sunlight shone in through the front windows of the shop, but the narrow hallway leading to the rear door remained mostly in shadows. She could see into the store but not all the way to the front windows. A light breeze blew back her hair, telling her the front door was either open, or the display windows were shattered. Neither one boded well for the chances of the store being empty. The part of the store she could see lay in disarray, shelves knocked over, canned goods scattered, the sunlight glittering off broken glass strewn across the floor.

Susan's stomach rolled over and growled as her eyes lingered on the cans of food just waiting for her to pick them up. "Okay, we're going in, stay close," she whispered.

"Staying close," Jeremy whispered back.

She crawled through the doorway and slid aside to make room for Jeremy. Once he crawled through, she grabbed the door by the push bar and gently pulled it closed. The door clicked shut loudly and she winced. With her gun pointed out towards the open store, she waited. Her vision grew blurry, and realizing she was holding her breath, she let it out in a hushed whoosh. Nothing lumbered into view searching for the source of the noisily closing door, and after a few agonizingly long minutes, she let herself relax slightly.

Susan glanced back at Jeremy, held a finger to her lips again, and gestured for him to follow her. Together they crawled to the end of the rear exit hallway and turned left into the back of the service counter. Susan carefully stood on her knees and peeked over the countertop. Only jagged, gaping openings remained of the front windows. The entire store looked like a hurricane had blown through, but as far as she could see; it was mercifully empty of walking dead shoppers.

She sat back on her legs and smiled at her hungry son, "Looks like we're going shopping." She reached up, pulled out two of the stores hemp shopping bags, and handed them to Jeremy, then grabbed a few for herself. "Stay right next to me and keep out of site from the front windows," she instructed. "Fill your bags with light dry box foods; anything you want. I'll get the heavier can stuff and then we'll make a run back home."

"Okay," Jeremy said and smiled.

She smiled back at him, then led him out into the store. The bags filled gradually, and an hour passed by as they moved slowly from aisle to aisle. Susan found a box of honey-nut granola snacks, opened the box, handed one to Jeremy, and then opened one for herself. They grinned sheepishly at each other as they chewed. Susan opened a bottle of grape flavored vitamin water and gave it to Jeremy before taking a drink herself.

The bright sunlight shimmering through the front of the store faded as overcast clouds rolled in, and the clinking clatter of breaking glass interrupted their feast.

Susan's eyes widened, and she swallowed hard and almost choked. With trembling hands, she spun up into a crouch and brought her pistol up. Slowly she slid up to the edge of the aisle and gingerly peered around the corner...and saw her husband.

Covered in blood and ragged bite wounds on his gray-fleshed face and neck, he was still clutching the aluminum baseball bat in his right hand. Justin stood just inside the front entrance of the store, swaying drunkenly at the head of the center aisle.

And he was looking right at her!

A gasping cry of horror-stricken grief exploded out of her mouth before she could stop it. Justin's dead, expressionless eyes locked onto hers and he spewed out a guttural, snarling groan as he lumbered forward. His free hand reached out to embrace her as the bat clinked and bounced alongside him. She lifted the pistol and centered the sites on his forehead. At almost point blank range she couldn't miss. Her finger tensed on the trigger as the hammer started to pull back, but she couldn't shoot him.

"Shit!" she spat.

Spinning away from her undead husband, she bent and snatched up the grocery bags. "Run!" she screamed at her wide-eyed son. "The back door!"

Thankful that Jeremy was spared the sight of his walking dead father, she ushered him out into the alley and slammed the door behind them. "He'll be able to push the door open," she gasped as they ran towards the Main Street exit from the alleyway. "We have to run, honey, run fast!"

"I'm runnin' fast, Mommy," Jeremy gasped out as he struggled with his bags of groceries.

"Not fast enough," she grunted as she scooped him up and ran out into the street. Luck was with them, most of the dead shambled blocks away in either direction. Only a few stragglers stood between them and the condominium apartment complex. Susan ran directly at them, dodged the few that she could, and cleared the others with her .45. As the reverberations of her gunshots echoed across the dead metropolis, a collective groan began to rise up out of the city streets, growing louder with each passing second until it seemed to vibrate the very concrete beneath her running feet.

Gasping for breath, she dashed through the massive concrete arched entrance to the Riverwalk Luxury Condominiums atrium lobby. The empty lobby looked normal despite the shattered glass of the entrance doors. All of the flowering plants and tropical trees still flourished beneath the domed glass ceiling, birds fluttered from tree to tree, chirping happily as if the world was still alive below them. Susan bypassed the dead elevators and ran down the corridor leading to the north stairwell they had used to get down to the parking garage. She skidded to a stop at the stairwell door, lowered Jeremy to the floor, then stood frozen at the doorway as a shocked expression spread across her face. "The key!" she cried out as she patted the pockets of her pants, knowing were empty.

From the inside, the heavy steel doors opened with a gentle push, but outside of the stairwell a key was required to gain entry. Only residents had keys, and hers were out in the overturned SUV in the middle of the street, still tucked safely within her purse.

"Mommy," Jeremy said and tugged on her pant leg.

She glanced down at him and saw his hand pointing back the way they had come. She spun and her eyes fell upon her dead husband, who was now blocking their only way out.

"It's Daddy!" Jeremy cried. "He's a walkin' dead man!"

"Oh, God," Susan sobbed. She pushed Jeremy behind her and lifted the gun. Her hand wavered, but she knew she had to kill him. She had to get back out to the Escalade and get those keys. "I love you, Justin," she said as she took aim on his forehead.

* * *

"I love you, Justin," the woman said to him as she lifted something in her hand and pointed it at him. The words were only sounds that meant nothing to him, yet they cut through his burning desire to eat her and battered his mind like a hail of bullets.

He reeled from the impact of the spoken words and staggered to a halt. The living flesh he needed so badly stood almost within reach, but he couldn't move. He had pursued the mother and her child to the lobby, and now, when he had them both trapped, something held him back. He had no memory of her besides the moment he saw her in the store, and she had abandoned a perfect opportunity to kill him, choosing to flee instead.

* * *

Though he longed to rend and gnaw the flesh from the woman and boy's bones, the world suddenly brightened into a blinding white light and his prey faded from view. Like a divine light shining into his eyes, a powerful memory from his past life overtook his senses.

As if some unknown power miraculously transported his undead mind across space and time, he no longer stood swaying before the woman and her child. The light shining into his eyes became the bright mid-day sun, and he shielded his eyes from the glare as a green landscape came into view.

"It's beautiful up here," he said. The words came from his mouth, but he didn't understand what they meant. His confusion mounted as he took in the greenery of the trees and wild growth surrounding him. Above him, colossal white clouds drifted lazily across the expansive blue sky. Beneath him, something shifted and the animal he sat upon whinnied and snorted with impatience.

"We have to dismount and walk up from here," a voice said. He turned his head to see a gray haired man dressed in blue jeans, a flannel jacket, and a white cowboy hat. The man jumped down from the animal he rode upon and tethered it to a wooden hitching post. Without effort, as he was a bystander in this vision, Justin nodded and followed the man's example.

He followed behind the older man as they climbed up a steep, narrow, rock-strewn path. After a few minutes, they both stepped into a clearing at the end of the path and beheld a breathtaking view. A brisk wind blew back their hair as they stood on a colossal stone outcropping on the side of a mountain. Justin carefully edged up to the precipice, and glanced down at a sheer drop of several hundred feet.

He whistled softly. "That's one hell of a drop, sir," he said as he stepped safely away from the edge. Green valleys and distant mountains both green and snowcapped commanded the majestic vista as far as he could see.

"My father brought me here when I was a boy," the man said as he gazed out at the horizon. "He used to come here to clear his mind and reflect on important decisions. The man turned his intensely bright blue eyes on Justin, "Over the years, I've come to do the same. This is the only place where I can think without distractions."

"I can understand that," he said as he felt himself begin to wither under the man's severe gaze. He steeled himself and returned the powerful stare with one of his own.

"Susan tells me she loves you, son, and she thinks you feel the same," the man said without breaking eye contact.

"I do, sir," he answered.

The man held his gaze for a second longer and then gestured to the valley below them. "You see that town and the surrounding valley?"

Justin looked down on the valley and nodded slowly. "Yes, sir."

"The valley and the surrounding mountains, including the one we're standing on, have been owned by my family for generations, handed down to my father by his and to me by him." The man took a deep breath as if the mountain's air itself were a prized possession. "This land means more to me than almost anything else in the world." The man turned his withering gaze upon Justin once more. "But I would burn it all to the ground, sacrifice my own life, walk through the fires of Hell itself, and spit in the Devil's face for my little girl," he said vehemently. "That, my friend, is love."

Justin lowered his head and then looked back into the man's hard eyes. "I love her, sir. I want to spend the rest of whatever time I have on this world with her."

"I don't doubt that, son, but what I need to know is will you die for her?"

"Sir?"

"When it comes down to the wire and your back is against the wall, will you put your life on the line? Would you give your life for hers?" The man's gaze cut into Justin's eyes like a laser.

Justin held his eyes steady and answered without hesitation. "Yes, I would give my life for her, and sacrifice everything and anything. If I died, I would claw my way straight out of Hell to protect her."

Susan's father looked deeply into his eyes. Searching for insincerity or deception and finding only truth, he smiled and held out his hand. "Then welcome to the family, Justin."

Justin took the offered hand and shook firmly, "Thank you, sir, it's very important to Susan, and to me, that we have your blessing."

"Consider it given, Justin, and you can call me Mike for now." Michael Warner said warmly and slapped Justin on the back. "C'mon, they should have dinner ready by the time we get back."

Michael's last words echoed across Justin's mind as if spoken from a great distance, then the vision faded to black.

Once again, he stood before the woman and her child. His mind reeled as he realized that he remembered the man from the vision.

His boss, Mr. Warner, was Susan's father!

Susan!

He knew this woman! He remembered her, and his promise to her father. A promise he had been about to break. He remembered who he was, and what he had become. His sluggish undead mind formed another thought, *I'm dead, oh God, I'm dead!*

A cry of undiluted anguish erupted from his soul.

* * *

Susan looked down the sight of the pistol at the thing that possessed Justin's body as her finger tightened on the trigger. She could hear more zombies coming, and knew she had to shoot him!

Why isn't he attacking us! she wondered.

Justin stood swaying in the center of the lobby, his face hanging slack though his lips moved as if in the middle of reciting a silent prayer. She gazed deeply into his vacant eyes, and somewhere in the blank emotionless emptiness, she saw something beginning to awaken.

Susan's trigger finger relaxed, and with a sob, she lowered the gun. "Oh, God, Justin," she cried out softly.

At that moment, life flooded back into Justin's vacant eyes and he looked at Susan. He looked at her and she saw recognition in his living dead eyes! His slack face came to life and twisted with unfathomable pain. He threw back his head and howled a cry to the heavens that sent shivers creeping down her spine. The groaning zombies coming through the shattered revolving door answered his cry with one of their own.

Justin lowered his head and looked at her again, his face still a dead mask of agony. His mouth worked, but he only managed a wet gurgle. His pale, gaunt face scowled with frustration, and he looked at her again with sorrowful haunted eyes.

"Daddy!" Jeremy shouted as he ran past Susan.

"No!" Susan cried franticly. Reaching out, she missed her son's arm as the little boy ran from her. "Jeremy, stay away from him. Jeremy!" Susan ran forward, reaching for her boy.

Jeremy ran to his father with his arms thrown wide. "Daddy, Daddy." Jeremy reached him and threw his arms around his father's legs, hugging tightly.

Justin gazed down at the boy, then rested his bloody hand on Jeremy's blond head. Jeremy looked up at his father with unconditional love and a clumsy smile spread across the dead man's bluish gray lips.

"Jeremy!" Susan cried out nervously as she came up behind her son wrapped in his undead father's arms. She held up the pistol and pointed it at Justin's face, then she reached out and grasped Jeremy's arm. "Come on, honey," she whimpered softly. "Come on away from him, baby." Hot tears ran down her face as she gently pulled Jeremy away from Justin.

"But, Mommy, he's okay," Jeremy protested as she drew him into her arms and stepped back slowly, keeping the gun trained between Justin's eyes.

Justin looked up at the gun pointed at his face and then into Susan's wet eyes. "*Suzy*," he said with a wet, strangled grunt.

"Justin," Susan sobbed. She lowered the gun, still backing away slowly. Her crying eyes widened as she raised the gun again. Another dead man groaned hungrily and staggered around Justin, reaching out his one remaining arm. Half of the thing's face was torn away, one eye socket holding nothing but a bloody-black emptiness.

Justin's head turned and his opaque dead eyes widened as the dead man shuffled past him, reaching for his family. "*No!*" he grunted and stiffly took off after him. Justin staggered up behind the zombie as he raised the baseball bat still dangling from his hand. He brought it down without much force onto the zombie's shoulder.

The zombie stumbled sideways and then turned and glanced back at Justin.

Justin stared at the bat, then wrapped his other hand around it and lifted it high over his head. The undead man gave Justin a curious glance, then dismissed him. Justin's atrophying muscles remembered how to use the bat even if he didn't. Moving in slow motion, Justin stepped up close and swung the bat down with all his might. The bat landed on the back of the zombie's head with a satisfying crunch and the dead man fell to the marble-tiled floor, this time dead for good. Justin gazed down at the corpse with the bat held high, ready should it move again.

"Justin!" Susan shouted. The dead man that had once answered to that name snapped its head up and looked at her. "There's more!" she shouted, gesturing behind him.

Understanding her, Justin turned and if he had still been a living man, his eyes would have widened in terror.

Dozens of hungering, undead forms clamored through the bottlenecked entrance of the building, with hundreds more behind them. The desperate groaning of the mob cast deep, foreboding echoes throughout the cavernous lobby.

Had he still lived, Justin would have calculated the odds of surviving and known it was hopeless. However, his dead mind saw things in a simpler light. These things wanted to kill his family, to eat their flesh. He couldn't allow that horror to pass. He felt no trepidation; no thoughts of failure crossed his dull mind. He felt only a deep sense of purpose, and a mission clearly defined. With a battle cry that would have wilted the courage of even the bravest battle-hardened soldier, Justin waded into the oncoming hoard while swinging the bat.

Susan watched in utter amazement as her undead husband moved into hand-to-hand combat with his living dead brethren. Diligently, he charged into the mass of walking dead, swinging his bat like a scythe as if he were Death himself returned to claim the souls of the undead.

He moved like a machine, and not seeing him as a threat, the undead did nothing to stop him. Still, there were far too many for him to destroy, but every one of the zombies that escaped Justin's merciless bat, fell under the fire of Susan's gun. Justin would have been proud of her marksmanship as almost all of her rounds found targets. Heads exploded, spraying their black remains into the air and the starving dead joined the bodies scattered upon the killing floor.

The air hung thick with the harsh stink of gunpowder, the stench of putrefying flesh and the congealed blood and brains spilled copiously upon the floor. Hundreds of rotting bodies littered the marble tile, and still they came. Justin's cries of rage and defiance joined the groans of the dead. In the chaotic echoes of battle, Susan's gun fell silent.

"Close your eyes, honey," Susan whispered softly to her son as she slid in her last clip of ammunition.

"Mommy," Jeremy whimpered.

Susan laid her free hand gently over Jeremy's eyes. "It's okay, we're going to be okay." Her breath caught and she cried silently. Susan gazed at her undead husband fighting so valiantly to save their lives in vain, and felt the familiar grasp of sorrow gripping her heart. "I love you, Jeremy," she sighed.

There were so many, but the numbers didn't concern him, Justin's arms performed far better than they would have in life, for now he was tireless. As his gore-dripping bat crunched into skull after skull, his eyes constantly tracked his next target and the one after that. He moved with a graceful beauty that transcended the death and carnage around him. Purposeful, pure, and undiluted by lesser base emotions, un-death and his renewed consciousness had altered Justin into a perfect killing machine. There were so many bodies littering the floor that he stumbled and tripped over them as he pursued new skulls to smash. The numbers were dwindling, and he should have felt a sense of hope as he inevitably drove the mob of zombies back and through the lobby's main entrance, but his mind was free of such clutter.

The sudden report of a solitary shot cut through his focus, and he spun just in time to watch his son's body slump to the floor. Susan's horrified scream cleaved his dead heart and he screamed with her as Jeremy bled out on the floor.

"*Susan!*" he growled. Abandoning his war of zombie attrition, he staggered over the bodies strewn across the bloody floor as Susan fell to her knees beside Jeremy's body. His son, sweet little four-year-old Jeremy, was now a bloodied, motionless body before Susan's knees. Susan sobbed heavily and let loose another wretched scream that twisted Justin's undead soul into bloody knots. Before he could reach them, Susan's hand came up in a detached mechanical motion, bringing the pistol up under her chin.

"*Susan!*" he howled. Dropping the bat from his bloodied hand, he staggered forward with his arms reaching for her like a love sick Frankenstein's monster.

She glanced up at him from only a few yards away, and her eyes were as dead as his were. Her empty sodden eyes hooded over, her eyelids coming down leisurely like the final curtain of a theatrical tragedy, and she pulled the trigger for the last time.

Blood, bits of skull, and brain matter splattered across his gray face as he fell to his knees at the foot of his family's massacre. "*No!*" he bellowed, his dead voice dripping with tortured anguish. Susan's body slumped to the floor, and the gaping wound in the back of her head leaked her life's fluid, the blood forming a bloody halo around her shattered skull.

"*Susan,*" he sobbed. Had his dead eyes been capable of shedding tears, the river would have washed them all away. He reached out a trembling hand and gently stroked the bloody mop of hair on what was left of his wife's head. "*Died for you,*" he gurgled out painfully, his dead face writhed and twisted, and a grief stricken roar erupted from his dead soul, stilling the gathering zombies in their tracks. The congregation of Hell's faithful minions stopped around their screaming brother and his dead family, swaying back and forth as if moved by a gospel of the living dead.

The assembled hoard stared in confusion as the zombie kneeling before the warm meat gathered the freshly killed humans in his arms, sobbing tearlessly as he pressed his gray lips to their serene and bloody faces.

When he pulled his wife and son's bodies into his arms, he heard a clatter as Susan's gun fell to the floor. With his family's blood staining his lips, he lifted his head and glared down at the gun. Glancing over his shoulder, his milky eyes scanned across his audience of the living dead, who seemed to be waiting for him to show them the way.

He would not disappoint them.

Justin shifted around until he lay against the wall between the two loves of his life. Ever so gently, he gathered them onto his lap, lovingly wrapping their arms around each other. Again, his face contorted and his lifeless lungs hitched with soft, silent sobs.

"*Love you, Susan,*" he choked, as reverently as a dead man could. "*Love you, Jeremy.*" Reaching out, he grasped Susan's gun in his bloody hand and placed it so the muzzle was under his chin, the metal pressed into his dead flesh.

His faithful followers bore silent witness as Justin pulled the trigger, and joined his family in the next world.

* * *

Outside, the overcast sky broke open fleetingly, and the bloody orange setting sun burned through the cloud cover. The life giving light shimmered through the lobby's atrium windows, bathing the three corpses in its crimson glow.

A collective groan rose up from the dead flock. One stepped forward from the mass and approached the trinity of hallowed corpses. Still wearing the tattered uniform of the public servant he had been in life, the dead cop bent over and pried the gun from Justin's gore splattered hand. The gun felt good in his hand, familiar and comforting.

His opaque gaze slid off the gun and dropped to the trio of bodies at his feet. So peaceful they appeared, chaos purified. He looked to the gun again, and groaned pitifully as something glimmered in his dead mind, a face, a beautiful, smiling, laughing face.

"I love you, Robert," the woman's face whispered as she stood on her toes to kiss him. The vision faded, leaving the dead cop once named Robert gasping for air he didn't need to breathe.

Mimicking Justin's example, the zombie cop's arm lifted the gun up and placed the muzzle beneath his chin.

"*Love you, Rebecca,*" he growled gutturally as his finger searched for, and found, the trigger.

The gun spoke its sermon and another imprisoned soul passed through the veil of unearthly dead flesh.

As the cop's body slumped to the cold marble tile floor, the next seeker shambled forward, reaching for salvation.

ABOUT THE WRITERS

David Bernstein, a.k.a. MacabreZombie, is still writing horror for various anthos and magazines, but has finally made major progress on his zombie oriented novel--Amongst the Dead, which the first two, maybe three by the time you read this, chapters are available online at Tales of the Zombie War. He is also proud of winning the MacabreZombie award for best horror fiction of 2009 and feels he'll win it again in 2010. He lives in the NYC area with his girlfriend of eight years.

Sheri Gambino works as a full time Sales Manager and a part time Horror Writer. Current publication's in "Vicious Verses and Reanimated Rhymes" by Coscom Entertainment. "End of Days 2" by Living Dead Press. She has several horror short stories coming out in the Library of the Living Dead: Vampology, Horrology, Ladies of Horror, Baconology, Zombology III, Letters of the Dead, Zombonauts, Zombie Feary Tales, Zombology VI, Zombology VII, Tales from the Cauldron. In her spare time when not writing, she enjoys playing with her three dogs and reading. She currently resides in Kansas City.

Anthony Giangregorio is the author and editor of more than 30 novels, almost all of them about zombies. His work has appeared in Dead Science by Coscomentertainment, Dead Worlds: Undead Stories Volumes 1, 2 , 3, & 4, and an upcoming anthology (Zombology) by Library of the Living Dead Press and their werewolf anthology titled Wolves of War. He also has stories in End of Days: An Apocalyptic Anthology Volumes 1 & 2, and 2 anthologies with Pill Hill Press. Check out his website at www.undeadpress.com

Michael D. Griffiths focuses primarily on writing Horror and Science Fiction, but has dabbled in odd Fantasy and even, gasp, literary works. He has won the Withersins 666 award, and several contests at Golden Visions. In the past, Mike has published two underground zines, been on over a hundred road trips, and has had his Skinjumper Series published in M-Brane magazine. He is currently a part of Abandoned Towers and Innsmouth Free Press magazines.

Sean Grigsby writes scary stories in central Arkansas where he lives with his wife, Whitney. His other work can be found in "Christmas is Dead: A Zombie Anthology". You can reach him on Facebook or at grigsbycomedy@yahoo.com.

Tom Hamilton is working on editing three novels along with short stories, poems and plays which have been widely published. You may have read some of his stories in the Dead Worlds Series and Chiristmas is Dead from Living Dead Press. He is getting ready for the winter along with his wife Mary Theresa and their three small daughters, Tiffany, Hope and Catalina. He lives in Loves Park, IL

Mark M. Johnson enjoys writing as a hobby. By the grace of good editors, his short fiction has appeared in Bits of the Dead, and Vicious Verses Zombie Poetry, from Coscom Entertainment, Zombology 1, from Library of the Living Dead Press, and the upcoming Horrorology from Library of Horror Press, Dead Worlds, Volumes 2 & 3, and Book of the Dead Volume 2, from Living dead Press. Born and raised in Detroit , he currently resides in Warren MI with his awesome, loving, and supportive wife Cindy, one college daughter, one high school son, one dog, three cats, and a python.

Keith Adam Luethke is the author of Dead House: A Zombie Ghost Story and has a short story in the Christmas is Dead zombie anthology published by Living Dead Press. He has a handful of other books for sale on Amazon.com and loves to talk to new fans.

Jessy Marie Roberts lives in a "haunted" house in Western Nebraska with her husband and their two dogs, Tucker and Snags. She grew up in Morgan Hill, California, where she danced on chairs to "Son of a Preacher Man" with the best friends a girl could ask for. She has several short stories published by Living Dead Press. Visit her online at jessymarieroberts.weebly.com.

Rob Rosen, author of the novels "Sparkle" and "Divas Las Vegas", has had short stories featured in more than eighty anthologies, most notably: Through the Eyes of the Undead, Zombology VI, Dead Christmas, Zombonauts, The Middle of Nowhere: Horror in Rural America, and Horror Through The Ages. Please visit him at his website, www.therobrosen.com, or email him at robrosen@therobrosen.com

Spencer Wendleton is a horror writer whose first novel is entitled "The Body Cartel" under his penname Alan Spencer. When he's not writing, he's walking his dog, Raymond, or watching horror movies. The author welcomes e-mails at alanspencer26@hotmail.com.

Marc Wiggins has been an avid lover of post-apocalyptic fiction ever since he saw his first zombie movie in seventh grade. He has always loved the written word and favors zombie novels over movies.
Marc lives with his loving wife and kids in Southern California. He has many stories published with Living Dead Press, the others being in Dead Worlds: Volumes 1 & 2, Christmas is Dead, Book of the Dead Vol. 1 & 2, & End of Days: An Apocalyptic Anthology.
He is presently working on his first zombie book due out next year.

BOOK OF THE DEAD 2: NOT DEAD YET
A ZOMBIE ANTHOLOGY
Edited by Anthony Giangregorio

Out of the ashes of death and decay, comes the second volume filled with the walking dead.

In this tomb, there are only slow, shambling monstrosities that were once human.

No one knows why the dead walk; only that they do, and that they are hungry for human flesh.

But these aren't your neighbors, your co-workers, or your family. Now they are the living dead, and they will tear your throat out at a moment's notice.

So be warned as you delve into the pages of this book; the dead will find you, no matter where you hide.

CHRISTMAS IS DEAD: A ZOMBIE ANTHOLOGY
Edited by Anthony Giangregorio

Twas the night before Christmas and all through the house, not a creature was stirring, not even a. . . zombie?

That's right; this anthology explores what would happen at Christmas time if there was a full blown zombie outbreak.

Reanimated turkeys, zombie Santas, and demon reindeers that turn people into flesh-eating ghouls are just some of the tales you will find in this merry undead book.

So curl up under the Christmas tree with a cup of hot chocolate, and as the fireplace crackles with warmth, get ready to have your heart filled with holiday cheer.

But of course, then it will be ripped from your heaving chest and fed upon by blood-thirsty elves with a craving for human flesh!

For you see, Christmas is Dead!

And you will never look at the holiday season the same way again.

DEAD HOUSE: A ZOMBIE GHOST STORY
by Keith Adam Luethke
Welcome to Dead House

The old mansion on the edge of town, aptly named Dead House, has a history of blood, pain, and death, but what Victor Leeds knows of this past only scratches the surface of the true horrors within.

But when his girlfriend is attacked by a shadowy figure one rainy night, he soon finds himself caught up in a world where the dead walk and ghostly wraiths abound.

And to make matters worse, a pair of serial killers are fulfilling carefully made plans, and when they are done, the small town of Stormville, New York will run red. The last ingredient to open the gates of Hell, and plunge this small upstate town into madness, is rain.

And in Stormville, it pours by the gallons.

The Zombie in the Basement

by Anthony Giangregorio

Illustrated by Andrew Dawe-Collins

The spooky house at the end of the street was the one all the kids avoided. With its overgrown shrubs and weeds, the place was a modern day haunted house. Especially at night. So when Ricky sneaks into the yard to retrieve his favorite ball, he comes across something he'd only seen in movies and bad dreams. He sees a zombie in the basement window of the old house, but when he tells his friends, no one believes him. Ricky knows what he saw, that something lurks in the old house, something that isn't supposed to exist.

With his best friend Eric by his side,   Ricky will find out the truth and prove to everyone that zombies are real. And when the night is done, every-one will know about the zombie in the basement.

Note: This book is for young adults and for those who are young at heart.

DEADFREEZE

by Anthony Giangregorio

THIS IS WHAT HELL WOULD BE LIKE IF IT FROZE OVER!

When an experimental serum for hypothermia goes horribly wrong, a small research station in the middle of Antarctica becomes overrun with an army of the frozen dead.

Now a small group of survivors must battle the arctic weather and a horde of frozen zombies as they make their way across the frozen plains of Antarctica to a neighboring research station.

What they don't realize is that they are being hunted by an entity whose sole reason for existing is vengeance; and it will find them wherever they run.

VISIONS OF THE DEAD
A ZOMBIE STORY

by Anthony & Joseph Giangregorio

Jake Roberts felt like he was the luckiest man alive.

He had a great family, a beautiful girlfriend, who was soon to be his wife, and a job, that might not have been the best, but it paid the bills.

At least until the dead began to walk.

Now Jake is fighting to survive in a dead world while searching for his lost love, Melissa, knowing she's out there somewhere.

But the past isn't dead, and as he struggles for an uncertain future, the past threatens to consume him. With the present a constant battle between the living and the dead, Jake finds himself slipping in and out of the past, the visions of how it all happened haunting him. But Jake knows Melissa is out there somewhere and he'll find her or die trying.

In a world of the living dead, you can never escape your past.

DEAD MOURNING: A ZOMBIE HORROR STORY
by Anthony Giangregorio

Carl Jenkins was having a run of bad luck. Fresh out of jail, his probation tenuous, he'd lost every job he'd taken since being released. So now was his last chance, only one more job to prevent him from going back to prison. Assigned to work in a funeral home, he accidentally loses a shipment of embalming fluid. With nothing to lose, he substitutes it with a batch of chemicals from a nearby factory.

The results don't go as planned, though. While his screw-up goes unnoticed, his machinations revive the cadavers in the funeral home, unleashing an evil on the world that it has not seen before. Not wanting to become a snack for the rampaging dead, he flees the city, joining up with other survivors. An old, dilapidated zoo becomes their haven, while the dead wait outside the walls, hungry and patient.

But Carl is optimistic, after all, he's still alive, right? Perhaps his luck has changed and help will arrive to save them all?

Unfortunately, unknown to him and the other survivors, a serial killer has fallen into their group, trapped inside the zoo with them.

With the undead army clamoring outside the walls and a murderer within, it'll be a miracle if any of them live to see the next sunrise.

On second thought, maybe Carl would've been better off if he'd just gone back to jail.

ROAD KILL: A ZOMBIE TALE
by Anthony Giangregorio
ORDER UP!

In the summer of 2008, a rogue comet entered earth's orbit for 72 hours. During this time, a strange amber glow suffused the sky.

But something else happened; something in the comet's tail had an adverse affect on dead tissue and the result was the reanimation of every dead animal carcass on the planet.

A handful of survivors hole up in a diner in the backwoods of New Hampshire while the undead creatures of the night hunt for human prey.

There's a new blue plate special at DJ's Diner and Truck Stop, and it's you!

DEAD WORLDS: Undead Stories
A Zombie Anthology Volume 2
Edited by Anthony Giangregorio

Welcome to a world where the dead walk and want nothing more than to feast on the living. The stories contained in this, the second volume of the Dead Worlds series, are filled with action, gore, and buckets and buckets of blood; plus a heaping side of entrails for those with a little extra hunger.

The stories contained within this volume are scribed by both the desiccated cadavers of seasoned veterans to the genre as well as fresh-faced corpses, each printed here for the first time; and all of them ready to dig in and please the most discerning reader.

So slap on a bib and prepare to get bloody, because you're about to read the best zombie stories this side of Hell!

THE DARK

by Anthony Giangregorio
DARKNESS FALLS

The darkness came without warning.

First New York, then the rest of United States, and then the world became enveloped in a perpetual night without end.

With no sunlight, eventually the planet will wither and die, bringing on a new Ice Age. But that isn't problem for the human race, for humanity will be dead long before that happens.

There is something in the dark, creatures only seen in nightmares, and they are on the prowl. Evolution has changed and man is no longer the dominant species. When we are children, we're told not to fear the dark, that what we believe to exist in the shadows is false.

Unfortunately, that is no longer true.

SOULEATER

by Anthony Giangregorio

Twenty years ago, Jason Lawson witnessed the brutal death of his father by something only seen in nightmares, something so horrible he'd blocked it from his mind.

Now twenty years later the creature is back, this time for his son.

Jason won't let that happen.

He'll travel to the demon's world, struggling every second to rescue his son from its clutches.

But what he doesn't know is that the portal will only be open for a finite time and if he doesn't return with his son before it closes, then he'll be trapped in the demon's dimension forever.

SEE HOW IT ALL BEGAN IN THE NEW DOUBLE-SIZED 460 PAGE SPECIAL EDITION!

DEADWATER: EXPANDED EDITION

by Anthony Giangregorio

Through a series of tragic mishaps, a small town's water supply is contaminated with a deadly bacterium that transforms the town's population into flesh eating ghouls.

Without warning, Henry Watson finds himself thrown into a living hell where the living dead walk and want nothing more than to feed on the living.

Now Henry's trying to escape the undead town before he becomes the next victim.

With the military on one side, shooting civilians on sight, and a horde of bloodthirsty zombies on the other, Henry must try to battle his way to freedom.

With a small group of survivors, including a beautiful secretary and a wise-cracking janitor to aid him, the ragtag group will do their best to stay alive and escape the city codenamed: **Deadwater.**

DEAD END: A ZOMBIE NOVEL
by Anthony Giangregorio
THE DEAD WALK!

Newspapers everywhere proclaim the dead have returned to feast on the living!

A small group of survivors hole up in a cellar, afraid to brave the masses of animated corpses, but when food runs out, they have no choice but to venture out into a world gone mad. What they will discover, however, is that the fall of civilization has brought out the worst in their fellow man.

Cannibals, psychotic preachers and rapists are just some of the atrocities they must face.

In a world turned upside down, it is life that has hit a Dead End.

DEAD RAGE
by Anthony Giangregorio

An unknown virus spreads across the globe, turning ordinary people into bloodthirsty, ravenous killers.

Only a small percentage of the population is immune and soon become prey to the infected.

Amongst the infected comes a man, stricken by the virus, yet still retaining his grasp on reality. His need to destroy the *normals* becomes an obsession and he raises an army of killers to seek out and kill all who aren't *changed* like himself.

A few survivors gather together on the outskirts of Chicago and find themselves running for their lives as the specter of death looms over all.

The Dead Rage virus will find you, no matter where you hide.

DEADTOWN: A DEADWATER STORY
by Anthony Giangregorio

WORLD OF THE DEAD

The world is a very different place now. The dead walk the land and humans hide in small towns with walls of stone and debris for protection, constantly keeping the living dead at bay. Social law is gone and right and wrong is defined by the size of your gun.

UNWELCOME VISITORS

Henry Watson and his band of warrior survivalists become guests in a fortified town in Michigan. But when the kidnapping of one of the companions goes bad and men die, the group finds themselves on the wrong side of the law, and a town out for blood.

Trapped in a hotel, surrounded on all sides, it will be up to Henry to save the day with a gamble that may not only take his life, but that of his friends as well.

In a dead world, when justice is not enough, there is always vengeance.

The Lazarus Culture
by Pasquale J. Morrone

Secret Service Agent Christopher Kearns had no idea what he was up against. Assigned on a temporary basis to the Center for Disease Control, he only knew that somehow it was connected to the lives of those the agency protected...namely, the President of the United States. If there were possible terrorist activities in the making, he could only guess it was at a red alert basis.

When Kearns meets and befriends Doctor Marlene Peterson of the Breezy Point Medical Center in Maryland, he soon finds that science fiction can indeed become a reality. In a solitary room walked a man with no vital signs: dead. The explanation he received came from Doctor Lee Fret, a man assigned to the case from the CDC. Something was attached to the brain stem. Something alive that was quickly spreading rapidly through Maryland and other states.

Kearns and his ragtag army of agents and medical personnel soon find themselves in a world of meaningless slaughter and mayhem. The armies of the walking dead were far more than mere zombies. Some began to change into whatever it was they ate. The government had found a way to reanimate the dead by implanting a parasite found on the tongue of the Red Snapper to the human brain.

It looked good on paper, but it was a project straight from Hell.

The dead now walked, but it wasn't a mystery.

It was The Lazarus Culture.

END OF DAYS: AN APOCALYPTIC ANTHOLOGY VOLUMES 1 & 2

Our world is a fragile place.

Meteors, famine, floods, nuclear war, solar flares, and hundreds of other calamities can plunge our small blue planet into turmoil in an instant.

What would you do if tomorrow the sun went super nova or the world was swallowed by water, submerging the world into the cold darkness of the ocean? This anthology explores some of those scenarios and plunges you into total annihilation.

But remember, it's only a book, and tomorrow will come as it always does. Or will it?

DEADFALL
by Anthony Giangregorio

It's Halloween in the small suburban town of Wakefield, Mass.

While parents take their children trick or treating and others throw costume parties, a swarm of meteorites enter the earth's atmosphere and crash to earth.

Inside are small parasitic worms, no larger than maggots.

The worms quickly infect the corpses at a local cemetery and so begins the rise of the undead.

The walking dead soon get the upper hand, with no one believing the truth. That the dead now walk.

Will a small group of survivors live through the zombie apocalypse?

Or will they, too, succumb to the Deadfall.

JUST BEFORE NIGHT: A ZOMBIE DUOLOGY

By Joe Tonzelli & Anthony Giangregorio

On one fateful night, humankind found itself battling hordes of the living dead. From diners to highways to farmhouses, the dead assaulted the living and consumed their flesh along with their lives.

Among them were Duane, a reluctant hero, trapped with strangers in a diner; the Hardman family, led by Karl, the antagonistic husband and father fighting for control; and young lovers Keith and Judy, fleeing through the dark woods with the dead close behind them. And caught in the middle of the madness was Sheriff Kosana, a simple, small-town lawman intent on controlling the situation himself.

Though their fates have already been written by the hands of time, their struggle for survival is one of agonizing suspense as they battle to escape the outstretched arms of the undead pursuing them.

Experience the terror in *Just Before Night*, a zombie anthology of gut-munching, bone-snapping stories that chart the origins of the living dead.

For when night falls, the dead will walk.

BOOK OF THE DEAD
A ZOMBIE ANTHOLOGY
VOLUME 1
ISBN 978-1-935458-25-8

Edited by Anthony Giangregorio

This is the most faithful, truest zombie anthology ever written, and we invite you along for the ride. Every single story in this book is filled with slack-jawed, eyes glazed, slow moving, shambling zombies set in a world where the dead have risen and only want to eat the flesh of the living. In these pages, the rules are sacrosanct. There is no deviation from what a zombie should be or how they came about. The Dead Walk.

There is no reason, though rumors and suppositions fill the radio and television stations. But the only thing that is fact is that the walking dead are here and they will not go away. So prepare yourself for the ultimate homage to the master of zombie legend. And remember... Aim for the head!

DEAD TALES: SHORT STORIES TO DIE FOR

by Anthony Giangregorio

In a world much like our own, terrorists unleash a deadly dis-ease that turns people into flesh-eating ghouls.

A camping trip goes horribly wrong when forces of evil seek to dominate mankind.

After losing his life, a man returns reincarnated again and again; his soul inhabiting the bodies of animals.

In the Colorado Mountains, a woman runs for her life, stalked by a sadistic killer.

In a world where the Patriot Act has come to fruition, a man struggles to survive, despite eroding liberties.

Not able to accept his wife's death, a widower will cross into the dream realm to find her again, despite the dark forces that hold her in thrall. These and other short stories will captivate and thrill you. These are short stories to die for.

REVOLUTION OF THE DEAD
by Anthony Giangregorio
THE DEAD SHALL RISE AGAIN!

Five years ago, a deadly plague wiped out 97% of the world's population, America suffering tragically. Bodies were everywhere, far too many to bury or burn. But then, through a miracle of medical science, a way is found to reanimate the dead.

With the manpower of the United States depleted, and the remaining survivors not wanting to give up their internet and fast food restaurants, the undead are conscripted as slave labor.

Now they cut the grass, pick up the trash, and walk the dogs of the surviving humans.

But whether alive or dead, no race wants to be controlled, and sooner or later the dead will fight back, wanting the freedom they enjoyed in life.

The revolution has begun!

And when it's over, the dead will rule the land, and the remaining humans will become the slaves...or worse.

KINGDOM OF THE DEAD
by Anthony Giangregorio
THE DEAD HAVE RISEN!

In the dead city of Pittsburgh, two small enclaves struggle to survive, eking out an existence of hand to mouth.

But instead of working together, both groups battle for the last remaining fuel and supplies of a city filled with the living dead.

Six months after the initial outbreak, a lone helicopter arrives bearing two more survivors and a newborn baby. One enclave welcomes them, while the other schemes to steal their helicopter and escape the decaying city.

With no police, fire, or social services existing, the two will battle for dominance in the steel city of the walking dead. But when the dust settles, the question is: will the remaining humans be the winners, or the losers?

When the dead walk, the line between Heaven and Hell is so twisted and bent there is no line at all.

RISE OF THE DEAD
by Anthony Giangregorio
DEATH IS ONLY THE BEGINNING!

In less than forty-eight hours, more than half the globe was infected.

In another forty-eight, the rest would be enveloped.

The reason?

A science experiment gone horribly wrong which enabled the dead to walk, their flesh rotting on their bones even as they seek human prey.

Jeremy was an ordinary nineteen year old slacker. He partied too much and had done poorly in high school. After a night of drinking and drugs, he awoke to find the world a very different place from the one he'd left the night before.

The dead were walking and feeding on the living, and as Jeremy stepped out into a world gone mad, the dead spotting him alone and unarmed in the middle of the street, he had to wonder if he would live long enough to see his twentieth birthday.

www.ingramcontent.com/pod-product-compliance
Lightning Source LLC
Chambersburg PA
CBHW070947180726
48291CB00004B/1185